The Mo Man's Christmas Bride

STAND-ALONE NOVEL

A Western Historical Romance Book

by

Hannah Lee Davis

HANNAH LEE DAVIS

This is a work of fiction. Names, characters, places, and incidents are either products of the author's imagination or are used fictitiously. Any resemblance to actual events, locales, or persons, living or dead, is entirely coincidental.

Copyright © 2025 by Hannah Lee Davis

All Rights Reserved.

No part of this book may be reproduced, duplicated, transmitted, or recorded in any form—electronic or printed—without the prior written permission of the publisher. Unauthorized storage or distribution of this document is strictly prohibited.

Table of Contents

The Mountain Man's Christmas Bride 1
    Table of Contents 4
    Letter from Hannah Lee Davis 6
Prologue 8
Chapter One 19
Chapter Two 32
Chapter Three 41
Chapter Four 49
Chapter Five 60
Chapter Six 67
Chapter Seven 80
Chapter Eight 86
Chapter Nine 93
Chapter Ten 101
Chapter Eleven 109
Chapter Twelve 118
Chapter Thirteen 126
Chapter Fourteen 135
Chapter Fifteen 142
Chapter Sixteen 150
Chapter Seventeen 157
Chapter Eighteen 164
Chapter Nineteen 171

Chapter Twenty..179
Chapter Twenty-One 189
Chapter Twenty-Two 197
Chapter Twenty-Three..............................204
Chapter Twenty-Four 211
Chapter Twenty-Five 218
Chapter Twenty-Six...................................225
Chapter Twenty-Seven 233
Chapter Twenty-Eight 243
Chapter Twenty-Nine................................257
Chapter Thirty 265
Chapter Thirty-One 274
Chapter Thirty-Two 280
Chapter Thirty-Three................................292
Epilogue..306
  Also by Hannah Lee Davis 317

Letter from Hannah Lee Davis

As my beloved husband, my school sweetheart, Mister John Bennett, would say:

"Life is like a bowl of soup—you've got to stir it once in a while, so all the good stuff doesn't settle at the bottom."

Hi y'all, I'm Hannah Lee Davis, a spry 65-year-old widow who's finally gotten around to doing what I've dreamt of for years—writing stories that touch the heart and soul. I was born and raised in the heartland of Indiana, where the cornfields stretch as far as the eye can see, and where folks still know the value of a hard day's work and a kind word. But these days, I find myself out in Colorado, sharing stories and sunsets with my darling sister, Janice.

Why did it take me so long to put pen to paper, you ask? Well, life happened, sugar. I spent most of my years caring for my family, raising kids—after years of trying, mind you—and looking after my aging parents. My husband's ailment needed time and dedication from my side. Don't get me wrong; I wouldn't trade those days for anything. But there were nights, oh yes, many nights, when I'd sit in my knitting chair, crocheting blankets or scarves, and my mind would wander. Each stitch was like a sentence, each row a paragraph, and before I knew it, I'd crocheted whole stories in my head.

Crocheting, you see, is a lot like weaving stories. You've got to have the right pattern, the right tension, and above all, the right yarn to make something truly beautiful. It's a labor of love, one stitch at a time, just like life.

So why now? Why have I decided to become a published author at this ripe old age? Well, darlin', it's simple. I've got stories in me that are yearnin' to be told—tales of love that burns like a prairie fire, and courage that stands as tall as a mountain. I write because I want to wrap you up in a narrative as comforting as one of my homemade quilts, a story that'll make you feel at home, no matter where you are. I write because this is what makes sense for me: imagining worlds where my husband, John, would admire, worlds where brides find the love of their lives in the most unexpected ways.

I write because this is what John made me promise before he passed away.

So, grab a cup of hot cocoa, settle into your favorite armchair, and let's journey through the wild frontier of human emotions, one story at a time.

Until next time,

Hannah Lee Davis

Prologue

Green River, Wyoming — 1872

It was the fiercest winter Evelyn Rhodes had seen in a long time. The "blizzard of the century" was what some folks around town were calling it, and Evelyn could certainly believe that. The snow was so heavy it battered the windows harshly as hail.

Inside the small sitting room above her tailor shop, pressing a cool washcloth to her cousin Arabella's forehead, Evelyn felt her hands tremble as she tried to bring down the fever that had been climbing steadily for the past three hours. The young woman's face was flushed red, and damp with sweat and water, her breathing shallow—but so rapid as her chest rose up high and fell low, quicker than if she'd just run miles.

A tear fell down Evelyn's cheek. Arabelle was so sick…

And was only getting sicker.

Next to the two women was a cradle, where one-month-old Mason cried with desperation that tore at Evelyn. It was as if he was pleading with her to help his mama. Help that Evelyn wasn't so sure she could provide.

She'd been trying to break this fever for a long time.

"Hush, sweet boy," Evelyn cooed as she reached over to rock the cradle with one hand while still keeping the cloth pressed to his mother's burning skin. "Just a little longer. Your mama needs to rest."

But the boy wasn't having it.

His cries only got louder, demanding attention no one had been giving him. Attention Evelyn could not fully give while tending to Arabella. And attention, Arabella was too sick to give him.

Truthfully, Evelyn felt pulled in two different directions, taking care of both mother and son. She was overwhelmed.

"Ev?"

"I'm here," she said sweetly, leaning in close to her cousin. "But I really need for you to save your strength."

But her cousin's eyes had opened, and she started to stir, despite the heat radiating from her body. Despite her disorientation, she turned her head slowly, weakly, to the sound of the baby crying. And she smiled.

Through the pain, the fever, the weakness—she was smiling.

"Bring him to me," she whispered. "Please."

"Arabella, you need to rest—"

"Please." She partially sat up, her voice stern.

Evelyn hesitated, wanting to argue, but knew that if Arabella sat up at a time like this and demanded it, there had to be a reason. Carefully, she lifted Mason from his cradle. The baby's cries intensified briefly as she moved him, but the moment she laid him beside Arabella on the bed, something changed. His mother's arm came up to shakily curve around her son.

"There's my boy," Arabella whispered softly, soothingly. "There's my beautiful boy."

Mason's cries softened to whimpers, then to small hiccupping sounds. His unfocused eyes seemed to find his mother's face anyway, and he made a soft cooing noise that sounded pleased with himself. A sort of happiness brought tears to Evelyn's eyes. Because even though he was looking at his mother's beautiful face, she was far too sick to be happy. But he didn't know that. He just saw his mama.

Arabella laughed weakly. "You see? He knows his mama. He knows—" She coughed. A harsh rattling sound came from her chest, and then her entire body convulsed with it.

Evelyn quickly grabbed for Mason to set him back down in his cradle and helped her cousin sit up to support her shoulders.

"It's okay," Evelyn cooed, swiping at the girl's hair. "It's okay...shh..."

When the spell finally subsided, Arabella slumped back against the pillows, clearly exhausted. And yet, her eyes remained open, fixed on Evelyn. The intensity behind that gaze made Evelyn's stomach clench and churn. She was dreading what she knew was on her cousin's mind.

"Evelyn," Arabella said, clearing her throat. "I need you to listen to me now and promise me something, when this takes me home, I need for you to take care of Mas—"

"Don't talk like that. You're going to be fine. The fever will break."

"No," she repeated. "No, it won't. I can feel it. The Father is calling me home."

"Stop it." Evelyn choked on a sob. "Stop talking like that. You can't leave him. You can't leave me. I need you, and Mason needs you."

"That's why I need you to promise me you'll take care of him. That you'll protect him. That you'll love him like he was your own."

"Of course I will, but you're going to be here to—"

"Promise me!" she cried desperately, her grip pinching Evelyn's skin. "I can't find peace unless I know he'll be safe. Unless I know you'll do whatever it takes to keep him safe. Promise me, Ev. Please. Take him in like you took me in."

Evelyn had loved having them there, truth be told. When she was just nineteen, her parents had died in a robbery gone wrong, at the hands of a bunch of good-for-nothing scoundrels with nothing better to do than to hurt people. She'd inherited the tailor shop when they passed, and it had been all she'd had to help her through her grief.

She'd worked hard to keep the business running, but hadn't had a life. No one to talk with, to share good times with, to laugh with. But with Arabella's presence, she felt taken in. She felt friendship. They had needed each other. For different reasons.

Arabella had been hurting the night Evelyn found her sobbing outside her door, too scared to knock, after her father had kicked her out of the house. It had been months ago, and Evelyn could still remember it like yesterday. There weren't any exterior wounds, but there were plenty in her soul. She'd been crying so hard she could barely breathe. All because she was pregnant out of wedlock.

Tears streamed down Evelyn's face. She wanted to refuse, wanted to insist the promise Arabella wanted was unnecessary because she would get better. She would live to raise her son herself. She wouldn't need Evelyn at all. Or anyone, for that matter. But looking into her cousin's fever-bright, tear-filled eyes, seeing the despondency all over her face, she knew she had to give in.

Even if Evelyn didn't want to voice it aloud because that meant giving up. And she wasn't willing to do that. Not now, not ever. She wouldn't give up on her cousin. She wouldn't give up trying to help rid her of this fever.

"I promise," she said. "I promise I will protect him. I will do whatever it takes to keep him safe."

Arabella's hands loosened, and her eyes closed as a smile pulled at her lips. "Thank you," she breathed. "Thank you, Evie. You've always been more sister than cousin to me. More family than my own family ever was."

"You are my family," Evelyn responded through a choking sob.

"I love you," Arabella said weakly. "Tell Mason... tell him his mama loved him. Tell him I fought to bring him into this world. Tell him..." Her breathing changed. Became shallower. More labored.

"Arabella?" Evelyn leaned closer, panic rising in her chest as Arabella's grip loosened entirely. Then, a soft sigh left her...And then no other breaths came.

"No!" Evelyn cried, launching herself on her cousin's chest. "No, no, no. Please. Please don't leave me."

But she had. She'd left. Arabella was gone.

Mason began to cry again, as if he could somehow sense his mother's absence. The sound pulled Evelyn from her grief just enough to somewhat function. She gently kissed Arabella's forehead, closing her eyes with trembling fingers before turning toward Mason.

She lifted him from his cradle.

"I'm here," she whispered to the baby, holding him close as she rocked him. "I'm here, sweet boy. I won't leave you. I promised your mama, and I don't take too kindly to broken promises."

She walked to the window, moving Mason gently from side to side, and looked out at the raging storm. Somewhere out in that cold, white fury was her uncle, Arabella's father, the man who had disowned his own daughter when she needed him most. The man who had refused to help refused to even acknowledge Arabella's existence after learning of her pregnancy.

And suddenly, anger filled every crevice within her. She never planned on seeing him again, but now she would have to. She would have to tell him that his daughter was dead.

The thought of it made her stomach turn. But she had no choice. There would need to be a funeral, a burial. Arabella deserved that much, at least. Deserved to rest in the family plot beside her mother, no matter what her lousy, fool of a father thought.

Mason cooed in her ear.

Whatever it takes.

That promise started to lie heavy on her shoulders. How was she supposed to take care of a baby?

She had no money. No family besides her uncle, who would most definitely turn her away. He had turned his own daughter away, after all.

She had nothing. And no prospects other than the very tailor shop downstairs. It had been her father's. The only thing left to her, and now it was her only means for survival. But it had been a bit of a stretch taking care of Arabella and a baby, too. Since Arabella had gotten ill, Evelyn had to slow down her work, and money had been tight for weeks.

The baby couldn't help out with dresses or suits, like Arabella could help earn a little extra money. But it didn't matter. She had made a promise to a dying woman. A woman she loved more than anyone. And Evelyn Rhodes did not break her promises.

Whatever it takes.

***

She heard the harsh rap on the door first, then, "Evelyn!"

She'd sent word through a neighbor boy. Just a simple word: *Come quick. It's Arabella.* She had hoped that the urgency might scare him into coming. That he might be afraid to lose his daughter and come quickly. But he hadn't come quickly at all. It had been several hours since she'd sent word, despite him only living on the other side of town.

"Where is she?" he demanded as soon as she opened the door. "Where's my daughter?"

She looked to the floor.

"Out with it, girl!" he barked, his spit flinging.

She looked up through heavy lids, her eyes raw from crying. "She's back there," she said, gesturing to the little room.

He pushed past her without waiting, his boots heavy on the stairs. Evelyn's eyes closed, and she said a silent prayer that Mason wouldn't awaken, then followed him.

When she found him, he was beside the bed, staring down at his daughter. She could have sworn she heard a strangled cry come from his throat, but he quickly cleared it, and when he turned around to face her, there was only anger in his eyes.

"When?" Just one word fell from his lips.

"A few hours ago. The fever wouldn't break."

"This is what comes of sin." His voice was flat, emotionless. "This is God's judgment on a woman who brought shame upon her family."

Evelyn winced, then glared at him, anger momentarily drowning out the grief. "How can you say that? She was your daughter. She made a mistake, yes, but she repented. She was a good Christian woman who—"

"A good Christian woman does not bear a bastard child!" He spat the words like poison, and Evelyn felt the burn off every one of them. "She made her choice. Now she can face the consequences in whatever afterlife she has coming to her!"

"I need to arrange a funeral. A proper burial in the family plot beside Aunt Mary. Arabella deserves to be—"

"She deserves nothing!" He turned away from me. "I will not pay for a funeral for a daughter who brought nothing but disgrace to my name, and definitely not next to my wife! Let the church bury her in a pauper's grave, if they will even accept her. That is more than she deserves."

"You can't mean that!" Evelyn cried, her voice shaking. "She was your child. Your only child. You can't do that!"

"I can and I will." His eyes were hard, cold. "I disowned her when she refused to give up that baby to another family, and I refuse to claim her in death."

Evelyn looked down at her younger cousin's peaceful face and thought how blessed she'd been to have her, and how devastating it was now that she was gone. This was the woman who had been there for her through everything. A true sister. She had laughed with her, cried with her, stood beside her through her parents' deaths.

She had never hated anyone, but in that moment, she thought of what a wicked man her uncle must be. To refuse to bury his only daughter? To give her the dignity of the burial she wanted—and not only her, but the burial her mother, his wife, would have wanted her to have?

It seemed evil.

She almost spat at him, but she didn't. God would not have wanted it for her. The Lord would have wanted her to forgive him, and although she wasn't sure she would be able to in that moment, she did choose to do one thing: bite her tongue.

She chose to not tell him what she thought of him. What kind of man she thought he was. Instead, the promise she'd just made was at the forefront of her mind. *Whatever it takes.*

"I will pay for it, then," she heard herself say. "I'll give her a proper burial. A decent grave with a headstone."

Her uncle's expression shifted, a smirk pulling at the corner of his lip. "Will you now? And how exactly do you propose to do that? Last I checked, that tailor shop of yours barely turns enough profit to keep you fed."

"I'll find a way!"

"I have a better idea." He moved closer, and Evelyn instinctively stepped back. "I've had my eye on that shop of yours for some time now. I think it would make a fine addition to my holdings."

"No," she said, shaking her head. The notion was horrifying. That was the only thing she had to her name.

"Yes." He smiled, evilly. "Sign over the shop to me, and I'll see to it that Arabella gets her proper burial. Family plot, headstone, the works. I'll even pay for the service in exchange for the shop."

"This shop is all that I have! It's my home and my work!"

"And your cousin's funeral is hanging in the balance," he returned, in a voice so pious and detached it nearly made a cold chill run through her. "Surely you wouldn't deny her a

Christian burial out of selfishness? What would she think of you, putting your own comfort above her final rest?"

The manipulation was blatant. It was so obvious she wanted to smack him across the face and turn the tables on him by asking the exact same questions. But she didn't bother. It wouldn't matter. This man's cruelty and his coldness was too far gone.

Evelyn's eyes fell past him, on Arabella. She had no choice.

She had to be buried, and they didn't have long to make the plans.

Whatever it takes.

"When?" she asked quietly.

"When what?"

"When would you arrange the funeral?"

His eyes widened in shock and surprise, and he looked almost... happy. That thought disgusted her.

"Three days." He laughed. "That will give time to contact the minister, prepare the grave. You'll sign the shop over to me before the service, of course. I'll need assurance you won't back out."

Of course, he would. Evelyn swallowed hard, fighting back tears. The shop had been her father's dream, his everything. It was her family's legacy and her only inheritance. It had been the only thing to keep a roof over her head, and Arabella's. And now it was going to be the only thing that got Arabella buried.

She had promised to protect Mason. That included honoring his mother with a proper burial, even if it cost her everything she had. He deserved a spot to visit her when he was old enough. And she deserved the dignity of being buried next to her beloved mother.

"All right," she whispered. "I'll sign over the shop. But I want your word—your solemn word before God—that you'll give Arabella a proper burial. Family plot, headstone with her full name, and a Christian service."

"You have my word." He extended his hand. "We have a deal."

Deal.

The word shook Evelyn to the core. Her uncle's plan wasn't much of a deal at all...but the word had prompted Evelyn to remember something she'd nearly forgotten. A deal of a different sort...and a possibility.

Arabella had made an arrangement before she passed away. She had been corresponding with someone about becoming a mail-order bride, planning a new life out west where she and Mason could start fresh, away from the judgment and shame of being an unwed mother.

Now, for Evelyn, that deal took on a whole different meaning.

Once her shop was gone, there would be nothing left for her here. Perhaps she could take her cousin's place, honor the agreement Arabella had made with the man expecting a wife.

It was a desperate plan. A silly one, in truth. But it was the only one she had, the only way she might have to keep her promise.

Whatever it takes.

Chapter One

Evanston, Wyoming — 1872

The ear-piercing sound of the train's whistle cut through the night, even over the howling wind, as Evelyn Rhodes clutched her three-month-old cousin, Mason, tightly against her chest.

She sighed as he nuzzled into her arms, and the locomotive finally shuddered to a halt. Through the frost-glazed window, she could barely make out the weathered sign that read *Evanston Station*. The letters had become obscured in the snow.

Evelyn wasn't so sure that the sky itself wasn't falling.

"End of the line, ma'am," the conductor called. His voice sounded sympathetic, although it didn't make her feel any better. She nodded quietly and stood as the slender man made his way through the empty car. "Best get yourself somewhere inside quick. This storm's only getting worse."

Maybe she wasn't the only one thinking the sky was about to fall.

She nodded again, although her limbs felt frozen in place. Stiff. Cold. And completely unsure of what to do from here. Was she crazy? Coming out to do this? Meeting a man, agreeing to be his wife, without even knowing him?

Three days she had traveled. Three long, exhausting days. Three days full of delays and bitter, blustery cold that had done nothing but chap her and Mason's cheeks. Which had also done nothing for his incessant crying. Crying that had drawn disapproving glares from every person within earshot.

People said it was colic.

But she knew it was something else. Hunger. Nothing but pure hunger. The milk she had brought was running thin, so she was rationing. As much as she wanted to fill up his belly, she knew that if she didn't ration it, and she couldn't get more in time, his cries would be even worse. And she wasn't sure if her heart could have taken hearing it raw and anguished in desperation and starvation. She wouldn't have been able to bear it. Still, he'd cried enough already that he'd exhausted himself, which was the only reason he was in slumber now.

"Ma'am," the conductor said again, a heavy sigh at the tail end of his words.

She nodded again, gathering up her worn carpet bag with her free hand before wobbling out into the aisleway on unsteady legs. She was hungry herself, exhausted, cold. She felt like the entire world was tilting. Dizziness consumed her. She wasn't sure if it was from the lack of food, or fear.

Whatever it was, she knew that she couldn't keep going like this.

Three weeks ago, she had owned a thriving tailor shop. She had a home, friends, and a livelihood. A future. One that she could almost predict. Now, everything had changed.

Now she owned nothing but the clothes on her back, a few spare garments in her bag, and … Mason.

She wasn't ready for a child, no, but she would have never told Arabella no. Not to something like that. And the truth was that Mason was already Evelyn's greatest love. He was half Arabella. He was blood.

Family.

The wind hit her like a whip across the face as soon as she stepped down from the train steps onto the snow-covered platform.

Her cloak and bonnet pulled away from her body, and Mason stirred, clearly just as bothered by the cold as she was. He whimpered. So did she. But she bounced him gently, shushing softly, hoping to lull him back to sleep. At least until she could get settled.

Where was he? The man who was supposed to become Arabella's husband?

Would he be disappointed when he saw her? She wasn't Arabella, after all. Arabella was so beautiful and eloquent in words. She was sure her letters had impressed.

She hadn't had time to write and tell anyone she was coming in her cousin's stead. But she thought it would be better than letting someone feel stood up. Beyond that, without her shop, Evelyn had nowhere to go.

She had ostracized herself after her parents' death. Her family had a successful business, and her parents had made a lot of friends over the years. But Evelyn had been too grief-stricken to entertain friends. Instead, she focused on work until Arabella had come along and forced her out of her shell. Forced her to coexist and to love someone other than just herself. Forced her to find her way outside of work. But allowing an unwed pregnant woman in your home wasn't the best way in Green River to make a good impression.

She'd wondered if Arabella had mentioned her baby. She tried to recall some of the letters. She'd remembered Arabella struggling with it. She'd remembered her being afraid and embarrassed. Ashamed. Not of Mason, but of how he was brought to be. She was a good Christian woman.

She'd just made a mistake and trusted a man she shouldn't have.

It would have been easy for Evelyn to fault her, but she knew Arabella's heart. Probably better than anyone else...

"Miss Armstrong?" a man's voice sounded, causing her to whirl to the left with a gasp. Armstrong wasn't her last name, but it certainly was Arabella's.

He was older than she expected, perhaps in his late fifties, with a bit of a weathered face. He was tan, tanner than all the white snow spilling out all around him. His eyes were blue and kind, and had little remnants of crow's feet.

"I'm Sheriff Cade McCrae," he said, touching the brim of his hat, pulling it down slightly just before his kind eyes fell to Mason.

They closed all of a sudden, and then they looked up at her. "You've brought a child," he said, clearly a bit irked.

It wasn't a question. It was a statement of dismay.

Evelyn's stomach dropped.

"Yes," she said, lifting her chin despite the trembling that had seized her entire body. "This is Mason. He is my late cousin's son." But she cleared her throat, confused. "Sorry, who did you say you were? You're not Travis Baldwin?"

He sighed. "No, ma'am, I'm here in his stead."

She laughed nervously. "Well, I'm Evelyn Rhodes, and I'm actually here in my cousin's stead. She passed away a few weeks ago now."

Sheriff McCrae took a deep breath, fiddling with the brim of his hat nervously. "Your cousin didn't have a baby..."

"Well, this is her child," Evelyn replied sternly, despite her panic. "She just must not have said she had a child. But she certainly did, and now I do."

Fear arose in her chest, and she clutched Mason tighter.

"I see. McCrae sighed. There was sympathy there. "Well, this certainly complicates things."

Her lips clattered together as she held Mason tighter, bundling the blankets and her own cloak around him. It was so incredibly cold that her cheeks and lips were going numb.

"I can work," she said desperately as Mason began to stir harder. It was only a matter of time before he started wailing. "I am an excellent seamstress. I ran my own shop back in Green River. I can sew, I can cook, I can keep house. Really, anything!" She moved closer to the man. "Whatever is needed. Please, Sheriff. I have nowhere else to go."

McCrae sighed again, and his eyes fell to the ground. For a long moment, he looked like he was about to apologize, to tell her he couldn't help her. But when he looked up at her again, he nodded. "Come on, then. Let's get you out of this wind. We'll figure something out."

"Thank you!" Relief nearly buckled her knees. "Thank you, Sheriff."

"Don't thank me yet," he said grimly, taking her bag. "Travis Baldwin is...well. He's a good man, but he's been through hell and back. I arranged this behind his back, you understand. He doesn't know you're coming and a baby...it's not goin' to go over well at first."

Evelyn's relief curdled into a fresh sort of dread. "He doesn't...?" she stammered. "Wh-what do you mean?"

McCrae shook his head. "Come on." He led her toward a wagon hitched nearby. He tossed her belongings in the back of the buckboard and helped her up onto the bench in front before climbing up beside her.

He clicked his tongue and breathed heavily, like a load had suddenly weighed him down.

"Travis lost his wife and son three years ago. House fire. Killed 'em both." His voice was flat, matter-of-fact, but Evelyn could hear the pain beneath it. Like he'd been close enough to this Travis Baldwin that he'd felt sorry for him.

"He's been living like a ghost ever since. Nobody sees him. Won't come to town, won't socialize, won't do anything but work himself near to death on that ranch of his. I thought..." He paused, snapping the reins. The horses neighed and lurched forward.. "I thought if I could just get a good woman out there, someone to bring life back to that house, he might start living again."

"But he did not agree to this," she replied slowly, horror mounting with each word. She couldn't even imagine having unexpected guests—let alone this arrangement!

"No, ma'am. He did not."

They rode quietly as he navigated through the snow. She wasn't necessarily sad for it, but it did leave her in her thoughts. It also made Mason's cries that much louder, which had become continuous now, a thin wail that cut through even the wind's howling. Evelyn tried to soothe him, but it was to no avail. After all, what comfort could she really offer? She wasn't his mother. She didn't make milk. She had no money to afford milk. She wasn't warm. She had nothing for him. Just promises she wasn't even sure she could keep much longer.

Before leaving town, McCrae stopped the wagon at the general mercantile, insisting they pick up a small tin of cow's milk. Evelyn protested weakly. She had brought milk; she had been rationing carefully. Mason was not starving, but the sheriff waved her off and paid anyway.

"Babies don't understand rationing," he'd muttered, handing the parcel up to her. "A little warm milk'll do him good for the road."

Mason had taken a few slow swallows before drifting back to sleep, his tiny body relaxing against her. That brief bit of warmth in his belly soothed them both, and she sighed, relieved.

What a kind man.

She could barely see through the storm and could only hope that the sheriff knew where he was going. Because she certainly didn't. The one thing she did know, though, was that going against the wind like this wasn't good for Mason. She turned her body to sit backwards on the bench, her back to the wind.

The cold was brutal, seeping through her cloak and dress so heavily that it practically settled in her bones, causing her to ache. McCrae hunched over as he steered his horses, his jaw clenched tightly, his breath visible.

"How much farther?" she asked, having to raise her voice to be heard over the wind and hoof sounds.

"Another mile or so. The ranch is up in the foothills. Beautiful country when you can see it."

Beautiful or not, Evelyn could only imagine what awaited them when they got there. A man who had agreed to nothing. A man who was mourning his dead wife and child. A man who, by all accounts, would want nothing to do with her or her situation.

She just hoped she could convince him otherwise. Although she wasn't sure how she was supposed to.

The absurdity of it struck her suddenly, and she might have laughed if she wasn't so close to weeping. This was all craziness! Truly, pure madness. Ridiculous. She should turn around, go back to Green River, and throw herself on someone's mercy!

You made a promise.

She was going to keep it.

The wagon lurched suddenly, and through the snow she could make out the dim shape of buildings as they came to a halt. There was a house and a barn on either side of them.

A faint light through a window showed through the gray evening. A light that looked warm and welcoming through the window. Oh, how she longed to be inside that house.

"Stay here," McCrae grunted as he threw the reins down and hopped down. "Let me go in first and talk to him."

But Evelyn shook her head.

And before he could protest, she was already climbing down, Mason clutched tightly in her arms. If anyone could plead their case, she would do it. Sheriff McCrae didn't know her. And besides that, she couldn't bear the thought of Mason catching a cold. They needed warmth, shelter, and some way to feed this child past today. If talking to this man was the only way to make that happen, that's what she would do.

She pounded her way up the porch, McCrae hot on her heels to catch up. "All right, then," he sighed, resigned. "I reckon you ought to brace yourself, though."

He pushed open the door without bothering to knock—something that would have gotten a man killed in Green River.

But she took a deep breath and walked in, grateful for the sudden heat in the room.

Two men looked up from where they sat near the fire. The older one, gray-haired and gaunt, stared at her and Sheriff McCrae with nothing if not open hostility. But it was the younger man who caught her attention. He stood up slowly from his chair, his eyes wide.

He had broad shoulders and muscular arms, a body built for hard labor. His hair was sandy brown, a little long, like he hadn't had it trimmed in some time, and his eyes were dark. He looked like a man who might have been very handsome with a little more care. His eyes moved from her face to Mason, who was shrieking now, fussy from the long journey. Pain flashed over the man's face, a pain so raw she took a step back.

"Travis," McCrae began, so nervously that even Evelyn heard it. "This is Miss Evelyn Rhodes. She's come from Green River to—"

"What is this, Cade?" His hands gripped into fists. He was looking straight at the sheriff, no longer paying any attention to Evelyn or Mason. "What have you done?"

"Now, Travis, just hear me out—"

"You brought a woman here?" He tossed his hands in the air, taking a couple of steps forward. "To my house? After I told you not to? You did this after being told I didn't want anybody here?" Travis Baldwin's voice rose with each word he spat out. "Have you lost your mind?"

"You need help," McCrae said firmly. "You can't keep living like this. Your father would be ashamed."

"Don't you dare!" he yelled, striding toward them. "Don't you dare bring my father into this."

The older man by the fire stood now, his face twisted with anger. "This is an outrage, McCrae. You had no right. No right at all. This is Travis's house, not yours! And this woman ain't his wife!"

"She's gone!" McCrae shot back. "And the two of you sit here and wallow every day!"

"Please," she began tentatively, at first. "Please, everyone, just lower your voices."

But her words had no effect. She was only something standing in the room. No different than the chair or the fireplace. Even Mason's cries had faded into the background.

But on that, something within her snapped.

"Enough!" she shouted, stamping her feet, and startling even Mason into momentary quiet. She turned to face Travis Baldwin directly, drawing herself up to her full height—which, she was mortifyingly aware, still only brought her to his shoulder. "I understand this is not what you wanted. I understand that Sheriff McCrae has meddled where he had no business meddling. But here I am, and here is this child, and we have nowhere else to go. You might not have been the one that sent for us, but someone has."

Travis stared at her, his dark eyes unreadable. Distant.

"I am not asking for charity," she continued, her voice shaky. "I can earn my keep. Look around you." She gestured at the cluttered, neglected room that they were standing in. "Your house is in shambles. I can clean it for you. When did you last have a proper meal? I can cook. Those pants there, with the rips in the knees? I can mend them."

"That is none of your business," Travis growled, but she went on.

"I can be your housekeeper. I can cook, clean, organize, anything you need. In exchange, you provide room and board for myself and this child until such time as I can secure other employment." She spoke with a lot more confidence than she had, but she had no other choice. "I ran a successful business for four years, Mr. Baldwin. I am organized, capable, and hardworking. You will not find better help, I promise you that."

She forced herself not to look away when he stared at her, though her heart was pounding so hard she feared it might burst from her chest. She had never had a confrontation like this in her entire life. Never had a confrontation at all before Arabella passed away. The first one was with her uncle, and she'd given in to his demands.

This, though, seemed different.

Just like she was looking out for Arabella with her uncle, she was looking out for Mason now. She had to give him everything he deserved. To fight for him and give him a family. To fight for herself.

"The baby," the older man huffed from beside the fire. "We don't want a squalling infant here."

"Royce is right," Travis said, his voice cold. "There is no place here for a woman and her child."

"He is not my child," Evelyn found herself muttering, as if it was any of their business. "He is my cousin's son. She died three weeks ago. Named me as his guardian. I have no one else, Mr. Baldwin. Neither does he."

The man opened his mouth to speak, but then immediately closed it again. His eyes scanned from Evelyn to McCrae and back again. There was something there. Was it sympathy? Understanding? But it was gone before she could even remotely identify it, replaced by coldness once more.

"With this weather, they can't leave tonight anyway," McCrae interjected. "For God's sake, Travis. Let them stay until the storm passes. Then we'll work something out."

Travis's jaw clenched, the muscle jumping beneath his skin. He looked at Mason. For a moment, Evelyn thought he might refuse to help. She thought he might order McCrae to take her back out into the cold, back to town, and put her on another train she couldn't afford.

But then he exhaled, long and slow.

"Fine. Until the weather clears. But that is all, Cade. Do you understand? When this storm breaks, you will find them another place to stay. You sent for them. It's your responsibility."

It wasn't exactly acceptance. But it was enough for now. A warm place. Maybe even some food.

"Thank you," Evelyn whispered, and she felt her legs beginning to shake with relief and exhaustion. "Thank you, Mr. Baldwin."

He didn't seem to acknowledge her gratitude. For which she couldn't exactly blame him, having things sprung on him like this. He turned and walked out of the room, his footsteps heavy on the wooden floor. A door slammed somewhere in the house, and Evelyn flinched.

"Well," McCrae said after a moment, rubbing his face with one hand. "That went about as well as I expected."

The older man, the man Mr. Baldwin had just called Royce, glared at Evelyn before stalking off toward the back of the house.

A door slammed again, and she winced at the sound.

"Mr. McCrae, could I change him?" she asked. "I don't intend to be rude, but he's eaten and now needs to be changed…"

The sheriff nodded and turned to walk toward the back of the house. "Go ahead. You ain't bothering nothin'."

Evelyn stood alone in the center of the cluttered room with Mason crying in her arms, snow melting off of her boots into puddles around her feet. Part of her felt guilty, tracking all the snow in, but as she looked around, she knew it didn't matter.

She had bought herself time. A few days, perhaps, to prove her worth. To find some way to convince Travis Baldwin that she and Mason belonged here. That they belonged…somewhere.

She had made a promise to Arabella. She couldn't let her down. She wouldn't. She was going to make this happen. But first, she needed to change this baby.

Chapter Two

Evanston, Wyoming — 1872

"What in tarnation was he thinkin'!" Travis muttered.

SLAM!

He shut the barn door behind him with enough force to rattle the hinges, then stood for a moment in the relative quiet, his breath coming hard and fast. He needed to calm down. But he wasn't sure he could. He wasn't even sure he could control his breathing, let alone the anger that poured through his entire body. It even hurt to breathe, the cold biting at his lungs, but still his breath was ragged and hard like a raging bull.

The sound of that baby had gotten to him.

He pressed his palms against his eyes, trying to block out the memory, but it was practically useless. That doggone infant's wails had pierced Chap, tearing open wounds he had thought had scarred over by now, at least enough that he wouldn't be in full panic. Three years. Three years of trying to drown out other people.

And Cade had the gall to bring a woman *and a baby* right up to his door.

A low whine drew his attention downward. Max, his loyal white and black shepherd dog, sat at his feet, dark brown eyes fixed on Travis, head cocked to the side. Travis reached down absently to scratch behind the dog's ears.

"What has he done, Max?" Travis muttered. "What in God's name has that meddling old fool done?"

Max had no answer. He just panted, his tongue out, happy to be given attention. Travis sighed and bent down to scruff Max's ears before moving deeper into the barn, the dog on his heels.

The horses nickered softly as he pushed his way into one of the stalls. These animals were the only things keeping his sanity. This is where he had purpose. These animals depended on him. Trusted him. And he might have failed himself, but he wouldn't fail them.

Not like he had failed Bonnie and Troy.

He grabbed a brush on the top of the railing and looked at Butterscotch, one of his mares that needed a bit of a brush down. "Hey, ol' girl," he said to her, running his hands over her flank.

Suddenly, the door to the barn burst open, and a rush of ice-cold wind flooded into the doorway of the barn.

"What in the world!"

When he turned, another man was standing in the doorway, dusting his shoulders and hat off.

Barrett Lawson was his foreman, a man of thirty-five, and strong as a mule. He was quiet but competent. In truth, he'd become almost what Travis might consider a friend.

"I saw McCrae's wagon," Barrett said. "Heard there was some commotion up at the house."

Travis returned his attention to the mare, his jaw tight. "Cade brought a woman here. And a baby. Like this is some sort of charity…"

Barrett cleared his throat. "I see."

"Do you?" Travis's hands stilled on the brush because it didn't sound like that, from where he was standing. "Do you see how he had no right? How he had no business interfering in my life?"

There was something about the way Barrett looked that Travis shot him a look of warning. *Careful.*

"I see a man trying to help a friend," Lawson muttered. "In his own bull-headed way, anyway."

Travis threw the brush down, startling the mare—and even Max, who whined softly.

"Help? He calls this help? Bringing strangers to my house, expecting me to...to...." He couldn't even dare finish the sentence. Expecting him to what? Take on a wife? Raise another man's child? Replace Bonnie and Troy as if they had never existed? He wouldn't do that. Not now, not ever.

"What did you tell them?"

"I told them they could stay until the storm breaks. Then Cade will find them some other place." Travis grabbed the brush up once more and did his best to speak without cussing. "I don't want anything to do with it, or *them.*"

Lawson leaned against the nearest stall door. "The woman must be desperate to come all this way in the middle of a storm like this. Must not have anywhere to go."

"Her havin' nowhere to go is not my concern."

"And that baby?"

Travis's hands clenched on the brush. "Especially not the baby. It ain't my baby. Just another bastard—"

"Travis!"

"No." The word came out harsh, final. "I ain't gonna talk about it anymore. I've been fair enough! I let them stay because it's stormin'. I ain't a monster and couldn't live with myself if I forced a woman and a baby out in the middle of a blizzard, but that's the extent of my charity. When that storm breaks, they are out of here!"

Lawson hung his head, shaking it with disapproval. "You may not want a wife, that's fine, but I think you should give the woman a chance, and McCrae a chance at helping you out a little around here. It ain't a secret you and Royce have a tough time." When Travis didn't say anything else, Lawson continued. "Y'all can't hide out here forever."

"I am not hiding." But even as he said it, he knew it for the lie it was. This ranch had become a great excuse. A great refuge. But it was also the only thing he knew. "I'm surviving, Lawson. And this ranch is all I can manage to do right now."

"Is it?" Lawson pushed away from the stall door and stuck his hands in his pockets. "Because you got me and Hartwell, both, and I got a whole crew of ranch men coming in and out of here. You ain't gotta do too much here lately. So, is it all you can handle, or are you just afraid of handling much more?"

Anger flared hot in Travis's chest. He gripped the brush at his side so tight it might snap. "Afraid of what?"

"Of gettin' out of this place for a little bit. Of having fun without them..."

Travis growled. "Don't." He liked Lawson, but he didn't take kindly to someone trying to push his buttons. Especially when it came to his wife and son. "Don't do it."

"You gotta let someone in sometime, pal," he said. "Otherwise, you're just a coward."

"You don't know what you're talkin' about."

"Oh, yeah?" Lawson met his gaze squarely, daringly, and Travis had the uneasy feeling these men had been talking about him behind his back or something. Planning something. "I know what it is to lose someone. Maybe not the way you did, but I know loss. And I know that shutting yourself away from the world ain't the way, so it may be worth it to just give somethin' else a shot."

Travis wanted to start swinging. It was what he was good at. Did everyone have to poke the bear today? Travis and Cade had been friends for his entire life, Lawson had been a good worker and a nice enough guy, but both of them were crossing the line.

His fists pumped at his side, his teeth gritted.

But he couldn't hit Lawson.

This man had stood by him during the worst part of his grief, and he never abandoned him or even judged him. Even when he couldn't pay him a decent wage. He owed this man. He owed both him and Cade, truth be told.

He couldn't explain what was happening to him. The fury he felt. The pain. Travis wasn't sure he could ever explain, or even put into words, the terrible ache that had climbed up in him the moment he saw that baby.

All he could think about was Troy. His first cry. His tiny little fingers wrapped around his thumb, the small little weight in his arms.

And then the sound of him and Bonnie screaming...

It was a pain so fierce that he nearly crumpled over just thinking about it. His throat got tight, tears burned the brims of his eyelids. He turned away and pressed his forehead against the mare's flank.

"I can't stop thinkin' about it, and what I should have done—"

"It wasn't your fault," Lawson said.

Travis ignored him.

"It wasn't," his friend said again.

"You all can say that all day, every day, but if I had been here..." he started, but Lawson cut him off.

"You would have died, too." He found his friend's hand on his shoulder. "And you know that's the God's honest truth. The fire spread too fast. There was nothing anyone could have done."

Travis shook his head. He knew he could have done something.

He would have figured out a way.

The guilt ate at him. It was too familiar these days. Too much a part of him. He'd never stop feeling guilty about what happened. Without it, what was he? Nothing. Not anymore, anyway.

He wasn't a father. He wasn't a husband. He was just a man in an empty house, mourning everything he'd lost.

"Give the woman a chance," Lawson said in a breath when Travis didn't turn toward him or say anything else. "If not to give yourself a break, to at least help someone else."

"I have already told her she can stay until the storm passes," he grumbled. "That's help enough."

"You know that ain't enough."

Travis scowled and pulled his shoulder away from his friend's grip, only to catch another sigh. When he turned to the man, Barrett tipped his hat.

"I'll leave you to it. Try not to freeze to death out here, will ya?"

And with that, he turned around and headed back out into the cold.

He stayed out in the barn for another hour or so, trying to busy himself until he was clear enough to go back in and talk to the woman. He groomed horses that didn't really need grooming, checked tack that really didn't need to be checked, and unstacked and restacked hay that didn't need doing, either.

But eventually it was cold, and he was ready for a fire. He had half-hoped that Cade had taken the woman and child back to town despite the storm. His wagon had gone, after all.

But when he peeked in the window, he saw her there on the rocking chair. Shaking his head, he rounded up the steps of the front porch and pulled open the door, stomping the snow off his boots before walking over the threshold. He was hoping he could slip past to his room without anyone noticing or talking to him. But sure enough, they were all still in the sitting room.

That baby had finally stopped crying, at least, and the woman sat on the rocking chair next to the fire, the infant cradled in her arms. She had removed her cloak and bonnet, revealing dark brown hair pinned back in a simple style, and a face that was pale with exhaustion.

She was a lovely woman. Beautiful. Young. Petite, with kind blue eyes. Truly pretty. But it was her expression that caught him the most. It was fierce. Strong. The devotion she had for a child that wasn't hers was admirable. And the look of love as she looked down at the sleeping child was apparent. She looked at that baby as if he was the most precious thing in the entire world.

Travis was taken by her beauty. He was angry with himself for even the thought, but he wasn't blind. This woman was unmistakably beautiful, and she was even more beautiful when she looked at the boy. It was exactly how Bonnie used to look at Troy.

Travis wasn't sure he'd ever felt a pain quite like the one he'd felt when he lost them until now—seeing this happening in his house. Another woman. Another baby...

He must have made some sort of sound, because abruptly, the woman's head snapped up, her eyes wide and her mouth open.

"Mr. Baldwin," she gasped quietly, clearly trying not to wake the baby. "You startled me."

"Where is Cade?" He already knew he had gone, but he truly didn't know what else to say.

"He left some time ago. He said the storm was easing enough that he could make it back to town,"—she shifted the baby slightly—"but asked that we stay here. We almost didn't make it up this far. It was too cold for him."

Travis nodded, finding his gaze drawn against his will to the baby boy's face. So small. So fragile.

"He said he would come back in a few days to take us back."

Travis grunted, forcing his eyes to look away. "You should take the child down the hall to that back bedroom. It's not prepared or anything, but you'll find a few blankets in the chest at the foot of the bed and"—he cleared his throat—"an old bassinet in the corner of the room."

It was the one they'd gotten from Royce when Troy was first born. It was a piece of junk, but it had sentimental value. It had been Royce's when he was a boy. He'd kept it for Bonnie when she was a child, and it became Troy's. Until Travis had carved him a special crib when he'd gotten a little big for the bassinet. But surely it would suffice for such a small baby for a few days.

"Thank you." She rose carefully from her chair. She rested the baby against her shoulder, looking at Travis through heavy-lidded eyes. "Mr. Baldwin, I want you to know—"

"No." That was all he could say. He didn't want to hear a thank-you. Instead, he moved past her toward his room, needing distance, needing walls between himself and this woman and her baby. "Good night, Miss Rhodes."

He didn't wait for her response, but he felt her eyes on him the entire length of the hallway. It wasn't until he closed his door that he was able to breathe. He shut his eyes and leaned against the door, his breath ragged, his chest heavy.

This was a mistake. Having them here was a terrible mistake. He could already feel himself unnerved by their presence. He should have had McCrae take them back to town. Or to a neighbor.

Anywhere but here.

He shook his head. It would be a long few days until they left. But he would just have to get through it. He'd been through worse. He could bear a couple of guests for a few days.

Chapter Three

She groaned as soon as the light hit her eyelids. She wasn't ready to be awake. She was tired. More than tired. More than exhausted, even if the sleep she'd gotten in that bed was the best one she'd had since she left home.

She lay perfectly still beneath the thin blanket she had found in the chest, trying to orient herself. She'd barely remembered where she was at first, but as soon as she felt that soft blanket, she remembered how surprised she was to find it in the dusty old chest.

Sitting up, she looked around the room. It was small and sparse. Nothing but a narrow bed, a washstand, and a single chair in the corner with an old metal bassinet next to it. It was warm, though.

Well, maybe "warm" was overstating the case. It was at the end of the hallway, the room furthest away from the fireplace, so it had a chill. But with the blankets on the bed, it had been comfortable enough.

Then Mason stirred, causing her to move faster. Slinging her legs over the side of the bed, ignoring the loud creak as her weight shifted, she hopped to the chill wooden floor and traipsed across the room to the bassinet. The boy's face was pinched and red, his little fists waving in agitation. She knew that look. He would be screaming any second, ready for milk she barely had. She knew she'd have to ask for more soon. From men who clearly didn't want her there.

"Shhh," she whispered, lifting him up and holding him against her bosom, hoping to soothe him. "Please, just a little longer. Let me think."

But he was far beyond soothing. His whimpers escalated to full-throated wails that seemed to roar through her entire body and bounce off the walls. She tried bouncing him, rocking him, doing anything she could to make those sounds stop. But nothing helped.

He was hungry, and he wanted the rest of the milk that she had.

She couldn't blame him. By the way he'd taken the last bottle, she knew she was being a little too stingy with the rations. He'd gulped it down so frantically she was afraid he would make himself sick. He'd been that hungry. Fortunately, he hadn't made himself sick. But the milk was gone.

She thanked her lucky stars that she at least got a full night's sleep after he'd drank himself full. But she had no idea where she might find more.

She needed to get downstairs. Surely there was a cow or a goat on the property somewhere. She really knew next to nothing of ranching, but every farm had some source of milk, did it not? She would have to ask Mr. Baldwin, though the thought of it made her stomach clench with nerves.

He wasn't the most gracious man she'd ever met. Not that she blamed him, given the circumstances. But still, he didn't incite comfort. He had looked at her and Mason with barely controlled fury, anger that stemmed from pain. Sheriff McCrae had told her about the fire. About his wife and his son.

What had she been thinking, coming here? What had McCrae been thinking, bringing her here? It was obvious there was too much hurt here. Not just on his part, but on the part of the man he called Royce, too.

McCrae had told her a bit about him as well when he had helped her get warm upon their arrival. Royce Hartwell. Travis Baldwin's father-in-law. The father to his late wife.

It was no wonder both men were so put off with her arrival. She didn't necessarily blame them, but she didn't know what else to do. She knew only one thing: Mason needed milk.

His cries intensified, cutting off her spiraling thoughts. She needed to act, not wallow in her discomfort or her nerves. They'd allowed her to stay. Surely, they would understand the boy would need to eat!

"Stop that infernal noise!" Royce shouted from outside the room, banging loudly on the door, the sound only causing Mason to scream louder from fear. Royce appeared, his gaunt face twisted with fury. "I can't sleep, I can't think, I can't have a doggone moment's peace with that baby screeching!"

"He's hungry," Evelyn said, her voice shaking. "He is an infant. He can't help—"

"Then you should have thought of that before you came here." Royce stepped into the barn, pointing an accusatory finger at her. "We didn't ask you here. And as far as I'm concerned, you have no business here!"

Evelyn dressed as quickly as she could manage while holding Mason, pulling on the same wrinkled traveling dress she had worn yesterday. There was no time for vanity, no time even to properly pin up her hair. She twisted it into a loose knot at the nape of her neck and secured it with trembling fingers, then wrapped the baby in the thin blanket and hurried from the room.

The house was silent as she practically tiptoed down the hall, hoping not to disturb either of the men again. Although that was going to be for naught if Mason woke himself back up.

The main sitting room looked even more a mess in daylight. There were crates of booze, dirt clumps from boots, scattered papers, and leaves on the tables and floor. And dust was thick on every surface. How long had these men been living like this? How had they not gotten sick in such a squalor?

But she had no time to wonder about it now. She made her way to what she hoped was the kitchen, as it was usually in the back of a home. And when she did, she gasped, finding it in much the same state as the rest of the house. Only...worse.

Instead of just clutter–which there was plenty of—there was also filth. Unwashed pots. Plates. Half-eaten loaves of bread sat uncovered, hard as rocks. She stood in the middle of the room, Mason screaming wildly against her shoulder. Suddenly, she felt a deep, despairing unease fall over her.

How was she supposed to manage this? How was she supposed to clean and whip this household into shape, care for a baby, and somehow convince these men that she deserved to stay?

You promised Arabella.

The thought calmed her, at least for a moment. She took a deep breath and held it, deliberately, before letting it fall away. She hadn't come this far to give up now. One step at a time.

She needed to find milk for Mason, and once he was full, he would sleep a bit more, and she could start putting this house in order. Just one step at a time. And, hopefully, Mr. Baldwin could see her usefulness. Maybe he would let her stay.

She strapped Mason against her chest using a long strip of cloth she had fashioned into a sling, leaving her hands free. His cries were muffled slightly against her body, but still loud enough to wake the dead. She only hoped the men had both gone outside to work the ranch by now. She'd heard loud footsteps just moments ago, followed by slamming doors.

With any luck, they were busy enough that she could find something and not have to ask either of them for help. She needed to get to the barn. Surely there was something in there that had milk. Moving through the kitchen, she found the back door and pushed it open, gasping as soon as the cold air hit her.

Evelyn wrapped her cloak more tightly around herself and Mason, then stepped out into the snow. It came up to her shins immediately, soaking through her thin boots. She bit back a desire to cry out at the cold and pressed forward, each step more difficult than the last as she trudged through the thick white blanket.

She heaved open the barn door when she got to it, welcoming the warmth and the dryness it offered. It wasn't exactly toasty like the house, but it was certainly more comfortable than that biting wind outside.

The smell of hay filled her nostrils, and the sound of horses' snorts immediately greeted her.

"Hello," she called out uncertainly. "Is anyone here?"

No answer.

Evelyn moved deeper into the barn, searching for any sign of a cow or goat. Something that gave milk.

And then—there it was.

One singular goat lying in the straw at the end, past the horses.

"Oh, thank God," she whispered, hurrying over, holding Mason tight with one arm, and her skirt with the other. The goat raised its head when she opened up the stall and made a sound, but luckily, stayed still.

She had no idea how to even do this. She had never milked a goat before. But McCrae had to get the milk from somewhere, right?

And how difficult could it be?

She found a small stool and a pail nearby, which only meant one thing: someone was milking her!

She reached out to grasp the goat's teat, and the animal immediately kicked. "Ow!" she groaned as soon as its hoof caught her shin. She partially fell backward—and that did it.

Mason ripped awake, his throat gutting screams wailing out new pitches of distress she hadn't heard yet. She was just grateful the goat hadn't kicked him.

Tears pricked at Evelyn's eyes. She was cold, exhausted, desperate, and now bruised. The goat glared at her balefully, as if personally offended. Maybe it was harder than it looked. Maybe she had no idea what she was doing, but she would have to figure it out.

She couldn't let the boy starve, and if he kept crying like this, the men would surely kick them out in the cold.

"Please," Evelyn cried out desperately to the animal as if she could somehow understand her. "Please, I just need a little milk. For the baby."

"What in God's name are you doing?"

Evelyn's head snapped up. And there he was, Travis Baldwin. He stood in the doorway of the barn, silhouetted against the gray morning light. She hadn't even heard him come in; she'd been so upset. Her teeth began to clatter together from the cold.

She scrambled to her feet, wincing as her bruised shin protested. "I was trying to milk the goat. The baby needs—"

"That goat is twenty years old and hasn't given milk in five years." His voice was nonchalant. "She is practically a pet at this point."

Evelyn felt something inside her crack. "Then what am I supposed to do?" The words came out sharper than she intended, edged with panic and exhaustion. "Sheriff McCrae got milk from somewhere yesterday, but he's had nothing since this morning. He is going to starve if I cannot find—"

He sighed, almost in a growl. She wanted to slap him. How dare he treat Mason like some sort of a burden. He was a baby! A perfect, beautiful child.

"Then you should have—"

"What?" she demanded, cutting him off, standing up, one arm looped around Mason and one balled in a fist. "What should I have done, Mr. Baldwin? Let my cousin's child die? Abandon him to the mercy of strangers? She died in my arms, begging me to protect him. What would you have had me do?

"I was not trying to inconvenience you when I came here," she surged on, before he could even answer. "I wasn't trying to intrude on your grief or force myself into your life. I thought you had an arrangement with my cousin!" She stopped, swallowing hard. "I thought your sheriff had told you. I thought I would be a fine replacement to come in my cousin's stead!

"So I am sorry. You don't know how sorry. I didn't know that you weren't aware, and truthfully, sir, I have no idea what else to do. He's going to die if I don't give him enough food, Mr. Baldwin. Do you understand? This child is going to die if I can't find some way to feed him."

The words hung in the cold air of the barn. Mason's cries had weakened to pitiful whimpers. She knew she could give him just a bit of the little bit of milk she had left, but when would they get more?

She had to ration. She couldn't bear the thought of not having enough later.

Travis stared at her, his jaw clenching and unclenching. And then, he sighed heavily and abruptly turned on his heel and strode out of the barn.

She made way to follow him, to confront him even further, but he stopped her instead

"Get back in the house!"

It wasn't a request. It was an order. And, the fact was, she had no other choice.

With that, he disappeared from view.

Chapter Four

Evelyn stood in the barn for a moment after Travis walked away, Mason's whimpers the only sound besides her own ragged breathing. At first, she wondered if she could imagine someone being as hostile as Travis Baldwin and Royce Hartwell—but then again, she knew her uncle.

She couldn't stay here forever. The cold was seeping through her cloak, and Mason needed warmth, even if she couldn't get milk for him right now. With trembling legs, she hurried back to the house. Back to the warmth.

Inside, she tried to busy herself with the kitchen. Tried to do something, anything, to start making things better. No doubt, it was a feeble attempt. She had a vague hope that maybe if they saw her worth, they'd want to help Mason.

But she couldn't focus. She couldn't do much of anything. Her hands shook too badly to properly grip the dishes, and when he woke up, Mason's cries made it impossible to concentrate.

"I'm sorry," she whispered against his soft hair. "I'm so sorry, sweet boy. I'm trying. I promise I'm trying."

She'd attempted to fill his bottle with water, but he turned his face away. She wished she could make him understand that the milk had to last just a bit until she figured something out. She wished she could help him understand that he just needed to sleep for a while, and he could have more when he woke up.

But she couldn't. And she shouldn't have expected to.

With a defeated cry, she slid down the kitchen door and collapsed on the floor in sobs.

Mason had already cried himself back to sleep, and she only wished she could do the same. And maybe she did, because as soon as she laid her head back, she heard a faint knock at the door behind her. When she stood up, she saw Travis Baldwin retreating down the stairs.

All she saw was the back of his head as he stomped back toward the barn. What had he wanted? Why had he knocked? It was his home, after all.

But something caught her attention through the glass. Steam.

Craning her neck, she caught glimpse of a metal pail on the small porch outside. What in the world—?

She flung the door open, ignoring the bite of cold, and there it was!

Milk. Fresh milk!

She grabbed it quickly and fixed the bottle as fast as she could. Mason latched onto the bottle immediately with a desperate hunger that saddened her. But as he took it, and small grunts and groans left his little body, she felt herself relax.

She watched him, tears still streaming down her cold-chapped face. "We're going to be all right," she whispered, laying a tender kiss on his forehead. They would survive. Somehow, some way, they would survive this.

She wasn't exactly sure how, yet. She knew the truth. Travis Baldwin had helped them out of pure obligation, and possibly even pity. Not genuine kindness. And definitely not caring. She knew that when the storm passed, he would want them out. But for now, Mason had food. And they were warm. That would have to be enough.

***

A knock at the door sounded—another knock, firmer this time. It was followed by a woman's voice calling out, "Hello? Miss Rhodes?"

Evelyn stumbled to her feet, nearly tripping over her skirts in her haste. She looked terrible; she knew she did. She'd been on her hands and knees scrubbing floors all morning and tending to a baby who was catching up on food.

And she was almost out, all over again. But who knew she was here?

She hurried to the door, her hair falling from its pins, face blotchy from crying and exhaustion, dress rumpled and stained with God-knew-what. But she didn't care. Someone was here, and they needed refuge from the cold outside.

She wrenched open the door.

A middle-aged woman stood on the porch, bundled in a heavy cloak, her round face red and chapped from the wind. But it was what she held that made Evelyn's breath catch. A rope, at the end of which stood a goat, its udder so big it nearly dragged the ground.

"Miss Rhodes?" the woman asked, breathily, her voice warm. Evelyn nodded. The woman smiled wide and stuck out her hand. "I'm Marigold Price. I own the dressmaking shop in town, and my husband is a rancher just down the way there. I was told you might be in need of a good milking goat for an infant?"

Evelyn found herself trying to speak, but no words came out. Instead, she burst into tears.

"Oh, my dear," Marigold soothed.

Quickly, she tied the goat to the porch railing and darted inside, but not without pulling Evelyn into the warmest embrace she'd had in years. "There now, there now. Let it out. You've been carrying too much, haven't you?"

Evelyn found herself coming completely unwrapped, sobbing against this wonderful stranger's shoulder. Suddenly it felt like all of her fear and exhaustion were washing away, by way of tears—soaking through this poor woman's cloak. But Marigold gave no appearance of caring about that, simply held her, one hand rubbing soothing circles on her back, and crooned to her like a child.

"Bless your heart," the woman said against Evelyn's hair. "Let's get you fixed up."

"I—I can't—Mason needs—" Evelyn stammered.

"Hush, now. I know what he needs, and we're going to fix it right now." Marigold pulled back. "Let's go get the baby."

Evelyn led Marigold to him, sleeping in his bassinet. "He did eat earlier. Some milk Mr. Baldwin had brought."

"Yes, yes," Marigold said. "He walked over earlier and got it. All his cows were sold, so he doesn't have any cow's milk, and his goat is a bit too old to give any."

She watched as the woman cradled Mason against her bosom. For a moment, she worried because his cries intensified, but Marigold didn't waver. And it was in that confidence that the baby settled.

"Oh, you poor little lamb," the older woman cooed, swaying gently. "You're famished, aren't you? We'll fix that. Yes, we will."

She handed Mason back to Evelyn and moved with surprising speed for a woman of her robust size. "You sit right there and hold him. I'll be back in just a moment."

Marigold disappeared out of the room, down the hall, and she heard the front door open and close again. Evelyn could hear her outside of her window. Just barely. She was talking softly to what Evelyn could only assume was the goat.

Just a few moments later, she was back, with a pail of milk. "Let's boil a bit of this for him," she said sweetly.

Evelyn grinned, grateful, following the woman back to the kitchen.

"Do you have a pot? And a bottle?" Marigold asked.

"I—yes," Evelyn replied. She'd used one earlier that morning and last night from Sheriff McCrae. "The pot is there, and I have a bottle right over there." She pointed to it on the cluttered kitchen table.

Marigold clicked her tongue. "These men should be grateful you're here. This place needs a good cleaning, but I can tell you've already started." She gestured to the floors. Evelyn nodded.

"I've just done the floors. Mason was full enough from what Mr. Baldwin brought over, so he slept for a couple of hours."

Before she knew it, Marigold was testing the milk's temperature on her wrist. "That's perfect," she said, nodding and smiling. "There we are." She handed the bottle to Evelyn. "Go ahead, feed that precious boy. He's waited long enough."

Evelyn's hands shook as she brought the bottle to Mason's lips. He began drinking so frantically that Evelyn worried he might choke.

"Gently now," Marigold said, settling into a chair beside them. "He'll make himself sick if he drinks too fast. Pull that bottle away for just a second, let him catch his breath."

Evelyn did as instructed, and Mason immediately began to wail in protest. But Marigold was right; when she put the bottle back up to his mouth, he drank more slowly, and he began to relax.

"There's my good boy," Evelyn whispered, tears still streaming down her face. Tears of sheer relief. "That's it, sweet one. Drink. You're going to be all right. You're going to be all right." He was going to have milk for more than just a meal.

She looked up at the older woman, who was watching them with soft eyes. "I don't know how to thank you. You've saved his life. You've—" She knew she was about to start crying all over again. "I thought I was going to lose him. I thought I'd failed Arabella."

"Who is Arabella?" Marigold asked gently.

And somehow, with Mason drinking peacefully in her arms and this kind woman sitting beside her, Evelyn found herself telling the whole story as if this was a friend she'd known forever.

She told her about her beloved cousin. The pregnancy that led to her being cast out by her own father. She told her of Arabella living with her while she was pregnant, caring for her through childbirth. And then about the illness that took her away just a short couple of months later.

"She made me promise," Evelyn whispered. "Made me swear I would protect Mason, no matter what. I—" She sighed, nervously picking at her fingers. "I'm not so sure I made the right choice to give up my family's shop, but I did so she could get a proper burial next to her mother. It's what she wanted. It's what her mother wanted. But my uncle wouldn't have it unless I gave my shop. And because I'd given up my entire livelihood, I decided to come here in Arabella's stead. She'd been corresponding with Sheriff McCrae to come here for Mr. Baldwin."

The woman sat there, openly astonished. Evelyn took the moment to swallow hard and take a breath. "Now I'm here with a man who hates the sight of us, in a house where we're clearly not wanted, with a baby I can barely keep alive. And I don't know what to do. I don't know where else to go. I tried to feed him however I could, but ran out of money quick. I even tried to feed him myself." She flushed red hot. "I'd heard that sometimes women could, if the baby suckled enough, even if they hadn't given birth. But nothing happened. I felt so useless, so—"

"Stop that right now." Marigold's voice was firm but kind. "It doesn't happen often, dear. Very rarely, in fact. It's not your fault. None of this is your fault."

The words seemed to slap Evelyn in the face. Abruptly, she took a shaky breath. She hadn't realized how much guilt she'd been carrying. Guilt for not being able to feed Mason herself, and even guilt for coming here and disrupting Travis Baldwin's life.

Guilt for not being enough. For anyone.

"Thank you," she whispered to this woman she barely knew, yet felt safe with. "For saying that. For the goat. For everything."

Mason had already practically finished the bottle. He was blinking drowsily, his small body finally completely relaxed. And now, for the first time in days, Evelyn relaxed too. Because now she knew there would be future meals coming.

She pulled him away gently, and he gave a satisfied sigh before his eyes drifted closed. It warmed her heart so much she could barely stand it.

"Oh, look at him," Marigold said softly, her eyes welling up with tears. "Poor little lamb was just so hungry. He'll sleep well now, with a full belly. And there's going to be plenty more when he wakes up."

Evelyn held Mason close, breathing in his sweet baby smell, feeling his warmth against her chest. He was going to be all right. *They* were going to be all right. But then it hit her—

"The goat," she said suddenly. "Mrs. Price, I can't possibly afford..."

"It's a gift, dear," Marigold said, cutting her off with a wave of the hand. "Or a loan, if that makes you feel better. I have three goats, and this one just weaned her kid. She needs milking regularly anyway, and I'm getting too old to manage all of them myself. Husband doesn't like goats." Marigold smiled at her. "You'd be doing me a favor, really."

Evelyn didn't believe it for a second. She knew it was a kindness disguised as practicality, but she was too grateful to argue. "I'll take good care of her. I promise. And I'll learn to milk her properly."

"I'll show you before I leave. It's not difficult once you know the trick." Marigold stood, brushing off her skirts.

Before Evelyn could ask what she meant, the back door opened, and Royce walked in, his boots shuffling dirty snow all over the freshly scrubbed floors. Evelyn forced herself to calm, counting to ten, and took a deep breath. He stopped short when he saw Marigold, and Evelyn watched in amazement as his entire demeanor changed.

The harsh, angry lines of his face immediately softened, and his broad, tense shoulders relaxed. He even managed something that might have been a smile as he cleared his throat.

"Mrs. Price," he said, his voice gentler than Evelyn had heard it so far. "What a pleasant surprise. I didn't know you were visiting." He pulled his hat off and raked his fingers through his hair.

"Mr. Hartwell." Marigold's greeting was warm but measured. "I've just brought Miss Rhodes a milking goat for the baby. The poor dear was quite desperate."

"I see, I see," Royce's eyes flicked to Evelyn, then away all over again. "That was kind of you."

"How have you been keeping?" Marigold asked, taking a couple of familiar steps toward him. "I haven't seen you in town for some time."

"Well enough," he said, nodding. "The ranch keeps us busy." He moved further into the room, and Evelyn noticed he actually looked… normal. Almost pleasant. Nothing like the hostile, bitter man who had been making snide comments since she'd gotten there.

"I should show you how to milk the goat before I head back home," Marigold said, shifting her attention from Royce to Evelyn. "The snow is letting up a lot, but I still don't want to travel after dark." She smiled at Royce politely. "Miss Rhodes seems to have been through a terrible ordeal. Lost her cousin, gave up everything to care for that baby. She's a good, strong woman doing her best, but it's so good of you and Travis to open your home up to her."

Evelyn smirked. She knew what Marigold was doing, and she loved her for it.

Marigold patted Royce on the forearm, her hand lingering there for a brief moment. "I trust you and Travis will treat her with the kindness she deserves."

It was said gently, but there was steel beneath the warmth that seemed to make him look almost—ashamed? Evelyn hid a smile, knowing that had been exactly Marigold's intention.

"Of course," he mumbled with a sort of grunt. "We'll... we'll do right by her."

Marigold smiled at him wide. Beamed, actually. "I knew I could count on you. You're a good man, Royce Hartwell, even when you forget. You always have been." She tapped him a couple of times again on the arm, her lips smiling so hard large dimples showed in her rounded cheeks. "My husband always said that you and he were the best of friends, and he didn't like anyone. I know you got a heart of gold in there somewhere." And just like that, she stepped away and her eyes found Evelyn again.

"Come along, dear," she said in a sing-song voice. "Put that baby down and come outside with me."

And so she did. Evelyn trekked into the bedroom, put Mason down in the old metal bassinet, and walked back out. Royce had wandered off by the time she got back to Marigold, and she found herself grinning back at the older woman.

"Let's go do this," she whispered, elbowing Evelyn's ribs. And then she led her outside where the goat was still tied to the porch railing. "We'll want to get her in the barn, it's awfully cold out here. But that baby was more important. I'll show you how to do it once we get her in a warmer spot.

"She's a gentle thing," Marigold went on "Unlike some goats I've known. She doesn't have a stubborn bone in her body. As long as you're firm but kind, she'll cooperate with you. Milk her twice a day, morning and evening, and you'll have more than enough for that little boy."

What a wonderful woman, Mrs. Marigold Price. What a kind, and wonderful woman. Maybe Evanston wasn't such a bad place after all. With neighbors like Mrs. Price, there were surely nice people all around. If only Evelyn could somehow convince Travis Baldwin to let her stay a little longer and show her worth, maybe, just maybe, she could do something she'd not been able to do in the longest time—make friends.

After her parents were gone, she'd needed distance, isolation, silence. But Arabella's death was different. Having had someone again, someone to speak to, lean on, confide in, left her now with an ache. A lonely longing. Strange, how grief changed shape. Her parents' deaths had drained her, turned her inward, away from others. But losing Arabella made the world feel too quiet, too wide, as if she were standing completely alone. And, Evelyn Rhodes realized now—she did not want to be alone.

Chapter Five

Travis stood at the workbench in the barn. His work had been done at the ranch for at least an hour now. He and Royce had finished up repairing a fence that the heavy snow had broken, and Lawson was out with a couple of ranch hands looking for any other areas that needed repair.

Now that it was getting dusk, he found himself in his barn, tinkering. And he'd been fiddling with an old bridle for a lot longer than he normally would have. Usually, he could repair one with his eyes closed, but this time, he was distracted. And a part of him was definitely dreading going inside.

The leather was worn, cracked from age and weather, which was akin to almost everything else at this ranch. But it was still worth saving. Wasn't it…?

Then, the old leather split, ripping completely in half. Kind of like how his mind felt at the moment. He couldn't stop thinking about that woman. That doggone woman, and the fear in her voice when she said Mason was dying.

"Drat!" he muttered, to no one in particular.

Max pressed against his leg, easing him a bit. Travis loved his dog. Max was the one constant he had in this world, and the one thing he didn't mind having around. He reached down, leaving his work on the bench, and gave the animal a little scratch behind the ears.

Dealing with animals, he thought, was just so uncomplicated. It was simple. The way the rest of the world should have been but wasn't.

The barn door creaked open. The snow was finally letting up, but outdoors was still frigid. He looked up, and there was Barrett Lawson.

"We need to talk," his foreman said abruptly.

Travis's brows twisted. "If this is about Miss Rhodes—"

"It is." Lawson cut him off and moved in closer, his boots crunching the hay beneath his feet. "I heard raised voices out here earlier. Heard enough to know she is desperate, and you are..." He paused, seeming to search for the right word. "Struggling."

"I ain't talkin' about this right now, Lawson. What I've done is really all I can offer." Travis met his foreman's eyes. "And I'd warn you and McCrae not to ask for more."

Travis never called Cade by his last name, but right now, he wasn't feeling too fond of the man. No matter how many years they'd been friends. No matter how much he'd trusted him, even since he was a boy and McCrae had first been deputized.

"I ain't asking for more, at least not yet. But the woman's brave, Baldwin, and she deserves kindness."

"You ain't even officially met her yet," Travis growled. "You know nothin' about her!"

"I talked to McCrae."

Travis bit his tongue so he wouldn't say anything he couldn't take back.

"All I'm saying is that the woman clearly has courage. Courage enough to stand up to you and fight for this baby that ain't even hers. Courage enough to come all the way across the state to marry someone in her cousin's stead. Fulfilling a promise she didn't even make. She took in another woman's baby. And someone that strong, askin' for help, deserves a little."

Then he was gone, leaving Travis alone with his thoughts and his shame. He wasn't wrong. He knew that. He knew that if someone like Evelyn Rhodes was asking for help, there was a reason. He could tell by looking in her eyes that she wasn't a bad person. She was, actually quite honestly, likely a good one.

He just didn't need anyone else around, complicating things for him. He just wanted to live in his solitude, in his peace. Alone with his ranch and his men. Ever since Bonnie and Troy were gone, that's all he'd ever hoped for. And now he felt like his entire life was being trespassed against.

Scowling, he threw down the leather bridle and left the barn.

When he got back to the house, Miss Rhodes sat on the old rocking chair asleep, her head tilted back. For a moment, he was angry. This woman said she'd be cooking and cleaning, and she was napping?

But then, he looked around.

The house was clean. As clean as a whistle. And he smelled…stew?

He looked around the room and then back to the sleeping woman. She looked exhausted, from what he could see by the fire's light. Exhausted, and frightfully young.

She looked even younger like this, in sleep. He found himself unable to look away. Her dark hair had come loose from pins, and it fell in soft waves around her face. There was something about the curve of her cheek and the delicate line of her jaw…

She was just a young woman. As delicate as they came in figure.

And beautiful.

The realization struck him so hard, it felt like he'd been punched in the face. He didn't just find her attractive, but she was beautiful in a way that he had never seen before. And that in itself made him feel guilty. Because not even the mother of his child had carried that same look.

"You should try this." Royce shuffled through to the front of the house from the kitchen. "The woman made stew, and it's pretty good."

A soft cry came from down the hall, and Travis noticed Miss Rhodes hadn't moved. She hadn't heard him, clearly too tired from the day.

Royce looked ready to spit nails. "Just when I was startin' to not be so angry at the fact that they're here. The baby goes and ruins it."

Travis nodded, but then turned toward the back of the hall.

"What are you doin'?" Royce asked. "Wake her up."

Travis shushed him. "I'll just see what he needs so she can rest. She's done a lot today."

"And we ain't?" he growled.

Travis shook his head. "I'll be right back."

The baby stirred even more when he pushed the door open. He wasn't crying. Just "talking." That's what Bonnie used to call it when Troy was this age. Making little noises here and there.

He smiled, thinking about his own son, and found himself moving closer to the metal bassinet in the corner of the room before he could think better of it.

Mason. That was his name. Mason.

Bonnie used to get so sore with him for calling Troy "the baby" or "it" or anything other than his name. Looking over into the bassinet, the baby looked up at him. He was small. Probably too small for his age. Fragile.

He had dark hair, similar to Miss Rhodes, but goodness, he was so impossibly tiny. Travis's hands trembled as he reached down, some instinct he thought long dead driving him to lift the child from the crate. The weight of him was devastatingly light. He hadn't been eating well in a while, it seemed.

It made him glad that he'd asked the Prices for help.

Apparently, McCrae had enlisted their help the night before, too. They were more than happy to help. Good people. Overly nosey, though. Travis didn't like the attention it garnered, but he'd assured them it would just be a few days.

Mason cooed in his arms, and for a moment—it was Troy.

That was all he saw. His son. Alive, warmly snug in his arms. Real. Travis's vision blurred with tears that he wouldn't dare let fall. Tears that burned. He shook his head. That wasn't true. Troy was gone. This was Mason, a different baby, a different life. A baby that had no business being here.

The baby opened his eyes fully and looked up at Travis with nothing but wonderment. The eyes were bright blue. He grinned, and Travis's throat closed. He couldn't do this. He couldn't hold this baby and not remember everything he had lost. He couldn't look at this tiny, helpless life and not feel the crushing pain of not being able to protect his own son.

Someone else's son was in his home.

He was keeping someone else's baby alive, while he'd let his die.

"Mr. Baldwin?"

Her voice startled him. He whipped around to find her. She was awake, watching him with her own bright blue eyes.

"I—" Travis started, panicked, before clearing his throat. "The baby was stirring, and you were asleep. I thought—"

"Thank you." She crossed the room. "I must have fallen asleep. I didn't mean to."

"It's fine." He carefully put the baby to her arms, suddenly aware of how close she was. There was a soft scent in her hair that wafted. It was light, but lovely. Lavender and vanilla. It clung to her. "You probably needed rest. You've cleaned all day."

"So do you." Her voice was soft, tentative. "You look exhausted, Mr. Baldwin."

He didn't know how to respond to that. Didn't know how to explain that he hadn't slept in three whole years. Being exhausted was his normal.

"Mrs. Price brought by the goat, I see," he said. "I heard it's a good milker. My foreman, Lawson's idea." That was a lie, but she'd never know.

"I really appreciate everything," she said. "You all are truly saving his life."

He held up his hand and backed away. "I'm just doin' what I think is necessary, and a good Christian thing to do. Nothing more." The words were a bit harsher than he intended, but he was glad the point was getting across.

She cleared her throat and nodded.

"Did you get supper?" he asked.

She shook her head. "I was waiting on you both to eat before I had any."

He looked at her curiously, his brows twisting. Had she even eaten since she'd been there?

"Have you had anything to eat?" he asked. "You didn't make breakfast this morning, which is fine. I didn't expect you to, but you'd said you were on a train all day yesterday, and I didn't see you make breakfast. Did you have anything today?"

She shook her head. "I haven't eaten much in a couple of days, sir. A little dried meat that I packed."

Couple of days?

He felt a pang in his chest. Sharp.

"That's stupid," he said. "Get you some supper." He found himself choking on the words as he turned on his heel and headed to his room—but not before looking over his shoulder and saying, "I'm glad that baby's done screaming, though."

When he got to his room, he slung his boots off and dunked his head into the wash basin in the corner. Grabbing a towel, he scowled.

This was a mistake. All of it. Agreeing to let them stay, arranging for the goat, allowing himself even the smallest connection to these strangers and their troubles. They reminded him too much of what he'd lost. Just when he thought he'd numbed the pain—here was a reminder of it, deeper and sharper than he'd ever imagined he'd feel again.

Chapter Six

Mason stirred in the rickety old bassinet, a dusty, forgotten thing that looked as if it might collapse at any moment, but she was grateful for it, for any place to put the little boy—even if it was shoved in the corner of the room. She lifted him carefully, checking his diaper and marveling at how much calmer he seemed now that his belly was regularly full.

She couldn't thank the Prices enough for the goat. It had been a true godsend. Mason had slept for longer stretches than he had in days. He wasn't colicky at all through the night. She'd been overwhelmed with gratitude and had thanked God for her many blessings the night before.

He'd been looking awfully small. Frail. And she'd felt incredibly useless every time she held him. It had been a reminder of the poor job she was doing raising her cousin's beloved son.

But now, he giggled when she peeked over the bassinet, the first time in weeks. Another blessing.

"Good morning, sweet one," she said brightly to him, pressing a kiss to his soft hair. "Shall we see what today brings?"

She could only hope his good mood would last the day. That it would give her a proper chance at keeping house for the men, and hopefully convince them that it might be worth their time to keep her around.

Although she had to admit deep down, part of her didn't want to be around. Royce Hartwell was a bitter, angry old man. No matter what Marigold Price wanted her to believe, she wasn't sure she saw a whole lot of gentility or kindness in him at all.

Mr. Baldwin was a bit of a conundrum.

He'd seemed just as bitter, with small ounces of kindness poking out from the surface every now and then—only to be then contradicted by something hurtful.

She'd accepted his invitation to eat supper the night before, and just like Mason, she felt rejuvenated. It was amazing what a little food could do for the soul. And speaking of food, she needed to get Mason fed and breakfast on for the men.

But just as she went to prepare Mason a bottle, Travis Baldwin appeared in the kitchen doorway, his hat in his hands.

"Miss Rhodes," he said, nervously, not quite meeting her eyes. "The weather has cleared enough for a trip to town. We need supplies. You and the baby should come with me. I'm not so sure Royce will want y'all around, and I could use a hand."

Evelyn stared at him, surprised. "You want us to accompany you?"

"The general store carries items you might need, too. For the baby." He shifted his weight from carrying it all on one leg, then to the other and back again, clearly uncomfortable. "And yourself."

"I don't have money," she said sadly, shaking her head.

He held up a hand.

"If there's something you need, you can put it on my account."

She narrowed her eyes, trying to read him. He'd been so distant the night before, storming off to his bedroom without supper. She was pretty sure all he'd had was a few bits of bread all day and knew he would have been hungry. And she knew one thing was for certain: when she was hungry, she was ornery. So why was he offering for her to come to town? Why was he offering to buy her things?

This was a temporary stop, she knew that. He had made that clear. So why was he being so kind this morning? Part of her wondered if he was about to leave her in town, without any way back. But she remembered that Marigold had told her she worked in town as a seamstress. If she could see her again, thank her for her goat and her kindness, she would enjoy the chance. No matter if there was an ulterior motive or not. And, honestly, she wanted to shake herself for imagining such things. She was just being silly.

"I would like that very much," she said. "Thank you."

He grunted in response and turned away. "We leave in twenty minutes. Dress warmly. It's still awfully cold out there."

She hurried to get ready, giving Mason a bottle quickly before laying him back down in the bassinet for her to get properly dressed. She didn't have much, but she wanted to look her best.

She wrapped Mason in a couple of blankets and pulled out her best dress, which was sadly wrinkled from being packed in her carpet bag for several days.

Still, she did her best, pinching her cheeks for a bit of color. Although she was sure by the end of the ride to town, they would be chapped and red anyway.

Then, suddenly embarrassed, she muttered a curse at herself. *What are you doing? It's just a practical trip, nothing more. Stop fussing as if it's important how you look!*

***

A man came out of the barn just as Mr. Baldwin helped Evelyn into the wagon. He was a bit leaner than Travis, around the same age. He clicked his tongue at a horse he was leading out to the corral and grinned at her warmly. The sort of smile that crinkled the corner of his eyes.

"Enjoy town, Miss Rhodes," he said to her, his voice just as kind as that smile. "And don't let Travis rush you through it. You deserve a proper visit."

Evelyn found herself smiling at him. Unlike Travis's gruff terseness or Royce's open hostility, this man seemed to be truly welcoming.

"Who is that?" she asked Travis.

He only rolled his eyes, hopping up on the wagon. "That's my foreman, Barrett Lawson."

It was such a small thing, that smile and those few kind words. But after two days of feeling like an unwanted burden, it truly felt like a gift.

But then again, being taken to town was a gift, too. According to Sheriff McCrae, Travis Baldwin hadn't been to town himself in quite some time.

"Ya!" Travis yelled out before slapping his reins.

Evelyn couldn't help but smile as she held Mason close. The landscape was so beautiful. It stretched in rolling hills covered completely in sparkling white, broken only by dark strands of pine trees, heavy with snow, just like the ground. Fog hanging around the mountains in the distance looked like a painting.

Gorgeous. Truly gorgeous.

"This is so beautiful," she said, letting her thoughts become her words. "The mountains. The snow. All of it…"

"It is deadly out here if you're not careful," Baldwin replied, his tone flat and emotionless. "Beautiful things often are."

She didn't even know how to respond to that. And she didn't speak again—until they reached town.

"Oh," she breathed. "This is much more lovely than when I got off the train. I can actually see the town!"

Travis glanced at her, shaking his head. "It is a town. Nothing more."

Why did he even ask her to come if he didn't want her to speak? Or if he was just going to be such a grouch?

He finally pulled the wagon to a stop outside the general store, a tall, slender brick building with a painted wooden sign that read *Dawson's Mercantile* in white lettering. He climbed down and came around to help her, his hands warm and strong. Masculine. Firm.

For a moment, as he lifted her down from the high bench, they made eye contact. His hands lingered at her waist. Her breath caught. Then he stepped back quickly, as if the touch had scalded him. He pointed to the store's sign. "Get what you need. I have an order already."

He turned and walked into the store before she could thank him, leaving her standing in the snowy street with Mason in her arms and emotions she could not quite name swirling in her chest. What had that look been? He was an attractive man. But she'd met many attractive men before—yet had never felt quite like that.

Shaking her head, she pressed inside.

Don't even think about it.

The smell of caramel hit her instantly when they walked inside. And sure enough, there were jars of fresh candy all over the counter. She smiled, but then shook her head. They weren't there for candy.

Looking around the store, she was impressed with the selection. There were barrels of flour and sugar, bolts of fabric, tools, and tinned goods, and everything anybody might need. It was far more impressive than the general store she'd had back home.

"Baldwin! Good to see you in town. And who's this?" A tall, bearded man called out jovially from behind the counter. His eyes were fixated on Evelyn. True curiosity.

Apparently, people weren't as big of gossipers in Evanston as they were back home, because if a strange woman was at the ranch of a single man, arrangement or not, people knew about it almost the minute it happened.

"Miss Rhodes. She is... keeping house for me." Travis grumbled, his teeth tight. "She's goin' to be needing a couple of things. Her and that baby." He pointed to Evelyn's chest like she had a growth attached to her. As if Mason was an alien.

But Mr. Dawson didn't seem to catch it, and if he did, he paid no mind to it. He began pulling items from the shelves. Diaper cloth, a tin salve for diaper rash, a couple of nursing bottles. "Some flannel would be useful," she said hesitantly, looking over to Baldwin for approval. But he ignored her. "For warmer clothes for Mason. And perhaps... if it is not too much... some thread and needles? Mine are nearly gone." She was still hesitant, almost afraid. She felt he was already being too generous.

"Of course, of course." Mr. Dawson paced around the shop, heading toward the flannel. "You'll want buttons too, I expect."

"The flannel and thread will be fine," Baldwin interrupted in a gripe. "Add it to my account."

When they walked back outside, Evelyn found herself looking up and down the street. "Mr. Baldwin," she said carefully. "Would it be...that is, I noticed the dressmaker's shop across the street, and..." She'd definitely been looking for it. "Mrs. Price was so kind to bring the goat, and I would very much like to thank her properly. Might I...?"

His shoulders slumped. "Twenty minutes," he replied tightly.

"Thank you!" She broke into a smile. "Thank you, Mr. Baldwin."

She hurried across the street before he could change his mind, carefully navigating the packed snow, and pushed open the door to a shop with a sign reading *Price Dressmaking*. It reminded her of her shop, although bigger.

The smell, also, was a bit different. The smell of fabric was the same, with the bolts of cloth displayed along every inch of the walls, a large cutting table in the center of the room, and dresses hanging about. But it was warm, cozy, and smelled like cinnamon and apples and everything sweet and wonderful about winter. And there, behind the counter, was Marigold Price, her round face lighting up as soon as Evelyn walked inside.

"Miss Rhodes! And little Mason! How wonderful to see you!" Marigold came around the counter, arms outstretched. "Come in, come in. Let me look at this boy. Oh, he looks so much better already! That goat is working out well!"

"She is perfect," Evelyn said, emotion making her voice crack, her throat as thick as molasses. "Mrs. Price, I cannot thank you enough. You saved both of us, truly."

"Nonsense!" Marigold waved her hand dismissively. "I am glad to see you both looking so much better today, though. You have color in your cheeks."

Evelyn found herself blushing.

"Thanks to you."

"And to Mr. Baldwin!" Marigold laughed. "He arranged for me to bring the goat by. And..." She looked around, her neck craning to see out of the window. "Did he bring you to town?"

Evelyn nodded..

"Well, well. Perhaps there is hope for that man yet." The older woman laughed, patting Evelyn playfully on the shoulders.

"Oh! You must be Miss Rhodes!" a high-pitched voice sounded from behind her. When Evelyn turned, there was a petite young woman, around her age, with blonde curly hair. She was carrying a bolt of bright blue fabric. "Mama told me all about you." She set down the fabric and immediately launched her arms around Evelyn, pulling her into a hug. Mason protested, and she giggled, pulling back from Evelyn's bosom to rest gently at a half-arm's length. "I am Clara Price. It is so lovely to meet you properly," she said, grinning from ear to ear.

It was the friendliest woman Evelyn had ever known anyone to be.

"And you," she replied, drawn to the young woman's bubbliness.

"Mama mentioned you are a seamstress?"

"I am. Or I was." Evelyn felt a pang in her chest for the loss of her father's shop. His entire life's work. "I worked in my father's tailor shop in Green River. Men's clothing, mostly."

"Men's tailoring!" Clara's eyes lit up, her face absolutely beaming. "Oh, how I envy you. I can make a ball gown, but put me in front of a man's jacket, and I am hopeless. It's just a whole different skill."

"And I have only the barest knowledge of ladies' fashions," Evelyn admitted. "I can sew a straight seam and make basic alterations, but gowns like those...." She pointed to the dress forms to their right, displayed in the window. "That is way beyond anything I could ever do."

"Nonsense," Clara said. "You can do it. I'm sure of it." She clasped her hands together, bouncing up and down.

Evelyn couldn't help but wonder if Clara had gotten into Mr. Dawson's candy stash. She was hyped up on sugar or something. And whatever it was, Evelyn wished she had some of it. Because goodness, the woman was energized. There was also a child-like wonderment behind her eyes. One that Evelyn envied.

"This is just perfect," the young woman all but squeaked. "I've been buried in work. Everyone wants new dresses for the holidays. I could use help with the simple alterations, and I would love to learn proper tailoring for men's clothes. Would you like to work together?"

"Clara," Marigold said gently. "Do not overwhelm the poor woman." She closed the distance between herself and the other two women, pulling her daughter away from Evelyn for some breathing room.

"I am not overwhelmed," Evelyn said quickly, finding herself actually...excited. "I would love to learn. And I would be happy to help with alterations, truly. I need to feel useful."

Marigold's eyes started to glisten, and she nodded, her lips a tight line. "Then we will work something out," she said. "Clara can come visit you at the ranch and bring some patterns and fabrics just to show you a little bit of what we do. You can come to town some and work in the shop, and we'll pay you for your time."

Evelyn shook her head. "I could not possibly take any money after all you've done for me."

"You can and you will," Marigold scolded, pointing with her index finger. "Good seamstresses are rare, and this is business, Miss Rhodes, not charity."

"Thank you," she whispered. "I'm not sure you can know what this means to me."

"I think we can," Clara replied, her voice no longer high-pitched. And suddenly, Evelyn got the definite impression that both these women did, in fact, understand a great deal.

"I must go," she said reluctantly. "Mr. Baldwin is waiting."

"I'll see you soon! If the snow holds out, I can come by tomorrow." Clara waved as Evelyn made her way toward the door.

Evelyn waved back, already seeing Travis Baldwin across the street, kicking rocks next to his wagon. The look of him made her feel as if a rain cloud had just loomed above her.

"Get on." He spoke sharply, shortly, the minute she'd crossed the street. "We need to get back before the weather turns."

She could feel it in the air. It was getting colder.

"Is it supposed to snow more?"

He nodded. "I'm sure this is just a small break."

When she climbed up into the wagon, he hopped up beside her, his jaw tight. Silence. That's exactly what the ride was going to be. She could already tell it.

But then, as they got to the edge of town, he surprised her.

"What were you discussing?" he asked, almost hesitantly. "At the dressmaker's shop? With Marigold and Clara?"

Evelyn looked at him in surprise. His eyes were fixed on the road ahead, but his jaw was no longer clenched as tightly as it had been.

"Sewing," she replied carefully. "Mrs. Price and her daughter Clara are dressmakers. I used to own a tailor shop. Men's clothing, though. Clara offered to teach me about ladies' clothing, and mentioned I could help them. They said they would pay me."

An expression she couldn't quite decipher flashed across his face. "That is good," he said, nodding. "You can have work. Your own income."

"Yes," was all she said in return.

She had come here to find a place in this world when the only thing she had ever known had been ripped away from her. She had come here to start a new life with Mason. It didn't matter if that life meant she was married or not married, even if she'd originally thought she was coming to become a wife.

She hadn't had much interest finding a husband before when she had her own shop. She didn't care for the idea, actually. She'd preferred to be alone after her parents passed, wanting to bury herself in her own work.

But she hadn't had a child to care for then, either.

When they finally pulled back up to the house, Travis climbed down and came around to help her. With a gentle hand, he guided her down, and she held Mason firmly. He'd been so quiet the entire trip. So good.

But she knew if she didn't get him some milk soon, he would get fussy.

Just as she made her way to the porch, though, she noticed that Travis was rummaging in the back of the wagon for something. She turned, curious, despite knowing. the man didn't want her in his business. He'd just said they needed to get back before the weather turned, so she'd thought he would have hurried and led the horses back into the barn.

Instead, he pulled something large from the back of the wagon.

It was covered in a white canvas fabric.

"What is that?" she asked.

He didn't answer. Instead, he carried the covered object toward the house and past her. His feet were heavy against the porch steps, causing them to creak, and his breath seemed strained as he hoisted the door open and moved through the doorway. She followed him, her curiosity now higher than ever.

She paused only long enough, once inside, to breathe a sigh of relief at the warmth that enveloped her. The fire was popping gently, and Mason began to coo as she watched Travis move down the hall toward her bedroom.

She continued to follow him, although she held her distance.

What was he doing?

When she finally reached the end of the hall, she gasped. He stood right next to her bed, with the most beautiful carved cradle she'd ever seen.

"Mr. Baldwin," she breathed. "When did you get such a beautiful cradle?"

"That metal bassinet is darn near falling apart. That was Royce's when he was a boy. This will be better."

That was all he said in answer to her questions. She wanted to say more. To express how much that meant to her. But words failed her, and so did her sense of timing—because he was gone before she could gather a thought.

Heavy boots thundered toward her next, and Royce stopped at her doorway. His eyes went to the cradle, his face pale. His lip curled up, but then he cleared his throat, swiped his fingers through his hair, and said, "You went to town, I see."

And he sounded almost...*pleasant.*

"I'll let you get settled in and warmed up," he went on with a slight smile. "We'll catch up at supper on how you liked town."

She merely nodded, and he turned and headed back to the front of the house. Saying she was perplexed would have been a great understatement, but at least he wasn't shouting at her anymore. For the moment.

Carefully, she laid Mason down in his new cradle, adjusting blankets all around him. Perhaps Marigold was right. Perhaps there was hope here, after all. Perhaps these men weren't as unkind as she thought. Quickly, she wiped away unexpected tears and turned to the stove to fix supper. Tomorrow, Clara would come over, but tonight, she would simply be grateful for warm shelter, a beautiful cradle, and soon—a fed baby, set to take a nap.

Chapter Seven

Travis Baldwin trudged through the knee-deep drifts, his boots heavy with ice and the leather soaked through. His hands were numb, too, despite thick gloves. It had been a long day of work, and there was nothing to keep him from getting warm now.

He pushed open the front door and sighed in relief as the warmth from the fireplace hit him. It felt nice, but he knew it would take a long time before it thawed him out completely. It had been frigid outside, and it had been a long, grueling day out on the ranch. Some of their fencing seemed to be down in places he wouldn't have expected the wind to get to. And a whole lot of mending had to take place in conditions that were unforgiving.

His hands were lacerated with wounds and blisters that he hadn't even felt until now because those hands had been so numb from the cold.

The smell of burning wood mixed with the faint tang of iron and hay still clung like a stubborn mule to his coat. He paused, squinting toward the living room, and froze.

There she was. Evelyn. Kneeling on the rug just in front of the hearth, Mason cradled in her arms. She hummed softly as she rocked him, her lips gently brushing the baby's forehead as she continued to move back and forth.

Travis's chest constricted. It should have been ordinary, even mundane, but it wasn't to him. To Travis, it was almost unbearable to watch. It proved something to him that he'd known all along, that he didn't want to face. Life had continued moving. It was right there in front of him. And the softness Evelyn showed, the warmth, nearly crushed him. The weight of everything he'd lost came rushing back like it had just happened this morning.

He wasn't sure how much longer he could take these reminders.

He wasn't sure how much longer he could look at that baby, at his innocence, listen to his coos. He wasn't sure how much longer he could listen to Evelyn as she soothed him. She sounded like a life he wasn't allowed to have anymore. A life he'd thought he'd buried a long time ago.

He spun on his heel and left the room, not wanting to spend another moment watching what should have been.

He didn't even realize he'd quit breathing until he reached the bottom step of the attic stairs, his lungs aching like he'd run just run miles instead of walking twenty feet. But he didn't care. He needed to get away. Without thinking, he found himself climbing the attic stairs, boots creaking over the worn wooden steps. The attic door groaned at its hinges as he shoved it open, and the cold hit him harder than downstairs. He looked out through the slatted window at the winter storm that had returned with full fury. He had known it was coming all day and had worked to get the animals ready for another round of it.

Sheets of snow drove down and spread out on the ground as a whistling air tore against the house and rattled the siding. Deliberately facing away from it, he turned to the items he stored up there and felt his chest tighten.

Dust motes floated in the faint light streaming through the small window, and the smell of old wood and mothballs reminded him of the things up there that he'd tried to forget but never would. He sighed when the box caught his eye, tucked beneath a pile of blankets, almost invisible unless you knew it was there—and he certainly knew it was there. He knew before he reached for it that it was the reason he'd even come up to the attic in the first place. Like a man possessed, destined to hurt his own feelings.

He knelt, lifting the wooden lid, and there they were. Troy's things. The few little bits he and Royce had gathered up after the fire. A part of him wanted to slam the lid shut the second he saw the first hint of his son's things. But, feeling his breath catch, he went ahead instead.

There was a tiny knitted bootie, a darn-near worn-out wooden rattle, and a small carved horse that Troy used to hold and suck on the head. Travis grinned, thinking about it, then had to clear his throat as he felt it wanting to clench tight.

He picked up the bootie, fingers trembling. The fabric was frayed at the edges and smelled faintly of smoke, even still.

And the memories hit all over again.

So vividly it was like he could practically see them in front of him. The way Bonnie looked, leaning against the counter with Troy's little hands reaching for him. The smell of food cooking on the stove, bread in the oven. The sound of their laughter…

The way they both felt in his arms…

His knees buckled, sending him down to the floor with a thud. He clutched the rattle tightly and closed his eyes, and for the first time in a long time, he let himself feel.

But only for a moment.

Because that moment was far too long, and far too painful.

Quickly, he shoved the box shut with more force than necessary, his hands shaking. He slid it across the floor and took a deep breath to collect himself, only to catch sight of something that unraveled him all over again. It lay to the side of that box, a small bit of fabric. White. Lace. Part of the wedding dress Bonnie had worn for their wedding day.

What a perfect day that had been.

He wasn't sure he could ever go to church again because the image of her in that beautiful white dress was all he would ever see when he stepped foot inside.

"God help me..." he muttered sadly, as he scooted across the floor to grab the fabric and tuck it into his pants pocket. He could hear Evelyn singing from downstairs, and he scowled, grinding his teeth, suddenly angry, although he wasn't sure why.

He pounded heatedly down each and every step, his mind torn between grief and frustration. By the time he reached the kitchen, he saw her preparing supper, steam curling from the pot on the stove, and the aroma of cooking filled his senses. It smelled good; the logical part of his brain could decipher that, but he had the sudden want to throw something. To scream. To collapse.

Instead of doing any of that, he spoke in a loud bark, "Why wasn't this started hours ago?" His voice was sharp, slicing through the warmth of the room. "I'll be starved to death before supper's done! And the place isn't even organized like you said it would be! What exactly are you doing around here?"

The second the words left his mouth, he hated them. They tasted terrible, but he couldn't help himself, standing there angry because he refused to feel anything else.

She'd been startled—he could tell by the way she whirled around—but there was more than alarm in her face now. He saw hurt there, too.

"Travis," she began, "you know what I've been doing. I've been tending to—"

"Tending to what?" He cut her off, anger and pain mixing bitterly. "The baby? Don't tell me you've been wasting time while there's work to do. Are you incapable of taking care of a child and tending to a house? Women do it every day!"

"Incapable?" Her eyes blazed with anger as she took a quick step toward him. "I've been managing the house, keeping Mason safe, cookin' breakfast and dinner and supper every doggone day! Making this place a home. You have a short memory of what I started with, if you think I'm incapable!"

A sharp, high-pitched cry broke abruptly through their voices. Evelyn rushed to the baby, rocking him against her chest as she looked back at him through slitted eyes.

Guilt stabbed at his gut so hard that Travis nearly toppled over. He wanted to scoop the child up himself, to hold him and apologize. But not only was he far too broken for that, what right did he have?

He turned toward the back door, needing air, needing distance. Lawson was already standing there, in the doorway, his hat clutched to his chest, his face holding judgment. Travis shook his head. "I don't got time for this," he muttered, rushing past his friend and foreman.

He felt Lawson round behind him, hot on his heels, but he ignored it. He kept moving toward the barn, not slowing down even though he knew his friend was right there every step of the way. Looking at Lawson meant facing the truth. And the truth was an ugly thing tonight.

When he finally got to the barn, Travis pivoted, ready to lambaste his best friend. But Lawson only sighed and leaned against the barn post, snow clinging heavily to his coat. Travis hated how calm he seemed, how nonchalant, when it was clear he had something on his mind.

"Out with it!" he hissed.

But Lawson just shook his head. "That woman didn't deserve that. You know it just as well as I do. She was cookin' supper, and it was almost done. She'd even come out into the cold and told me to come on in to eat while you were up in the attic."

Travis's throat clenched.

"You're hearin' me?" Lawson asked, shoving himself off the post. "She ain't done nothin' wrong, and you know it."

Travis swallowed hard.

He already knew what Lawson was saying was true.

He just didn't want to admit it. To himself, to Lawson, or to Evelyn. But he knew it. He had been unbearable, and he knew that he was punishing her for something she had no control over. Reminding him of everything he had lost.

She had done nothing but step into his life in the middle of a storm, and he had lashed out at her for it.

"I know," he said, voice hoarse. He didn't know what else to say. Words failed him. Grief had carved up something nasty inside of him that he hardly recognized. "I just can't stand to see her, see Mason..."

Lawson nodded. "It ain't her fault, though," he said. "She ain't tryin' to hurt you by having that child with her. And she ain't tryin' to make you feel what you lost even more than you already do. You gotta cut her some slack on that. That woman's done everything to try and help since she's been under your roof. Have you seen your house?"

Travis sighed and looked back to the house.

She had made it start to look like a home. And maybe, that's what scared him the most.

Chapter Eight

Evelyn stood frozen long after Travis stormed out, her hands trembling as she continued to hold Mason. The baby whimpered against her shoulder, as if he somehow sensed the tension that still lingered in the air.

He was right. The humiliation was raw, as painful as the throbbing in her head.

"I'm sorry, sweetheart," she whispered into his fine brown hair as she rocked him. "You shouldn't have to hear that. Any of it." The trouble was, she could still hear it in her mind, over and over again, every harsh word.

He thought she was incapable. Wasting time.

She couldn't believe he'd said that. It felt like nothing she would ever do would be good enough, like she would never measure up to his expectations. She'd thought she'd gotten the hang of it. She'd cleaned the house, took care of Mason, made hearty meals that the men would feel satisfied with. She'd cleaned up after one as well.

She blinked hard, refusing to let tears spill. She'd cried enough in her life; she didn't need to waste more tears over thoughtlessness like this. No matter how deep it cut.

She'd been doing her best.

Trying so hard….

In the midst of her musings, a sharp rap at the door made Evelyn's heart leap, and her spirits lift in anticipation—although a visitor at this point was strange, given how late in the evening it was getting to be. She hurried across the kitchen, grateful that at least Mason was finally soothed after Travis's outburst.

She opened the door to find Marigold and Clara, bundled in thick coats, scarves wrapped tightly around their faces, cheeks rosy from the frigid cold. Clara carried a bundle tucked against her chest, and Marigold's hands were laden with a load of other things that Evelyn couldn't quite see yet.

"Evelyn!" Marigold called, breathless. "We made it!"

Something inside her loosened at the happy greeting. She hadn't realized how starved she was for a friendly face until now. The storm practically howled behind the women, but they brought warmth as they stepped inside. Evelyn laughed, even as tears pricked the corners of her eyes. "The two of you are crazy! You didn't have to come out here in all of this!"

"We are women of our word," Clara chirped as she stepped inside and brushed the snow from her shoulders. Her pale white hands were red from the cold, but she smiled brightly, seemingly unfazed. "Besides, we've got important deliveries." She set the bundles down carefully, and Evelyn couldn't help but grin at the sight. There were tiny shoes, swaddling blankets, little knitted hats, even a small wooden rattle. She felt herself smiling ear-to-ear.

"Oh, you didn't have to!" She held Mason up to let her friends fuss over him. The baby gurgled, reaching out for Marigold, who took him gently, settling him against her shoulder while she rubbed soothing circles on his back.

"Look at him!" Marigold swooned. "He's such a healthy little thing! Ol' nanny goat must be doing pretty good at feeding him."

"Absolutely, thanks to you," Evelyn said.

"Oh, dear, you don't give yourself enough credit. It's not easy taking care of a baby, even with enough milk. And this house!" The woman looked around, clearly appreciating her hard work.

Evelyn felt herself blush. "How've you been doing, juggling everything?"

"I try," Evelyn said, feeling the edge of guilt that came up. If she was being honest, trying to balance the house, the baby, and all the responsibilities had pressed down on her, especially after Travis's blow-up. He'd made her feel absolutely terrible about herself and the job she was doing.

Maybe she wasn't doing as much as she thought she had been. Maybe she wasn't as good at all of this as she thought she would be.

As if Marigold could read her mind, she snorted. "You do more than try, dear," she said. "You're doing a good job. Don't let anyone tell you different. Now, let me tell you about all of this we carried over here." Evelyn smiled as Mason giggled, clearly delighted at the notion himself.

And then, together, Clara and Evelyn moved to the table, as if they'd been there and visited a hundred times before. As if it were all familiar—but for Evelyn, it was not familiar at all. She wasn't used to fellowship quite like this, but she enjoyed it. Oh, did she enjoy it.

Spreading out the packages, Clara pulled out folded cloth and smoothed the pieces lovingly, while Marigold hummed a hymn under her breath and bounced Mason gently.

"I thought you could use some new patterns. Dressmaking is easier when you've got something new and inspiring to work with. And I brought some fabrics for Mason, too."

Evelyn brushed her fingers over the soft fabrics. They felt like quality. She smiled. She could tell that there had been so much care in each and every stitch. She loved when people took pride in their work.

"Clara, these are beautiful. I can't thank you enough. Mason will have the best wardrobe in town before long/" She smiled wistfully. "Even if he is growing way too fast. Every day, he surprises me. I can't believe how much he's changed in just a couple of weeks now. Growing out of everything. So you have no idea what it means to me that you've brought him these."

Evelyn couldn't remember the last time she'd had a moment like this, and although she was in a stranger's house, she felt at home all of a sudden. Mason babbled happily.

Evelyn's heart warmed.

Marigold chuckled as she bounced him lightly on her hip. "He's lucky to have you."

The conversation turned, naturally, to patterns, fabrics, and sewing techniques, with Clara offering advice, Evelyn asking questions, and Marigold chiming in whenever she could. They talked of men's clothes, too, and Evelyn's professional opinion. A thoroughly enjoyable conversation it was, "talking shop"—until Marigold paused, then asked a different question entirely.

"How are you and Mr. Baldwin getting along?" she said quietly.

Evelyn sighed. "He is…well, he's the most ornery, gruff man I've ever met."

Clara raised an eyebrow, a knowing smile tugging at her lips. "There's a reason for that," she said softly. "He didn't become that way overnight. You should know… the man has seen more tragedy in his life than most people will see in a lifetime."

Evelyn nodded sadly. "He lost his wife and child in a fire, and he's been left to pick up the pieces out here in the middle of nowhere."

Marigold nodded. "That's part of why he is the way he is. Harsh. But you know, he used to be really lively in town. A blacksmith."

A blacksmith?

A rancher *and* a blacksmith?

"Yes, he was both." Marigold went on, as if she'd heard Evelyn's silent question. "He loved it. Worked hard in town, and Royce and the hands took care of this place until Bonnie died."

"A blacksmith?" Evelyn repeated.

Marigold nodded. "His father was a blacksmith before him. He took over the business when he was a younger man. Just like you with your father's shop!" They blew heat into her hands, one by one. "When he married Bonnie, he was so smitten. Couldn't blame him there, she was beautiful, so beautiful. They got married, and Royce continued to take care of the ranch just like he'd done for years. You know, Royce and Sheriff McCrae were his father's best friends."

Evelyn's breath caught. "So he wasn't a rancher before?"

"The ranch became his sanctuary because he could shut everyone out," Clara said. "But he was a blacksmith through and through. His father owned the land because his daddy was a rancher. But they always had ranch hands work the land so he could blacksmith, and Travis followed in his footsteps until...everything happened."

Evelyn stared down at her hands, trying to process the hurt he must have felt. She knew what losing her parents was like, so she could relate to that—but losing a spouse and a child on top of it? She couldn't imagine the hurt.

She'd known about the wife and child, but she hadn't completely thought about the ramifications of it all until now. She hadn't thought about how much he was already carrying, and then to lose his wife and son and start all over again?

"So you see why he can be... difficult," Clara continued, as if reading her thoughts. "But if you stick around, you'll find that he's worth the effort. The man's not only handsome, but he's a hard worker, and he loves deeply. He's a good man."

Evelyn wasn't quite sure why they were even talking about all of this. He was just letting her stay. He didn't want to be betrothed. He didn't want another wife. And she couldn't blame him. "Yes, but I'm sure me and Mason will be sent on our way soon enough." She feigned a laugh, as if making a casual joke, to cover the cold fear that shot through her.

Clara smirked. "I wouldn't be so sure," she said. "You're helping them out a lot. Whether they want to admit it or not."

She'd no sooner spoken when heavy footsteps thundered toward the room, and Evelyn jumped, clutching the bundle of patterns tightly in her hand. It was Royce, carrying a satchel by its strap, and making an effort to hold it away from himself. The satchel was dusty and had strands of sticky cobwebs all over it.

"This all needs to go," he said firmly. "All of it is trash. Throw it away."

There was something in his tone, a sharpness she couldn't quite place, causing her to hesitate. Atop the satchel was a lovely white fabric that she nearly asked him to keep, but she knew better. Royce wasn't the type of man for that sort of question. Evelyn found herself looking to Clara, who smiled back at her encouragingly.

Still, Evelyn felt something strange. Not so much in the request itself, but in the way he'd said it. She forced a compliant nod, shoving down her unease, and hurried over to the hearth.

As the fire consumed the items, she couldn't help but feel a weight in her gut. It seemed like a waste. Burning items like that. In her experience, most things could be repurposed.

Clara watched her quietly, then smiled again. "You have the right spirit," she said. "Keep that, and people will see you just want to help out. Travis, too."

Marigold, still holding Mason, added, "And don't be scared of Travis and Royce. You will do just fine here."

Evelyn felt the warmth of their encouragement seep into her. She wasn't just a visitor here; she could contribute. She could help. Become a meaningful part of this household, just like she'd set out to be. Just because they likely would have her leave at some point didn't mean she couldn't make the most of it while she was here.

She glanced at Mason, who gurgled happily in Marigold's arms, and then at the patterns still laid out on the small wood table, and sighed happily. She would do everything in her power to make this place a home, for however long they were there. She would support Travis and—if he let her—help bring just a little light into the darkness that had settled inside him.

Chapter Nine

He had waited until Marigold and Clara left, not wanting to entertain the company, to go in and have supper. By the time he'd gotten his food, it'd been cold, and Evelyn had gone to bed.

Not that he blamed her.

He'd been a jerk.

He'd slept with the piece of fabric he'd gotten out of the attic before tucking it into a small box underneath his bed that next morning, along with Bonnie's locket, that he also kept safely hidden away. He knew he was coping about as badly as anyone could expect. He wasn't a stupid man. He could see it.

But he didn't know any other way to be.

Travis dragged a hand down his face and let out a long, exasperated breath.

The truth was, he hated coming home now. Not because of anything she did wrong, but because of what she did right. She almost made the house feel... lived in. Warm. Alive. And those were all dangerous things.

Those things meant a man could start hoping, and that was something Travis had sworn he would never do again. It was a mistake to hope for anything because no matter what, there was always going to be something out of his control.

The sound of her laughter earlier nearly undid him. Soft and beautiful, it followed him around like a ghost, taunting him. He had stood in his room for hours, listening to women's voices that night. Sounds he hadn't heard in years. Marigold and Clara had called on Bonnie that same way...

He scowled.

He didn't know how to move on. He didn't know how to be all right, knowing he hadn't been able to help them. That he hadn't been able to save them. And that he would have to live the rest of his life with that knowledge—and without them.

The next morning, breakfast had been on the table waiting for him, but still, no sign of Evelyn. He'd gone out to work the day, and it was still cold. Too cold. The wind, it cut through like a knife. Unrelentingly ruthless and cruel, it had shrieked through the trees like something alive all day. By the time Travis got back to the house, his coat was practically frozen stiff. His fingers ached around the reins of his horse, Buck. His body ached. His teeth clattered.

He paused on the porch, breath coming out as a white fog around his face.

A braver man could've apologized to her before bed. But the words were stuck in his throat, jagged, and he wasn't sure he could even swallow them.

Travis Baldwin wasn't even so sure he would recognize an apology if it came and knocked him in the head. He didn't apologize much. Men like him usually didn't. They just...endured.

The sky had gotten even darker, not just from the evening hours pressing in closer, but with the prospect of another round of snow, about to be dumped on top of him and his ranch. Every single part of him begged for warmth.

But when he pushed open the door, he froze from emotion, not cold.

Wooden boxes sat open on the floor, old papers and books spread across the rug. The faint scent of lavender and freshness filled the air, although he had no idea how. The entire ground was frozen, and not an ounce of lavender was in sight. And he didn't think he'd had dried lavender, had he?

He didn't even have time to contemplate it before his eyes fell on Evelyn.

She was bent over a crate near the window, her sleeves rolled up to her elbows. Her hair had begun to fall out of its bun in curls. The room, which for months had been nothing but a dumping ground for God-knows-what, looked halfway like a home now. One with a woman's touch. Curtains were drawn open, the fire was built high, and the clutter... it was almost completely cleared out.

At first, he could only stand there, his jaw tight, with nothing but the sound of his own breath in his ears. But she heard the creak of the floorboards and turned, startled.

Something in his chest twisted painfully at the sight of her. He looked around the room, at just how clean it was, and how pretty it looked in the fire's light. It all felt wrong.

But it also felt...God help him...*comforting.*

That made his anger flare again. He didn't want comfort.

"Oh, Travis! I didn't hear you come in."

Her smile was small, nervous. After his blow-up the day before, not a surprise.

He said nothing for a moment. His eyes drifted past her to the dresser table on the wall that led to the hallway. Atop of it was a vase. *The* vase. Porcelain. White. Delicate blue flowers that curled up over each side.

His wife's vase.

His breath caught in a gasp that trapped itself in his throat. It was the one thing he had left of her, aside from the locket he'd dug out from the ashes. Not much had survived the fire. The few things of Troy's he kept in the attic. The crib he'd given

Evelyn for Mason now. The locket. The fabric of Bonnie's dress...

Not much at all.

That was why he'd moved out here instead of rebuilding. This was a blank slate.

His old house was gone. Nothing but ashes that had washed away into the soil by now. He hadn't even remembered packing the vase, now that he thought about it. It had always been tucked away in that box, untouched. *Untouchable.* Now it sat in plain sight, polished and catching the light like it belonged there for everyone that came in the house to see. He shook his head, the air still not fully in his lungs.

"What's that doing there?" he gritted out at last.

She blinked, then followed his gaze, which still hadn't left the spot atop the dresser. "The vase? I—well, I thought it was lovely. I didn't see why it shouldn't be out. It brightens up the room so much..."

Travis's gut clenched. "Put it back."

Her brow furrowed. "I don't understand. I cleaned it. It was covered in dust. I thought—"

"*Put it back.*"

He watched as she shrank back, and part of him hated himself for it. But he couldn't stop. The anger wasn't really at her, but it was there. He turned and walked right past her, toward his bedroom. What else had she touched? "Where did all those boxes come from?" he asked, desperately.

"Travis," she said softly behind him, her voice barely rising above the crackle of the fire. "What did I do wrong this time?"

He didn't answer. He couldn't. He just bounded up to the attic, throwing open the door to find—nothing.

It was almost empty.

Completely.

He dropped to his knees toward the stack of blankets that were there—and Troy's things... they were gone! "No, no, no..." he muttered, frantically searching. Furiously throwing things out of the way.

Then he shook his head and pounded back downstairs, slamming the attic door behind him. He thundered to his room, scrambled to reach beneath his bed. The small wooden box where he kept Bonnie's things wasn't there.

A deep dread rose in him, sharp and panicked. "Where is it?" he muttered. He began pulling drawers open, moving stacks of papers, although he knew he hadn't moved it.

Evelyn appeared in the doorway, hesitant, stammering. "W-where is *what*?"

"The box," he barked. "It was here. Did you move it?"

Her lips parted, her eyes wide with confusion. "No," she said, shaking her head. He took a couple steps toward her.

"Really. Just tell me where you moved it!"

"I haven't even been in this room before!" she snapped back.

His hands froze, and he looked at her with ragged breath.

"Don't lie to me!" he yelled. "What about the boxes in the attic!"

"I'm not lying!" She stepped forward, her voice trembling. "I promise, Travis, I wouldn't go through your bedroom! I didn't even go through your attic! Just the sitting room and kitchen!"

He turned away from her, pressing a hand to the edge of the desk. The wood felt cold under his palm.

"I just thought," she continued, her voice quieter now, "I would go through some of the boxes in the sitting room and help organize some more."

He did mention that she hadn't done enough. He let out a long, uneven breath and looked at her. "I didn't mean to overstep," she finished softly, not looking at him.

He nodded. "That vase," he said, the words slow, heavy, "belonged to my wife."

"I'm sorry," she whispered. "I didn't know. I only thought it was beautiful."

He nodded once. His throat burned, and he felt as if there wasn't enough air in the room.

"But I really didn't touch any other things, especially not in your room. Maybe you moved it when—"

"I didn't move it," he said, cutting her off. Hard. Loud. Evelyn recoiled as if he'd hit her. Her lips parted, like she was about to scream, her lips trembling, but no sound came out.

"I'm sorry," she whispered again. "I'm sorry you lost her. I can't imagine what that kind of pain feels like. But I didn't take your box."

On that, she walked out of the room.

He just watched her leave, then followed with his eyes as she went down the hallway. He stood, frozen, as she moved to the sitting room and lifted the vase with a care that almost broke him.

She didn't slam it into a box. Didn't curse him for his temper. She just cradled it, her thumb brushing the painted flowers as though offering an apology to the vase itself. Travis leaned against the wall, suddenly drained as he watched her. The sight of her gentleness truly did something to him. This woman was kind. And she was honest.

He thought about the way she'd taken in that baby without a second thought, how she'd sung to him by the fire at night. He thought about how kind her heart must be.

And now he'd gone and shouted at her like some heartless fool.

When she passed across the other end of the sitting room and placed the vase back in its wooden box, her lashes damp, he felt a bitter guilt wrack through him. There was something about watching this woman treat the last remnants of his wife's life with such gentleness that cut him straight to the bone.

She handled the vase like it was something sacred. Like it mattered—like she mattered, although Evelyn didn't know Bonnie at all. She was tender. Kind and…

…and for one brief, traitorous moment, he thought—*she's beautiful.* Beautiful in a quiet, unassuming way that snuck up on a man. Beautiful in the way she cared, even when she shouldn't. Even when he didn't deserve the care.

He clenched his fists, furious with himself.

Not only because he'd caused her tears, but also because he had no right to think that way. No right to enjoy another woman's beauty. No right to any of it.

She turned back to him, her hands folded in front of her.

"I put it away," she said quietly. "Until you decide what you want done with it."

He nodded once, unable to speak.

Her eyes lingered on him. "Travis… I truly am sorry. For your loss. For everything."

He wanted to tell her that he could see that she meant that, but he didn't have the words. So instead, he turned back to his room, sinking down into the chair at his small corner desk. Sighing wearily, he pressed his palms to his eyes.

He didn't want to suspect Evelyn. He didn't want to suspect *anyone*. But someone had moved his things. Someone had been in his room.

If he trusted Evelyn, then…?

Chapter Ten

She wasn't entirely sure how long she could stay with Travis and Royce, at odds with herself and this entire ordeal. Trapped. She couldn't go. She didn't have money or any prospect. She didn't want to go for those same reasons.

But at the same time, she just wished more than anything she had any answers on when she would need to go.

Evelyn stood near the hearth, Mason in her arms, trying not to cry. Her fingers ached from the endless rocking. There wasn't a lot of milk left, and the nanny goat that Marigold had lent them had gone lame that morning.

Evelyn had gone out in the biting wind to milk her, only to be met with bellows and kicks that nearly sent the pail flying. She'd seen it immediately. The swelling. Felt the heat radiating off of it. It had to mean infection. Mastitis, by her guess.

She'd tried again and again, whispering soothingly to the animal, praying she would calm herself. But every touch seemed to bring out pain. Every touch brought another kick. The poor thing had practically gone wild with it, stamping and crying out. Not that it would have mattered anyway, her milk would have been tainted. Useless.

Now, Mason cried from hunger, and Evelyn's heart broke with every sound.

"I'm sorry," she whispered, rocking him. "I'm so sorry, little one. I'm trying."

She pressed her forehead to Mason's soft hair, her breath hitching painfully. She had never felt so utterly useless. She'd always been capable. Motherhood, though... that was something she felt completely incapable of doing.

Her arms ached. Her back throbbed. She hadn't slept more than a handful of hours. *What if Travis is right? What if I'm really incapable...?*

The thought cut deeper than she cared to admit.

She could do little now but wait until the men came back in from working. It wouldn't be long, with the snow picking up, they'd not been out long at a time.

She just needed Mason to sleep for a little longer. Nap just a while.

And then she could figure something out with them. Send someone into town. Something. Anything.

But he wouldn't sleep.

Her hands shook as she glanced down at her chest. The thought came again. It was a desperate, foolish thought, but she couldn't stop herself.

What if she *could* feed him herself?

She'd tried before, in those quiet hours when no one was looking. Still, she'd heard stories. Women who'd nursed children not born of them. It was possible. It *had* to be.

She sank down into the chair by the fire, pulling open the top buttons of her blouse. Mason rooted blindly, his tiny mouth seeking, and she guided him close, heart pounding with hope and shame and fear all at the same time.

But the moment his lips touched her skin, the hope that had shown up faded away just as quickly as it had come. Nothing.

The baby cried harder.

Evelyn bit her lip as tears stung her eyes. "I'm sorry," she whispered, her voice shaking. "I'm not enough. I'm not enough for you—"

Suddenly, the latch clicked behind her.

"Evelyn?"

She all but shrieked as she hurried to cover herself up. He pulled off his dripping hat, his eyes wide. "What's wrong with him?" he asked.

It was a simple enough question, but she felt it like a blow. "What's wrong?" Her voice rose with anger. "What isn't wrong?"

He blinked at her and took a half step back. But she wasn't going to let up. Not now.

"The baby's hungry," she said, standing now, still holding Mason close. "The goat's sick! Every time I try to milk her, she kicks and screams. I can't feed him. I can't do anything right. I should've just—" Her breath hitched, overcome with emotion. "I should've given him up. Let someone better suited take him. I knew families that would have loved him and done a good job as parents. I should have left him in Green River with a family!"

Travis didn't say anything. He just stared blankly at her.

She kept going, her voice cracking. "You think I'm useless, too. Maybe you're right." She laughed then, a laugh without humor, short and bitter. A laugh of pure exasperation. "I can't milk a goat, can't quiet a baby, can't even feed him the way a mother should."

Travis didn't move. Didn't speak. Just stood there as snow melted onto the floorboards at his feet. Her arms tightened around Mason. "Say something," she demanded, choking, her voice louder than she'd expected it to be. "Anything."

If Travis yelled back at her, she could handle it. It would be better than the unbearable silence. It yawned between the two of them, made her feel small and foolish.

But he said nothing, just turned and left, the door shutting behind him with a thud. For a moment, all she could hear was the wind and Mason's cries.

Evelyn rocked and shushed him.

There was a little milk left. Just a little. Maybe she would give him half now just to help him sleep.

***

She didn't have much, but she'd boiled off what she had, and it had been just enough to get him to sleep. She only dreaded when he woke back up, and there was nothing left.

Her eyes fixed on Mason's eyelashes fluttering as he drank, and she brushed a knuckle over his cheek. This little boy hadn't asked for any of this. For snowstorms, for hunger, for a mother who wasn't a mother at all…

Then, heavy footsteps sounded outside. Had they been this heavy the first time he'd come to the door? Nervous, she raised her head just as Travis stepped over the threshold, his breath ragged and in his hand, a pail. Half full of milk, steam rising up.

Evelyn's mouth fell open. "You—how—?"

He set it on the bedside table, pulling off his gloves. "Marigold and Gunter Price's ranch." Snow dripped from his hair in a melted puddle on the floor.

Her breath caught. She could see his shoulders sag, exhaustion all over him. "You went that far?"

He nodded. "I told 'em I can get her better, but I brought over another goat until she does."

"Travis..." she whispered. "I—I don't know what to say."

"You don't gotta say nothin'," he muttered.

She blinked away the tears threatening to spill out of the brim of her eyelids. She was grateful. So grateful.

Her heart fluttered as she prepared the bottle when Mason began to stir. Gently, she guided it to his lips, and he latched it greedily, sucking with a whimper.

"There you go," she whispered, smiling through tears. "That's it, my brave boy."

She sighed with nothing but pure relief. For the first time all day, she felt at ease. There was no sound except the sound of Mason drinking. Travis lingered nearby, gently taking off his hat, then his coat. Only then did she notice that he was soaked.

"Come by the fire..." she whispered to him, rocking Mason gently. He nodded, shivering slightly, before clearing his throat as if he was somehow embarrassed to be cold. But of course he was! He'd been outside for hours.

He breathed out in relief as soon as he got close, slinging the wet coat off himself completely and laying it on the rocking chair.

Neither of them spoke.

She kept her eyes on Mason, afraid to ruin the moment. Travis wasn't a man accustomed to sharing quietness with others. But she could still feel his eyes on her. Almost suffocatingly so. But not in a bad way. Just... different.

When the baby finished, Evelyn grinned. "Thank heavens."

Travis reached out then, his voice quiet. "Here, let me."

She blinked at him. "You?" He wanted to hold him?"

He gave a small, crooked smile. "I know how to burp babies."

There was something in his tone that told her he was sure. That, for the first time, he truly wanted to hold Mason. So she let him. She passed the full baby over, and he took him with an ease that startled her. One of his hands cradled Mason's tiny back while the other steadied beneath his head.

Travis began to pat gently, murmuring under his breath. The baby gurgled against his shoulder, and then a loud burp spilled from him. They both froze, then laughed. Real laughter, too. Honestly, the hardest laugh Evelyn had let out in the longest time. She pressed a hand to her mouth, her shoulders shaking. Travis, too. She wasn't sure she'd ever heard such a pleasant sound as his laugh.

Their eyes met, and when they did, the laughter faded away, leaving behind a hush that felt almost intimate. Dangerously so. She could hear the pop from the wood in the fire. She could hear his breath, slow and ragged.

Her pulse fluttered. His eyes dropped to her lips for half a second—barely long enough to notice, but she did. So much so that her own breath faltered, and she looked away first, pretending to fuss with the baby's blanket.

"Thank you," she whispered sincerely.

"For what?"

"For the milk. For... knowing what to do."

He shrugged. "Someone had to."

Mason stirred, and Travis glanced down at him, his thumb brushing the baby's tiny hand.

Evelyn swallowed, the room suddenly too warm. Travis never looked at anyone the way he was looking at Mason now. It made something inside of her ache.

"He likes you," she whispered.

Travis shook his head faintly. "No... he just likes being held." But the way his voice gentled gave him away.

Evelyn lifted her eyes. "You don't have to pretend."

His brow furrowed. "Pretend what?"

"That you don't care," she replied. "You came back with milk in the middle of a storm. You held him like you've done it a thousand times. That wasn't all just out of obligation."

He let out a slow, shaky breath.

"You did good," he said quietly.

Evelyn's heart thudded once, hard. She wasn't sure if he meant *her* or the child. Either way, she found herself smiling as Travis set the baby back into her arms. His fingers brushed hers, just barely, but it was enough to send a shiver down her spine.

She shifted Mason against her shoulder, but she couldn't ignore the warmth still lingering where Travis's fingers had grazed her skin. She tried to tell herself that it was nothing. A brush of hands. Nothing more than a tiny accident. And yet it unraveled her far more than she had ever been unraveled before.

"I should... get him settled," she stammered.

Travis nodded, but his eyes didn't leave hers. "Yeah. 'Course."

Even as she moved away, she could feel the roughness of his voice. But this hoarseness wasn't anger, or even irritation. More the sound of a voice that hadn't been used much for gentleness in a long time.

Maybe years.

Chapter Eleven

Travis had been up before dawn, as usual, but it was now near high noon, and he was still messing with the sick mare they'd found in the upper paddock. Sweetheart. The best and most beautiful roan in the lot. She'd been lying on her side, sweating despite the cold, breathing heavily.

"She was fine yesterday," Lawson said, kneeling to press a hand to her flank. "Wouldn't take her feed this morning. Looks like a fever."

Travis crouched down beside him. The mare's breathing was shallow, her coat dull. He sighed, sadly. Her eyes rolled in pain.

"Colic?"

"Could be," Lawson said. "But her gut sounds are near gone."

Travis clenched his jaw. If it spread, it would ruin them.

He rose up with a grunt, his back aching as he pulled his coat tighter to his body. "We'll keep her separated. Give her water, molasses, anything she'll take. I think Royce has some asafetida in case of colic. But if she worsens, we'll have to end it."

Lawson nodded grimly, shaking his head. The last thing any of them wanted to do was kill a horse. This was their bread and butter. They raised horses and sold them out. Good, hardworking, strong horses. Cowboys from all over would buy up their stock.

But the last year had been rough. Any horses dying now was dire, and Travis knew Lawson understood that as well as he did.

They stood in silence for a moment, the only sound the mare's labored breathing.

Finally, Lawson cleared his throat, as if something lay heavy on his mind. "You hear from the bank again?"

Travis's mouth hardened. "A letter yesterday."

Lawson looked at him and pursed his lips.

"They're threatening foreclosure," Travis said quietly. "Want the payment before month's end."

Lawson swore under his breath. "Vultures."

Travis didn't reply. He rubbed the back of his neck and blew out a puff of air as he stared out toward the ridge. The land stretched on for miles. He loved this land. Every inch of it.

It had been his father's land. And once he and Bonnie married, he'd moved Royce out to it, giving him the house they now both lived in. It was the main house. The house he'd given his father-in-law in exchange for Royce to work the ranch while he blacksmithed in town.

Royce had always worked that land. He deserved the house, as far as Travis was concerned. He was one of Travis's father's best ranch hands, and that was how he'd met Bonnie. She'd been his childhood sweetheart, and they'd made a life out here. After her death, he'd poured his all into the land his father had left him, even though he had to move into the house with Royce.

But now, they might not even have that house left.

Or any of the land his eyes were gazing out at that very moment.

The thought of losing it twisted something deep in his chest, and he kicked at the frozen ground.

"You know, I ran into Fletcher Kane in town last week," Lawson went on carefully. "He was askin' about you."

Travis's head snapped up in a scowl. "Kane?"

"Mm. Said he's still interested in buying."

Travis's eyes narrowed. Fletcher Kane left a bad taste in his mouth. "That man's been circling like a wolf for years. He'll not have this land."

Lawson clicked his tongue. "You know what he's after. He wants your ridge to sink another shaft. He said as much. But he would pay a pretty penny for it…"

"He won't get it," Travis said flatly. There was no way he was going to give up his land for a man like that. He didn't even want to do any good on the land. He didn't want to work it. He wanted to bleed it dry of its resources. And Travis would never forgive himself for letting it go for nothing greater than money.

"He's not the kind to take 'no' too kindly," Lawson replied. "You've heard the stories, I'm sure."

"I know what he is," Travis said, nodding. "A man who builds his fortune off other men's ruin. And I'll burn this place to the ground before I'll sell it to him."

***

The two men worked silently to lead Sweetheart into a horse-drawn wagon, then into the back of the barn. Travis set a fresh blanket on Sweetheart as soon as they got her into the last stall, and once they got her settled with water, they both leaned against the fence just outside.

Lawson looked at Travis, gesturing up to the house. "How's it going with the girl and the baby the last couple days?"

Travis shot him a look. "What do you mean?"

"You know what I mean." Lawson's grin widened. "Seems a bit quieter at the house the last little bit."

Travis adjusted the rope on the gate, not daring to look into his friend's eyes. He felt them fixed on him, but only shrugged at that. "It's fine. The baby's settled now."

"That so?" Lawson teased. "Well, maybe you'll keep her on, then. She's a fine girl, Travis. Sweet. Capable. Pretty as spring."

Travis stiffened. "She's been through a lot. Don't make light of her."

"Who's making light? I just said she's fine company. You could do worse. Maybe you should marry her and give that child a proper home."

Travis turned on him sharply. "That's enough."

Lawson chuckled as he raised his hands up in mock surrender. Travis felt himself anger even more at the condescension

"Easy, ol' pal. Didn't mean to rattle you up."

But he had. He had rattled him up. Travis could still feel his heart and the way it thundered the other night. The way she'd sounded when she laughed. The look in her eyes during their shared laughter. A sort of affection, something he hadn't seen in so long he almost had forgotten what it felt like entirely...

"She's ain't mine, ain't ever goin' to be mine," he muttered. "And it ain't any business of yours."

What Lawson might have answered, he didn't know, because then the sound of hooves pulled their attention to the road outside, covered in snow. Cade McCrae. Travis held his hand up in a wave, and the man came to a halt near them at the barn.

"Morning," he called, swinging off his horse. "Heard you had trouble with a horse today. Is that true?"

Royce had gone into town to get a few things for the horse, Travis thought. Must have talked to Cade while he was down there.

"Sweetheart's taken ill," Lawson said.

Cade gave a low whistle. "She's a good mare. Doggone shame." He looked at Travis then, eyes narrowing. "I saw Kane today, too. He's been asking around again. Says he's getting impatient and told a couple folks that he was gonna make sure you sell."

"My answer hasn't changed," Travis returned. "It's still no."

Cade nodded slowly. "He's pushing hard in town. Got the bank in his pocket."

Travis wondered if the letters were a coincidence or if Kane had something to do with them. Didn't seem to be much doubt on that.

"Listen, Travis..." Cade went on slowly. "I don't have much, but I could lend you something. Enough to get the bank off your back for now."

Travis looked at him sharply. "No."

"Don't be stubborn. It's a loan, not charity."

"I said no," Travis repeated, more firmly. "You've got your own place to keep. I'll manage it on my own."

"Manage how?" Cade asked him quietly.

Travis fought down the urge to snap back. The man was butting in to business that wasn't his. And he was making a habit out of it. He might have been one of his father's best friends, and he might have been like family to him, but Travis wasn't sure how much more of this he could take without losing his temper.

Cade shook his head. "You've got too much pride, you know that? One day it'll break you."

"Maybe," Travis retorted. "But that day ain't today."

The older man shook his head, muttering something under his breath before mounting up again. "Just keep an eye on Kane. He's not done with you. I gotta go out to the Price place and help Miss Clara out to town. Just keep an eye..." And with that, he clicked his tongue and rode off.

When he was gone, Lawson let out a long breath. "You sure about refusing him? That man means well."

"I won't take money from him or anybody else," Travis shot back. "I'll find another way."

Lawson clapped him on the shoulder. "You always do."

But as the afternoon wore on and the daylight began to fade, Travis couldn't shake the feeling that the world was closing in around him. Sweetheart, the bank, Kane. All of it. He was too near that breaking point Cade had talked about, and in his gut, he knew it. When he finally headed home, his boots as heavy as his mind, he saw Royce out on the porch. His arms were folded. His expression unreadable.

"Evening, Royce," Travis said, tying his horse.

Royce nodded. "Evening. You got a minute?"

Travis frowned. "What's wrong?"

Royce hesitated, glancing toward the house. "Everything all right with Evelyn?"

Travis raised a brow. "Far as I know. Why?"

"She's been different lately. Thought maybe—" He broke off, shifting uneasily. "Just wondering if everything's in order."

Travis studied him, puzzled. "In order?"

Royce looked away suddenly and sighed. "You notice anything missin' lately?"

Travis's gut tightened. "A box of a few things of Bonnie's I kept in my room. I've looked. They're gone. But Evelyn swore she never touched them."

Royce nodded slowly, his jaw tightening in what looked like anger. "That so?"

"What are you getting at?" Travis persisted.

Royce shook his head with a deep breath, then spat tobacco on the ground. "Things goin' missin',' and her alone in the house all day with the child?"

Travis felt a sudden chill that had nothing to do with weather. "You think she's a thief?"

"I'm saying it looks that way," Royce said with a shrug. "You know I've got no quarrel with the woman, but I don't take too kindly of my daughter's things going missing. First, my pocketknife, now you say Bonnie's things. I don't like it. None of it."

Travis's temper flared, but he couldn't tell if it was anger at Royce or at the suspicion that suddenly crept in of Evelyn. Things were getting better between the two of them. And as far as he was concerned, she was a good woman.

"She ain't a thief," he bit out, more defensively than he'd ever thought himself capable of. He didn't like this uneasy feeling, this sense of having to take sides.

"You sure about that?"

"Yes." The word came out as quick as a bullet.

Royce chuckled with a touch of malice. "You hardly know her!"

Travis's jaw clenched. "She lost her cousin. She took in the child. That's enough to know that she's a good and honest person."

"Maybe." Royce's voice went cold. "Or she could've killed the woman and stolen the child. You don't know any different."

"That's enough!" Travis rounded on him before he could stop himself, his fists clenching at his side. "Watch your mouth in my house!"

He sensed the irony in the words before they even fully left his mouth.

His house?

In truth, he'd given this house to Royce. Royce had deserved it for working the land so long. It was still Travis's land, and still Travis's property, but he wasn't the kind who'd rub another man's nose in that. Or at least he'd never thought himself that kind before.

Now, he wondered.

"All right!" Royce hissed, holding his hands up in surrender. "No offense meant. Just keep your eyes open, is all."

Travis didn't say anything else. He knew if he didn't end the conversation now, he'd say something else he regretted. So instead, he strode past his father-in-law into the house.

But Royce's words followed him, clinging and clawing at his back and into his head. The fire was roaring, carrying heat that thawed him as soon as he walked in. And the scent of stew wafted into his senses.

His stomach grumbled. He was hungry. But his nerves twisted in his gut. Had he been a fool for trusting her so blindly? What did he really know about Evelyn Rhodes?

Chapter Twelve

At last, the house gleamed.

Evelyn stood in the middle of the sitting room, her hands on her hips, biting her lip as she surveyed the room. Truth to tell, she was more than a bit stunned. All the clutter was finally gone, except for a couple of wood boxes of things Travis wasn't ready to unpack.

The floors were freshly scrubbed, the curtains completely mended and washed, and now hanging fresh in the windows. The windowpanes were frosted, icicles forming atop the window next to the dress she'd been working on for Clara and Marigold and their shop.

She was supposed to take it to them soon for their Christmas display.

Christmas, she thought suddenly, her heart feeling suddenly tight. *Good heavens... It's almost Christmas.*

How could she have forgotten?

Back home, before all the tragedy, Christmas had been the one day she looked forward to in the long stretch of winter. The church bells, the smell of roasted chestnuts, the sound of laughter, and carols spilling down snow-covered roads. She used to decorate her parents' small cottage with anything she could find. Pine boughs, ribbons, scraps of cloth—anything festive—and her mother would smile, giddy at her creativity.

How would the ranch take to decorations? She smiled wryly to herself. There were no ribbons hanging in this house. No laughter. Only wind and cold. And moody men.

Still, something in her refused to let the day pass unmarked. She loved Christmas too much, and besides, she wanted to give the very best to Mason. He deserved to have his first Christmas truly celebrated, even if they hadn't quite found their real home yet.

When Mason finally drifted back into another nap, she wrapped her shawl tightly around her shoulders, pulled on her old boots, and stepped outside. The sharp bite of the wind completely took her breath away.

The storm had passed again, but the air was still frigid, and the sun did very little to warm anything or anyone. Her breath puffed in front of her as she trudged toward the edge of the property. She gathered what she could of pine and holly, even a couple of tangles of mistletoe that found hanging from a low branch—which almost never happened! She remembered as a girl she used to climb up on her father's shoulders, and then hoist herself up to a branch higher than her head from there just to get a bundle of it.

By the time she couldn't take any more, her fingers stinging, her cheeks chapping, inwardly she was aglow, her spirits alight as she jogged back to the house. She could almost hear her mother's voice again, teasing her. But it warmed her heart, the thought of bringing life and color into this place.

When she got herself back inside, she shook the snow from her shawl, dropping the bundle of things from her arms on the wood table in the center of the room and tiptoeing to the wood-carved crib. Bless him, Mason was still peacefully napping. Good!

She grinned.

The house was clean. The baby was out. Time to get to work.

She placed the greenery over the mantle and on the windowsill of each window in the sitting room. She even hung the mistletoe in the archway leading to the sitting room and placed a few pine branches on the wood table in the center of the room.

She closed her eyes and took a deep breath, her lungs filling with the clean scent of forest and sap. With a stroke of good timing, she heard Mason begin to stir in his cradle from the room and started to go to gather him up, humming softly.

Maybe he would like the Christmas decorations as much as she did.

She hoped that Travis might approve. That he might, for once, see that she wanted this place to feel like a home.

But before she'd gone two steps, the sound of the door opening made her turn abruptly. Quickly, she brushed a stray strand of hair from her face. Heavy boots sounded before she saw him actually step inside.

But she did see how his eyes swept the room. At first, she thought he liked it, but then, his eyes falling on the mistletoe with bright red berries, he clenched his jaw and his nostrils flared.

"What is all this?" he demanded.

Evelyn blinked, taken aback. "It's—it's Christmas," she said softly. "Or nearly. I thought it would be nice to—"

"Take it down."

"What?" she asked, clutching at her chest.

"I said take it down." His voice was as harsh as it had been with the vase.

Her stomach dropped. "Why? I don't understand—"

"I don't celebrate Christmas," he said curtly, yanking off his gloves and tossing them onto the table, his jaw was set hard, eyes distant.

Evelyn stared at him, searching his face for something she might appeal to, some hint of warmth or reason. "Not celebrate? But why ever not?"

He didn't answer right away. He just waltzed past her, toward the hearth, staring into the flames. She wondered why she'd even asked. It was obvious. The man was hurting. He clearly didn't celebrate because he'd lost his wife and child.

Her chest ached at the thought, and at the fact that she was the reason he was now upset all over again, warring with himself over his feelings. "I only wanted to make it look cheerful," she went on, a bit shakily. "You've been working so hard, and I thought perhaps—"

He turned then, and she saw what looked like a scowl. "Royce told me today that he's noticed things goin' missin', too."

She blinked, startled. "What are you talking about?"

"You tell me."

Her mouth went dry. "You think I'm stealing from you? Is that what you're saying?" *After all I've done around here?*

"I think I don't know what to believe anymore," he said flatly. "You swore you didn't touch those things, but now, this—" He gestured around the room, pointing at the garland.

She felt her face heat up. "That doesn't make sense. This is what offends you and tells you that I'm some sort of thief? Decorating your home for Christmas?"

"I asked you once before to leave things be," he said, his tone rising. "This house is mine, and there are things in it that don't concern you! And you shouldn't be doin' things to my house without permission!"

"That's absurd!" she snapped back. "I've done everything I can to help you and make this place livable again, all the while caring for Mason! I told you I was going to organize and make it a home. This is how you show your appreciation? Accusing me of being a thief?"

Travis's expression didn't change. "How am I supposed to know what your intentions really are?" he said. "You're a stranger here. You came out of nowhere with a child that isn't yours. For all I know, you could—"

"For all you know," she cut in, trembling, "I might be trying my best to make a home where there was none. For your sake as much as mine and as much as this baby's. It's just a temporary home for me. I know that, but I'm doing everything I can to make it nice for you. To show you that I'm grateful to you for letting me stay here, even though all of this was thrust on you!" Her eyes burned. "You have no right to treat me this way. None."

He looked away first, jaw tightening, then turned and walked out the door without another word.

The garlands blurred in her vision. Her hands shook as she reached up and began pulling them down, one by one. She ignored the berries falling. Just continued to jerk everything down. Erasing it all. All her hard work, along with any sign of the Christmas holiday that was quickly approaching.

By the time she was finished, her chest hurt from holding back tears.

How could he not celebrate Christmas? How could any man be so cold, so unmoved by the season, or even by a simple kindness? And worse, how could he accuse her of stealing?

She pressed a hand to her heart. It was beating rapidly.

She understood shutting people out. She'd done that a lot after her parents passed away. It was partially the reason she was in the situation she was in. Being alone. Without a soul to help her, to shelter her, to give her aid with a newborn baby she hadn't been ready for.

But he had to know.

He had to know there was a better way.

She wanted to show him. She wished she could. Just like Arabella had shown her. Life was awfully lonely without anybody to share it with.

He had endured much, but so had she. Loss, hardship, the death of practically all her kin—but the way that man had just talked to her wounded her in a way she hadn't expected. Part of her had started to think that he was kind. That's what everyone kept telling her. How amazing he was before grief got in the way.

But she didn't see it.

Mason stirred in his cradle again, now crying softly, and she felt a jolt of shame at leaving him for so long. Kneeling down beside him, she hummed softly to soothe his upset. "Hush, Mason. Hush now, little love."

But she could hardly hear herself over the rush of her own thoughts. Over the question that had just hit her. One she disliked, but one she couldn't ignore.

Did Royce have something to do with all this?

Could he have planted the seed of suspicion in Travis's head?

Of course, he could have. Again, she hated the thought, but it wasn't impossible. She was told he was a good man, too, but she'd yet to see it. He seemed like the kind of man that hid behind a kind exterior to some, only to be mean and spiteful deep down.

He'd looked at her with disdain, and even worse, in his attitude toward Mason. A child! A little, innocent baby!

If that was what was happening here, she wasn't about to let it go on.

After settling Mason once more, she rose, her hands balled into fists, and hardly felt her steps going down the hallway. He'd be in the kitchen right about now. No time like the present.

"Royce," she said sharply, pushing her way inside.

He looked up, startled. "Miss Rhodes," he muttered. "What brings you—?"

"I'm not here for small talk," she cut him off, stepping closer. "I want to know why you've been spreading lies about me."

He blinked, feigning confusion. "Lies? I don't know what you mean."

"Don't play the fool," she snapped. "You told Travis that things have been going missing. That I might be responsible."

Royce straightened, resting his hands on the edge of the crate, and gave her a crude smirk. "Well, haven't they? Things *have* gone missing. He said so himself."

"That doesn't mean I took them!"

He shrugged. "You're the outsider," he said flatly. "You can't fault a man for putting two and two together."

She almost literally saw red. "You know full well that's not true. What's true is that you've had it in for me from the start!"

Royce's jaw flexed tightly, the only sign that she'd hit some sort of a nerve. He straightened his old back and looked at her with hardened eyes.

"You've got spirit," he muttered. "I'll give you that."

"I have truth," she shot back. "Something you seem to have misplaced."

His mouth twitched. "Careful, Miss Rhodes. You think cleanin' a house gives you ground to stand on, but you don't know this place. Or the people in it. You don't got a clue what I'm capable of."

"Lying is clearly the thing you're most capable of," she said. "And if you'd care to show me what else, then go ahead—show me."

He didn't say another word. He just grabbed his coat from the hook, shoved his hat on, and brushed past her with a cold shake of his head.

For a moment, she could do nothing more than just stand there, trembling. But then, she spoke aloud to the empty room. Needing to say it...to make it real.

. "I promise you this, Mr. Hartwell," she whispered. "I will show you both what kind of woman I really am!"

She wasn't sure exactly how she was going to make good on her promise—but she meant every word. And she'd find a way.

Chapter Thirteen

"Will this snow ever stop?" Evelyn groaned, her teeth chattering.

Snow had been falling all morning, soft as sifted flour, sparkling against the glow of the sun trying to poke gently through the clouds. By the time she and Barrett Lawson reached the town, her dress was completely covered in frost. The only thing redeeming this trip was her excitement at the chance to see Marigold and Clara in their shop. Climbing down from the wagon, she bundled Mason tightly against her chest beneath her shawl and beamed at her chauffeur.

"Thanks for letting me join you today!" she called out to Mr. Lawson. He flashed a half-smile at her and waved.

"Pleasure's mine, Miss Rhodes," he called back in reply. She flashed another smile his way and, clutching her satchel firmly, turned to head off while he watered and cared for the horses. "I'll come and find you soon."

The smell of Christmas, pine, cinnamon, and wood smoke, was all over town. It filled the streets, flooding from the storefronts that were open—not very many, from the looks of it.

Every window she passed, though, even in closed shops, was dressed for Christmas. Garlands of evergreen looped from door to door, big red ribbons placed beautifully every so many inches. The strands fluttered lightly in the breeze, and lanterns glowed warm and yellow behind the frosted glass of most of the windows.

Past the bakery, awash in the amazing smell of bread and sweetness, carolers were singing *God Rest Ye Merry Gentlemen.* Their voices dredged up memories Evelyn thought long forgotten, of Christmas seasons spent with her mother and father.

It had been so long since she had seen a place look so warm, so alive. And for a moment, Evelyn found herself feeling a surge of deep longing.

At the ranch, the world was still and gray. Nothing but clouds and snow and the mud-slushed porches. No decorations. No singing. No Christmas stories. Nothing but two grumpy men mostly ignoring her, for most of every day.

In town, families walked together—although not as many as she might have hoped for. Maybe because snow was still coming down fairly hard, and she couldn't blame people for staying indoors. Of course, there were a few hardy children out, wandering about, pressing their faces to the glass of the bakery and staring at the sugared treats in the window.

The small bits of laughter. Of togetherness. And the décor of Christmas did nothing but warm Evelyn up. She tightened her hold on Mason, pressing a kiss to the top of his woolen cap. "We'll just stop in quickly to show them the dress," she whispered against his head. "It'll be nice for you to see some friendly faces."

When she pushed open the shop door, the bell chimed overhead, and immediately she felt wrapped in a warm hug—only, no one was actually hugging her. The warmth of the shop, the smell of new fabric and sweet bread, like something was baking in the back, an aroma even better than the bakery had—it took hold of her. She smiled.

When Marigold saw her from behind the counter, Evelyn watched her entire face light up.

"Evelyn! Oh, you made it!" She bustled out into the open, wiping her hands on the small white apron wrapped around her waist. "You poor dear, you look frozen to the bone. Come in, come in!"

Evelyn smiled weakly, relieved to be met with such enthusiasm. "I'll admit, the weather nearly kept me away. But when Mr. Lawson said he was coming into town and offered to let me join him, I had to say yes."

Marigold reached to peek at Mason, her eyes absolutely brimming with happiness. "And how is this handsome fella?"

Evelyn grinned. "He's been eating well. I—well, we're managing."

Clara came out then from the back, her eyes just as bright as Marigold's, and Evelyn counted her blessings. It truly was a nice change of pace to be in the presence of people who enjoyed her and whom she enjoyed. Royce and Travis made things difficult, to say the least.

"Show us what you brought!" Clara called out in glee as she skipped over, gesturing to the satchel with the dress partially falling out.

Feeling eager, Evelyn opened her satchel carefully and pulled out the dove-gray wool with a high collar and tiny pearl buttons. She was proud of this work; it had been among her best. The stitching was delicate and neat, the hem trimmed in lace she'd salvaged from another older dress. But as she looked around at the dress shop, she hesitated slightly. Even this fine work was nowhere near as glamorous as what they already had on display—

Marigold didn't seem to agree, however.

"My word, Evelyn!" She gave a gasp. "This is beautiful!"

"Thank you." Evelyn watched as Clara brushed her fingers across the seams, nodding and smiling.

"It really is so beautiful!" she echoed. "Better than even what I could do."

Evelyn flushed at the praise. She wasn't quite sure about all that. Clara was incredibly skilled, and the clothes in the window were shining examples of that skill. But the compliment wasn't lost. She beamed at both of the women as a warmth spread over her chest. "You're kind to say so. I just followed what you showed me."

"Kind?" Marigold scoffed. "I'd say it's just recognizing true talent. You've got a gift for this, dear. I would hire you right on the spot."

Evelyn laughed nervously. She would have actually enjoyed that quite a lot. She would have her own income. Money to buy a place with her and Mason and stop feeling like a burden on two men who never wanted her there in the first place.

"You may yet have your chance," she murmured. She wasn't even sure why they hadn't demanded she leave yet. After all, the storm hadn't been so treacherous that they couldn't get to town.

As if sensing her silent question, Lawson had merely mentioned Travis being a man of his word—and in fact, the storm hadn't broken. The snow was still coming down. The ice was still on. She could stay until it passed. He told her, even just on the ride, that Travis would stick to that.

But she had no plans yet for after. Eventually, the snow would stop. Eventually, it would melt. And eventually, she would have no excuse to stay.

The door opened again. A gust of wind swept through the shop, along with the familiar scent of horses and leather.

"It's awfully nippy out there!" Lawson declared, then shook the fresh snow from his shoulders and took off his hat.

"Morning, ladies," he went on politely. His gaze lingered a bit longer on Clara than Evelyn anticipated. She caught it immediately and nearly laughed, but held back to watch Clara duck her head with a sly smile.

"Morning, Mr. Lawson," the girl practically giggled, and Marigold cleared her throat.

"How do you do this cold morning, Barrett?" Marigold asked.

"Cold," he laughed. "But doing better now that I'm with you, fine, beautiful women."

Evelyn watched as Marigold blushed, although there was still something lingering between Clara and Mr. Lawson even after both women laughed and waved him away dismissively. But then, seeing the look between the two of them, Marigold cleared her throat once more, harder this time.

"I think Mr. Lawson could use his shirts back," she said, rather pointedly, to her daughter.

"Oh, right! Yes!" Clara laughed breathily and skipped to the counter to grab a small bundle of shirts. She skipped back over and handed it to him. He smiled, taking them, looking through the pieces with wide eyes.

"You've outdone yourself, Miss Clara," he said. "I might start tearing my shirts on purpose if it means stopping by more often."

Marigold snorted. "Heavens, you two are enough to make a person blush."

Clara swatted at her mother playfully, but then, her teeth gritted, whispered just loud enough so that Evelyn and Marigold could hear. "Don't start, Mama."

Evelyn smiled faintly, her heart tugging at the sight. There was something so effortless about it. *How wonderful it must be to fall in love,* she thought, the ache deepening. *To be looked at like that...*

But she wasn't sure the good Lord intended that life for her. Quickly, hearing Marigold's voice again, she brought her thoughts back to reality.

"We were just about to ask Evelyn here how she was getting along at the ranch," Marigold chirped.

"Travis hates me," she blurted before she could stop herself. "And Christmas."

Lawson's brow furrowed. "*Hates* Christmas?"

She nodded, her cheeks burning, and she knew they were likely blushed red, but not from embarrassment as much as irritation. "I tried to decorate the house. Nothing fancy. Just some holly and evergreen. He came home and told me to take it all down. Said he doesn't celebrate Christmas."

Lawson rubbed the back of his neck. "Ah. I reckon that explains his mood..."

"Explains his mood?" she asked, confused.

"Travis hasn't celebrated Christmas since he lost his family," Lawson replied. "Bonnie loved Christmas. The whole house used to be covered head to toe with Christmas decorations. After the fire, well..." He sighed. "It's too much for him, I reckon. Reminds him of everything he's lost. He and Royce won't even touch that part of the property anymore. Me and a couple ranch hands have to take care of all that now. Anything that reminds them of her... It's too hard, I guess."

Evelyn felt her throat tighten. "I didn't even think about Christmas decorations hurting him," she whispered. "When my parents died, I was sad the first Christmas, but after a while, it felt more like I was keeping them alive by celebrating

Christmas the best I could. It was almost like they were there with me."

Lawson gave her a kind look. "That's a really nice way of lookin' at it. But he ain't like that." He laughed nervously.

Marigold sniffed. "It's about time he did start celebrating again. The trouble with that man is he can't let go of what happened. I hate to say it, but he needs to move on."

"Mother!" Clara cried, appalled. "He lost his entire family. You can't expect him to just forget."

"I don't mean forget about her," Marigold retorted, folding her arms. "None of us can do that…" The woman's voice started to crack as a tear fell down her cheek. She sniffled and then cleared her throat, the emotion behind her eyes obvious to Evelyn, who felt her throat clench. This was the first time she'd ever seen anyone's true emotions come out when it came to Bonnie Baldwin. "But that man needs to understand he's got to live. He's got to breathe again. Bonnie would want that."

Lawson shrugged. "I've tried to get him out, get him to join a supper or two at someone else's house, but he won't go anywhere except into town for an hour or two. He just stays on that ranch, buried in work."

"And he's not done any metal work, has he?" Marigold huffed.

Lawson shook his head. "No, ma'am. He doesn't even think about blacksmithing anymore. I don't think he's got a love for it anymore, either."

"Does he have a love for anything?" Evelyn asked.

Lawson chuckled. "Ma'am, he's a good man…He cares about people. He just ain't one to show it, especially not with all the hurt he's gone through. And he ain't goin' to admit it, but you bring a lot of that old hurt up. Your cleaning, cooking, rearing of that child, and those Christmas decorations…"

She swallowed hard. "He must think I'm meddling," she said softly.

Lawson frowned. "You're just doin' your best. You ain't doing a thing wrong."

Evelyn shook her head. "He doesn't see it that way. He's just so cold. Every time I think we make some sort of truce, he starts yelling at me."

Mason stirred, letting out a small whimper, and she rocked him gently until he quieted.

Marigold broke the silence at last. "You ask me, that man needs someone to kick him right in the rump and force him to quit moping."

"Mother," Clara warned again, though her cheeks flushed faintly.

Evelyn forced a small smile. "I think I've caused him enough trouble. I won't make things worse."

"I hate to break this up," Lawson said, looking over his shoulder out the window. "But Miss Rhodes, we should be getting back."

She nodded and said her goodbyes. "After this storm, and you can travel into town a bit more freely, I think you should come and join the shop." Marigold kissed the top of Mason's cap. "Dresses and men's clothes, too, if you'd like to bring your expertise. Clara's already doing big things with what you've shown her!"

Evelyn grinned wide. "I would very much love it."

Lawson opened up the door, the bell ringing in their wake, just as children ran past with their arms full of pinecones, ribbons, and what looked to be snacks. They were laughing, and carolers continued to sing just a few buildings down.

Christmas everywhere.

And yet she was about to return to a house stripped bare of anything Christmas.

"Thank you," she whispered to Lawson as she got back into the wagon.

He smiled faintly. "If you ever need anything at all, you just tell me."

She nodded gratefully, but her mind was on something else entirely.

It was on Travis Baldwin.

She knew he'd been through so much pain. So much that he couldn't find joy even in the most joyful time. *Please... let him find peace again.*

Chapter Fourteen

Even a couple of days since he'd lost his temper on Evelyn, Travis couldn't shake the guilt. He used to love Christmas, but now? Now it seemed like too much pain wrapped up in one single holiday. But even as he tried to acknowledge that, the suspicion of things going missing came back full force.

Things have disappeared. With no explanation.

What if he was wrong to trust her? What if Evelyn, as kind as she seemed, was meddling on purpose? What if she was taking things right under his nose?

What if it was her plan to come here and rob him blind slowly, but surely?

Stop it! He couldn't go against every ounce of instinct that he had. He knew better. There was no denying that the woman had a heart for Mason. And a woman with a heart wouldn't have stolen something she knew was important, would she?

His musings were interrupted by her voice, raised from the kitchen.

"I didn't do it! And you know good and darn well I didn't!"

Travis found himself hurrying to that room, its door already propped open to get the heat from the stove through the rest of the house. He could see down the hall that Royce scowled and tried to walk away from her, slamming his plate down on the counter. But she rounded on him, grabbing him by the forearm.

"Get off me, woman!" He yanked his arm away.

Travis paused. He wanted to intervene, but he also needed to hear just what on earth they were yelling about.

"You have to tell him the truth! I can't possibly spend Christmas with people who despise me!" Her voice was desperate, choked, like she'd been crying.

"It was necessary to make it look like you took those things!" Royce barked back. "You'll never take her place."

The words hit Travis like a blow to the ribs. *Never take her place. As if anyone could.* As if Evelyn had ever tried. Evelyn moved through the house as carefully as a church mouse. She tried to be delicate with the memories of Bonnie and Troy, not disregard them.

Hearing Royce fling Bonnie's memory out like a weaponed strike against Evelyn now?

Inexcusable.

All right. Enough was enough. Royce was not only crossing the line, but he'd lied. Bald-face lied.

Gut clenching, Travis cleared his throat and stepped closer to the kitchen's threshold. Evelyn turned at once, her eyes wide and shimmering with tears.

"I can't believe you lied like that," he said steadily. "She did nothing wrong. *Nothing.* Bonnie would hate to see you standing here, lying like a dog. In my house!"

There it was again.

Travis's house. He meant it this time, though.

Royce's face paled but quickly hardened. "Watch yourself, boy!"

"No." Travis didn't want to yell, but Royce made him feel like he had to. "You have no right. What did you do with them?"

He grabbed the older man by his shirt collar and jerked him toward him. Royce's face pinched into disdain. *Good.* Because Travis was feeling an awful lot of disdain in that moment himself.

"The locket and photographs are in my dresser drawer," Royce said slyly. "Some of it I had her burn, but she didn't know what it was."

Travis felt shock go through him. Burn it? He had her *burn* it?

"You need to get out of my sight right now, old man." He let go "Because if you don't, I'm goin' to do something I'll regret."

The older man couldn't even meet Travis's gaze. He muttered something under his breath and spun on his heel, storming out into the cold.

"I hope he had enough for breakfast," Travis finished with a growl. "I don't want him in here for lunch."

Evelyn's shoulders sagged in relief for a moment. Then, she launched herself at him full force.

"Thank you… for believing me," she whispered, clasping him around the neck. "I couldn't bear the thought of you thinking I did anything with them! Lawson said Bonnie's locket and photographs were missing, and a couple of pieces of fabric from her wedding dress. Lawson told me about it on our ride back from town, and I recognized that fabric—it was in a satchel he had me burn last week. I thought it was beautiful and wanted to ask him for it, but I couldn't bring myself to. I knew there had to be a reason he was throwing it out."

Travis grunted and pulled away. "And about…the other stuff?" He swallowed. "If decorating the house means that much to you, I reckon you can have at it."

He knew that this was coming out of nowhere, but it was the only thing he could think of. It was hard for him to offer even just that—the decorations, bringing the memories of Christmas with his family back—but it seemed like the right thing to do. It seemed only fair. He wanted her to enjoy Christmas there if she was to put in that much work.

And although it would be difficult to see all the decorations, after all Royce had done, the least he could do was to make her feel comfortable on Christmas. If decorations helped her feel comfortable, then so be it.

Her eyes widened, surprised. "I... I won't if it pains you," she said quickly, stumbling over her own words.

He let out a short sigh. "You don't understand," he said. Then, his voice softened, low and rough, as the memory clawed back to him. "The last Christmas I spent with Bonnie and Troy... before the fire. It was perfect."

"How was it perfect?" she asked him.

He smiled faintly. "Bonnie spent a week makin' candies. Peppermints and chocolate drops. I stole them every time I could, even though she made them for the neighbors and merchants in town. We went out together, cut a tree from the hill overlooking the creek. Rain comin' down so thick we could barely see each other. She kept fussin', sayin' we should've waited for better weather, but then she laughed and said she didn't mind if it meant holdin' on to me a little tighter." He swallowed hard. "It was simple. But it was ours. And I never thought I'd lose it."

Evelyn's expression softened. "I can't imagine your loss," she said. "But at least it was a perfect Christmas to remember..."

He could only nod, temporarily at a loss for speech.

She wasn't wrong.

At least it had been a perfect Christmas. A memory, he hoped, one day he could look back on fondly instead of with pain.

Evelyn looked down. "My last Christmas with my parents…" she began softly. "Mama baked gingerbread shaped like angels. Papa would play the fiddle terribly, so terribly, but he'd insist." She laughed. "He picked me up and let me put a star on the tree, and twirled me around 'til my feet kicked mama's lamp." Her smile faded. "I was a teenager. A little too big to be twirled around like that, I guess." She swiped tears from her face and cleared her throat.

"Come have breakfast," she said then, moving back to the stove.

He pulled out a chair and sat down, his stomach growling despite his nerves.

When she set a plate of bacon, eggs, and fresh bread before him, he practically salivated. Grabbing the fork she handed him, he dug in, then spoke with his mouth half-full. "Tell me about your cousin…Mason's mother."

He wasn't sure what prompted him to ask her that. He just suddenly found himself wanting to know more about her.

She turned around from the stove, eyes distant, as if she was dredging deep into her memory. "Arabella… she was like a sister. When her father found out she was expecting Mason, he disowned her. She had nowhere to go. I took her in, tried to care for her… and then she died. I gave up the store so she could be properly buried. She'd written Sheriff McCrae to become your bride…" She took a few steps closer, pulling a chair right next to him.

Travis chewed softly, swallowing hard. McCrae really was a meddling son of a gun.

"So, did you buy that tailor shop, or was it your parents'?"

"My father's pride and joy." She beamed.

His stomach sank a bit. He knew all about that. His father had owned this land and was a blacksmith in town. Travis had done his best to follow in his footsteps. His pa was the greatest man he'd ever met. But any man that raised a woman as good and kind as Evelyn Rhodes was likely just as good of a man as his father, too.

Travis looked down at her hands and marveled. How small they were—and yet he'd seen the dresses she made, and the way she cooked and cleaned. They were capable, and looking at them closer, he could see that they were callused from years of needlework.

"You walked away from all that?" he asked quietly. "From your father's work?"

Her smile wavered, a softness replacing it. "I needed money to bury Mason's mother," she said, shrugging. "A home can be rebuilt, and so can a business. A life, too. But a proper burial? You can't replace that. A place where her son can go visit? That's priceless to me."

Something in his chest pulled tight. He swallowed hard.

"You're a remarkable woman," he said finally, his voice almost reverent.

Admitting that felt dangerous. The moment it left his mouth, he knew he hadn't meant to say it. Not out loud, anyway. Not where she could hear it. He watched her fingers still on the table, watched the way she breathed in just a little sharper, and it rattled him. He shouldn't be noticing things like that. He shouldn't even be noticing her at all.

Their eyes met. It was always difficult when he looked her in the eyes, and this time was no exception. It was dangerous how time seemed to stretch.

Travis felt a pull like no other toward her, almost as though the world around them disappeared. All he saw was her. Her lips.

Are we about to...?

Then a sharp cry pierced the silence.

"Mason!" Evelyn gasped, rushing to the other side of the house, skirts swirling behind her. He could hear her, down the hall, as soon as she reached the cradle. "Shh, shh, little one..." she cooed, rocking him gently.

Travis sank back into the chair, his breath ragged. When she disappeared down the hall, he dragged a hand over his face, his mind going wild as a bucking bull.

What in God's name am I doing? What just happened?

He stared at the empty spot next to him.

God help me. I might actually be falling for her.

The realization hit him like a steam train. It was reckless. Dangerous.

And yet, he couldn't deny it, either.

Chapter Fifteen

He could still see Evelyn, staring at him like that at the kitchen table that morning. He couldn't deny the stir of emotion that had started moving in him when it came to her. Even though he wanted more than anything to push it deep down inside himself.

She'd looked lovely, wearing a dress she'd been working on. He'd watched her—far more than he wanted to admit— as she'd made two dresses.

One that she'd taken into town for Clara and Marigold, and one for herself.

The one for herself was a bit plainer, but beautiful, nonetheless.

She had done the same for Mason, too. He'd seen the tiny shirts and trousers she had fashioned, stitched neatly and carefully. She had worked day and night to craft them.

He grumbled, mad at himself for letting himself notice it all. And notice her.

He dragged a hand down his face. *Fool.* It was only a dress. Only a woman doing honest work. No matter how beautiful she was, and no matter how good at making the dress she was, it was still just a woman, doing honest work, and wearing a dress. Yet, he felt like he was unraveling bit by bit.

Her. Royce.

All of it.

His temper with Royce still burned at the back of his mind. Forgiving a grieving man was one thing. Living next to him and his bitterness was another. The whole house felt tight lately, like one wrong word might split it in two. And sure, he could blame Cade McCrae, but the truth of the matter was, it was only a matter of time before something would come between him and his father-in-law. Their grief went separate ways, and they lashed out at one another.

He could understand where the old man was coming from, though. Ever since the fire, since losing his daughter, he hadn't been himself. That was his daughter. His only child. His only grandchild. His legacy.

Gone.

They'd both experienced more grief than either one of them ever thought they would, and the truth was, they'd changed. Both of them. Maybe grief didn't just leave scars. It hollowed a man out until there was nothing left—or he'd changed into something he never wanted to be.

With a shake of his head, Travis pushed the thoughts aside. There were chores to do. There would be time to think about all the rest later.

After saddling up Buck, he mounted him and rode out toward the back stables, holding his reins loosely in one hand. Until he saw something that stopped him, abruptly.

Lawson.

He was running out of the stables, his arms flailing. "Travis!"

"What's the matter?" Travis clicked his tongue and kicked Buck's side.

"Come quick!" Lawson yelled back, turning back into the stables.

"Ya! Ya!" he slapped the reins roughly, and Buck's breath puffed white in the frigid air. Travis leaned forward in the saddle, gripping the leather reins as tight as he could.

One of the biggest reasons he'd left blacksmithing was because he'd found comfort in horses. There was something about a steady gait, leather cracking in his hands, hooves stomping against the dirt.

This, though, this moment right now, it did nothing to steady him. It did nothing to calm him.

"Focus," he muttered to himself, jaw tight.

He needed to focus.

On this. On the ranch. The ranch needed to be first. Always.

His father's land. The land he and his wife built a family on. The ranch first.

He all but jumped from Buck, launching himself toward the door of the stable.

When it groaned open, the smell hit him first. It was something rancid. Heavy. It clawed at his throat roughly, making him cough.

Sickness.

The smell of sickness.

His horses should've lifted their heads. Should've nickered. Stamped. Reached their long necks over the stall doors, eager for some grain like they usually did. But they didn't. This time, all he heard was shallow groans and weak shuffling of hooves against straw. He froze.

Nothing could have prepared him for this. The rows of horses, normally spirited and restless in the cold, lay almost still. All of them—their flanks heaving weakly, eyes half-lidded and dim. Just like Sweetheart.

A shiver ran down Travis's spine. His boots sank into damp bedding as he moved deeper into the stable, checking all the stalls, every step slower than the last.

Some of the horses were propped slightly with their legs trembling, too weak to stand fully. Others lay flat on the ground, necks stretched out, their ears twitching feebly.

"Lawson…" Travis's voice was hoarse. "What in God's name do you think this is?"

He had a notion, but he didn't dare say it. He'd never seen anything like that before.

Lawson's jaw tightened, and he didn't answer. Not immediately anyway. He just looked at the animals, his own breath ragged. All of them were sick. Some of them suffering. "It's the same as Sweetheart," he said. "Royce had to put her down."

He dropped to his knees beside the nearest gelding. Duke. He was a steady and gentle giant. A good horse, one of Bonnie's favorites. She always used to say that he would carry Troy to school one day. "No…" he whispered, pressing a hand to his neck.

It was burning up.

Hot as fire.

Duke's muscles twitched, and his breath came out fast

"Easy, boy," Travis whispered. His voice cracked. "I'm right here."

He hadn't cried since the fire, but now there was a sting behind his eyes.

"Poison," Travis said quietly. Reluctantly. "It's gotta be…"

'Who?" Lawson replied. "Who would do this?"

Travis only had one man come to mind.

Fletcher Kane. Of all the devils in Wyoming territory, Kane was the only one bold and dumb—not to mention heartless—enough to do something like this.

He wanted nothing more than to see this ranch fail so he could take it over for a cheap price. Especially since Travis had turned down all the 'fair' offers he'd seemed to have.

"That son of a gun…" Travis muttered. He wanted to say something stronger, but held back. Cursing wouldn't help now.

***

After securing the animals as best they could, Travis moved quickly and mounted Buck. The gelding tossed his head, sensing whatever it was that Travis felt—fear, anger, and everything in between. Horses knew. They always knew. He needed to check the fences. The water troughs. He needed to look for any sign of anything.

Of any tampering.

His body was tense, his mind a jumbled mess.

He came up on Royce, fixing a fence line. The old man's posture was hunched, eyes downcast, but focused on his work. Part of him wanted to ride past, leave the anger sitting, but the ranch wouldn't survive on grudges.

"Royce," Travis called out.

The old man stiffened at the sound.

"I… Travis…" He stood up and turned around. "I… I can't stand us bein' sore with one another. But I also can't see another woman in this home. It is too painful. Evelyn… she is a good woman. Pretty by all counts, a good cook, a good housekeeper. But she will never be my daughter. I can't—"

"She can't and won't ever replace her," Travis cut him off quietly. "She's here for her boy, and she's just tryin' to earn her keep. But right now, we have bigger fish to fry."

"What do you mean?" he asked.

Travis shook his head. "Doesn't look like Sweetheart's the only horse that we're going to lose. One of our stall-houses was completely wiped out with some sort of illness. Looks like they've been poisoned, to have that many down at once."

Royce's face fell. "Who you think?"

"I think Fletcher Kane may have an idea. He's been askin' for this place, and I've been sayin' no. And from what Cade says, he ain't too happy about it. Said he's gonna make sure I sell."

"Travis!" Lawson bellowed, running wildly toward them, his arms flailing, his legs skidding through the slick snow. "The horses... they've started to die!"

Travis's stomach lurched violently, the cold dread returning like a stone pressing down on his chest. He could barely process it before the panic started to rise up and suffocate him. He swung toward the stables. "Ya!" he kicked at Buck's side.

Every horse they had tended, every life he had been responsible for since foalhood, was all being threatened. All his hard work. His livelihood. Any chance he had at paying the bank back.

It was quickly fading.

He kicked Buck hard, heading for the barns. He had to fix this. He had to stop it before whatever it was took all the horses. And he had to make sure whatever this was—and whoever was doing it—didn't go unpunished.

He barely felt the cold as Buck tore across the land, kicking up snow in sheets behind them as they powered through the field. Travis's thoughts rattled. His ranch couldn't take another hit. Not the horses. Not the land. None of it.

They wouldn't survive it.

He moved to all the stables, feeling himself quaking.

"Whoa there!" he shouted, pulling back Buck's reins and forcing him into tight circles to slow as they approached the stable at the far east.

His boots hit the ground before Buck even managed to get fully stopped, and he ran hard, slipping on packed ice, catching himself on the stable door as he stumbled inside and moved frantically toward the stalls. He couldn't bear to think of the horses dying like that. He had to find out what was going on. Lawson scrambled beside him, catching up, and Royce was there, too, before Travis even got into the first stall.

"Lord help us..." Royce whispered, his voice cracking at the condition of the animals.

It looked like only Duke was left...

It felt like Travis's ribs were trying to splinter apart, like his lungs couldn't find enough air to keep him alive. This ranch was all he had left. His father's land. His wife's memories. What was meant to be his son's future.

He kicked an overturned bucket hard enough that it cracked against a post. Duke flinched weakly at the sound, and Travis immediately dropped beside him again.

"Easy, boy," he whispered, stroking the gelding's trembling cheek. "I'm here. I ain't leavin' you."

Behind him, Royce muttered, "If Kane did this... he's got to pay."

Travis didn't turn. Didn't want to see the shared grief in Royce's eyes, because in all honesty, it mirrored his own too just a bit too closely.

"He will," he answered, his voice low and cold as the wind shrieking outside. "But right now, we got to save whatever horses we still can."

Lawson brought fresh buckets, hauling water frantically. Then, all three of them propped Duke upright, rubbing his legs in hopes of keeping the blood moving. Travis prayed as hard as he rubbed...and he suspected the other two men did, too.

Chapter Sixteen

"Silent night... holy night... all is calm... all is bright..." Evelyn sang as she moved carefully, almost reverently, stringing the greenery around the hearth, tying small clusters of holly with ribbon along the bannisters. This made her happy. Decorating.

It was even grander than the last time, with permission from Travis, of course.

She hung up sprigs of mistletoe again, in just a couple of places.

She had clad herself in one of the dresses she had just finished fashioning by following Clara's instructions. This one was a bit simpler than the one she'd taken for them to look at. A side project of sorts, something for her to wear herself

It was a soft cotton, soft and gentle, like a tender touch. It was blue, like wildflowers creeping up in the plains at spring— both color and feel bringing comfort. And comfort it was, she thought, heart melting in gratitude.

She scooped Mason up, holding him close. She couldn't get enough of the warmth of his little body and the sounds he made. She found herself growing more and more attached every single day.

He looked like her.

Like Arabella.

He had the same blue eyes. The same smile, although his was a little bit gummier than Arabella's. She laughed.

There was something about him. His smile. His laugh. His noises. The smell at the top of his head—it filled her with a joy unlike any she'd ever had.

She wasn't sure how anyone could love anything this much. But she did. As if he were her baby boy, as if she had grown him inside her.

He'd quickly become her everything. Like it was her and him against the whole wide world. And she wanted nothing but to share the warmth of the Christmas season with him. She was so grateful to Travis for letting her decorate. For letting them stay for a time here without worrying where they were to spend Christmas.

She set Mason down gently in their bedroom, leaving him snuggled safely in his cradle before moving to the kitchen. It was time for his nap and her supper preparation.

It'd be a meal worthy of the season, if she had her way! She had noticed that Travis favored cottage pie, and so that would be the menu tonight.

For over an hour, she labored over the hot kitchen stove, peeling potatoes and mincing up meat. She'd felt her own stomach growl as the smell of herbs and roasting meat filled up the entire room. She smiled, noting how it mixed well with the piney, clean scent of the house and evergreen decorations

But as the afternoon waned, and supper started to cool, she couldn't help worry creeping in. Travis was late. Normally, he got back to the house by dusk; it was already dark now, and there was still no sign of him. Or Royce, either, for that matter.

She had already set the table, polished the forks, placed candles on the table oh-so-carefully, and adjusted the garlands she'd just put back up until she was certain they looked perfect.

Just as she was about to get up and head out onto the porch for any sign of him, however, the door opened, and Travis stepped inside. He looked at the ground, his cheeks flushed from the cold, but his face showed more than a little frostbite.

Her heart sank.

Something was wrong.

She wondered where Royce was. He usually beat Travis inside, but there was still no sign of him, either.

Not that she cared.

Travis didn't seem to notice, or at least he didn't acknowledge, anything. Not the decorations. Not the candles. Nothing. He just set his coat aside, atop the back of the rocking chair in the sitting room, and looked at her almost curtly before he moved to the back of the house toward the kitchen.

Evelyn's heart sank. She had worked so hard.

And he wasn't going to acknowledge it?

He began eating quietly. He didn't say grace. He didn't thank her. Nothing. He just started shoveling food directly into his mouth, paying her no mind at all.

"Travis..." she began almost timidly. "I... I hope you like the decorations."

He set down his fork and looked at her briefly, a frown pulling his face tight, then pushed his plate away. "Leave me alone."

And without another word, he stood. So abruptly that the chair skidded harshly against the wood floors. Then he brushed past her and headed toward his bedroom.

Her mouth fell open, the sting of rejection harsh. She waited for a moment, not sure what she might say to make things better. She wondered if she should leave him be. But then again, after Arabella, she knew it was usually better to have someone else right there with you. She sighed and quietly followed his steps down the narrow hallway to his bedroom.

She knocked lightly on the door. "Travis... may I come in?"

A curt, almost imperceptible grunt was the only thing that came, but that was permission enough as far as she was concerned. She pushed the door open slowly. The room smelled faintly of old leather and ink, the ledgers spread across the desk in the corner of his room. He was bent over them, pen in hand, scribbling something.

"Are those your ledgers? ... I could perhaps help," she ventured, stepping further into the room. "At the tailor shop, I did much of the bookkeeping."

Travis snapped the book forcefully and looked at her with cold irritation. "This ain't none of your business," he growled. "I already told you to leave me alone tonight!"

Evelyn froze for a moment, her lips parting, then closing again.

"I..." she began, voice trembling, unsure of what to say. "I only... thought—"

"Enough!" he barked, standing abruptly. His swiftness sent a small draft across the room, chilling her and gently ruffling the edges of the papers he had stacked up. "I said leave me be!"

Her shoulders slumped. She knew she shouldn't argue. Not now.

She had prayed for this man. So hard. Each and every day.

And she could only hope that he would find his way again, that he would learn to trust someone other than himself, and that he would let go of some of his pigheaded stubbornness.

But tonight was clearly not that night.

She sank back to her room, where Mason giggled and kicked his feet in the cradle. She smiled, gently gathered him up in her arms, and sat down on the bed. She kissed his forehead tenderly and smoothed the hair back from his face.

"I don't understand," she whispered to him, although she knew he couldn't answer. "We were... getting closer, weren't we? At least in a way that let us have an understanding. I don't get why he wants to shut me out so much."

She may not have known everything, but she knew one thing: A man who came in angry and upset and immediately went to his room to scribble down something on what looked like ledger books was a man scared to lose his livelihood. She wasn't going to push it anymore tonight. She would wait. She would bide her time. But she wasn't going to give up trying to help this man.

She was ready to see the Travis Baldwin everyone said was so grand and wonderful—the one she'd seen glimpses of now and again. And although she was tired of being hurt and disappointed, she knew she'd survived much worse.

Tomorrow, she promised herself, she would try again.

She was determined. This was going to be a nice Christmas. Not just for Mason, but for her, and for Travis Baldwin, too.

But as much as she tried to settle her heart with that promise, her mind remained restless. How would she make it a good Christmas for Travis if he wasn't willing to open up?

She sighed, laying Mason back down in the crib. She lingered there, a little longer than she should have, watching him breathe, loving the tiny movements of his lashes and the slow rise and fall of his chest.

He looked so peaceful.

So innocent.

He was so unaware of the heaviness she felt—the love she had for him, the worry she had being what he needed. But as she looked at him, she knew her resolve would never let her give up being the best mother she could be.

"Sleep well, little one," she whispered. "Mama's right here."

It didn't matter that she wasn't truly his mother. It didn't matter that the world would say different. Mason felt like hers and, in all rights, was going to be. She was all he had. And he was all she had...

With one last glance at the beautiful baby boy, Evelyn stepped quietly back into the hallway. Dim lantern light flickered along the wooden walls, and Travis's door remained closed. She could hear the faint scratch of a pen from inside his room.

She sighed and turned away toward the sitting room, even though it pained her heart to do it. He'd been up since before dawn, and he was still working, even inside. Clearly still angry. Clearly hurting somehow.

The fire had burned low in the sitting room, but it was still warm, and it looked beautiful with the garland that hung in the fireplace.

The mistletoe draped above the archway stirred slightly with the faint draft that moved from the windows. Why had she even bothered to hang that up? Any of it? Travis Baldwin was not fond of Christmas, and he'd made it known that he also wasn't so fond of her, either.

But... he *had* let her decorate.

That had meant something. It had to.

She lowered herself onto the rug near the fire, pulling her knees up beneath her skirt. The heat of the flames slowly seeped into her body, warming even her chilly fingers. Her eyes drifted shut as she listened to the fire and took deep breaths to soothe herself from the day.

Truth be told, she was exhausted. Bone-deep tired in a way she hadn't felt in years. Not only from the work—though there had been plenty of that—nor from caring for Mason. No. The additional burden was trying to navigate Travis Baldwin.

Trying to help him. Trying to understand him.

He confused her, even frightened her at times. But admittedly, he also, without even meaning to, made her heart swell.

She pressed a hand to her chest, feeling the steady beat beneath. Was she foolish? Probably. But she'd always believed hearts were meant to be foolish sometimes.

Shaking her head, she stood up and added another log to the fire. She watched as sparks flared upward, then faded.

She would keep trying. Not because she was weak or desperate. But because she believed in the possibility of something better. For herself. For Mason. And for Travis Baldwin.

And because Christmas—no matter if someone liked it or not—carried nothing if not hope. Jesus had come into the world on Christmas to save it; Evelyn decided to claim the hope that, perhaps, she could make Travis Baldwin smile and see the beauty in the day all over again.

Chapter Seventeen

Poison.

It had to be.

The wind had came in like a steam train, hard and fast. It shook the house. Rattled the trees. And it hadn't stopped all day. It was rough being in the middle of it atop Buck, trying to find the source of the horses being sick.

Lawson was with him, scanning the banks and the frozen creeks.

They had to stop any more horses from dying. Travis's gut twisted to a point where he thought he might be sick himself. What kind of lowlife would really do something like this? It had to be someone like Kane. A whole stock full of horses didn't get poisoned by accident. The problem only made sense to be coming from the water somewhere.

Travis tightened his grip on the reins

"Check the water again," he said, voice tight with resolve. "Every inch we can get. Look for anything that might have been dropped in, anything unnatural."

Lawson's gaze swept the banks carefully, eyes narrowing against the wind. It was drying both their eyes out, but Travis knew they had to keep going. It had to be Fletcher Kane. He was the only one wanting him gone, and the only one with enough evil tenacity to actually pull something like this off.

Travis had known the risk when he refused Fletcher Kane's repeated offers to buy the ranch. He knew what kind of man he was. Through and through.

Relentless.

Still, though, Travis hadn't known he would go this far this soon. He hadn't even put pressure on the bank to take the place yet.

The chilly wind made it so much worse being out here looking for what might have been left out here. But he had to push forward. His mind kept drifting to his horses. His faithful, strong, beautiful horses that he'd raised from nothing. He owed it to them and to himself to find the source.

These horses were meant to be alive for years to come, working land for whoever bought them. They were meant to be part of someone's legacy. Not killed in the middle of a harsh winter.

Then, abruptly, movement on the rise above the stream caught his attention. Two figures were advancing, their horses cutting a path through the frost-crusted grass. One was tall, broad-shouldered, and dressed in black and gray, a coat that looked far too fine for these harsh plains. The second was shorter, leaner, covered in grime, with the unmistakable look of a gunslinger. Even at a distance, Travis's jaw clenched. Fletcher Kane and his right-hand man, Amos Sharpe.

Travis's hand brushed the gun at his hip, and his fingers tightened around the handle instinctively. Lawson tensed up beside him atop his own horses, his eyes sharp, his face scrunched into a scowl.

"Travis Baldwin," Kane called, his tone mockingly polite. "I hear terrible news about your horses. Truly, it's a tragedy. Such beautiful creatures, lost so cruelly. I've heard… and I think it's time you consider your options. I don't think you'll be able to make it without every last one of your horses. I heard the bank's really having a tough time extending your loan."

Travis felt rage bubble in his gut. The man being there was enough of a threat to him. He had it in good mind to drop him where he was. But he didn't want that on his conscience. Not unless he drew first. "This is my property," he said instead. "You'll go on now."

Kane's thin smile was infuriating, as if Travis's anger amused him.

"You should sell, Baldwin," he said smoothly, tilting his head toward the stream. "Start over somewhere else. It seems inevitable, doesn't it? You're being ruined, whether by your own misfortune or by... circumstance. Why fight a battle you ain't gonna win?"

Travis's grip on the reins tightened further. The man had practically just admitted to being the culprit. But they had to keep following the stream to find the source of this. Eventually, he'd clear that stream up, and he'd find a way to keep the likes of Kane away from his water.

"I ain't ever gonna sell to you," he snarled. "Now get out of here before I shoot you where you are."

The smaller man, Sharpe, rode his horse forward a few steps, menacingly. His grimy eyes narrowed, his fingers brushing the rifle at his hip. He said nothing, but Travis felt threatened enough to pull his pistol from its holster.

Sharpe didn't flinch.

"Consider carefully, Baldwin. Even the strongest men must bow to circumstance eventually. It would be... *unfortunate* to see what happens if you insist on standing firm."

Travis's chest heaved with fury barely restrained. He wanted to ride forward, to make the threat tangible, to show Kane that he wasn't someone to be trifled with. His mind raced through the possibilities, ways to defend the ranch, protect the remaining horses, and make sure, once and for all, Fletcher

Kane wouldn't win. Lawson grabbed up his rifle. He knew that his foreman shared his same resolve.

"I said leave," Travis repeated, holding his gun pointed at Kane's forehead. "I won't say it again."

Fletcher's thin lips twisted into a smirk, which did nothing but make Travis's blood boil. He breathed out lazily and turned his horse. "Very well. But consider carefully. Stubborn men often pay a high price."

With that, Sharpe turned, too, and together they rode off.

Travis gritted his teeth, his father's words cutting deep into him. *It's the wild west, but we ain't got to be wild heathens.*

"They'll be back," Lawson grumbled. "And I'm willin' to bet that next time, they're gonna wanna do more than talk."

Travis nodded, staring after the men. He knew they may have only delayed the inevitable. Kane would surely push more. He had some kind of plan.

That smug smirk.

Travis wanted nothing more than to knock it straight off his face.

But he was trying to be civilized. He didn't want the blood of a man on his hands. But a man couldn't tolerate being pushed much further.

"We need to get with Cade," he said finally. "The Sheriff... he can do something. Surely there's a way we can get this figured out."

Lawson nodded. "Maybe," he said, spitting. "We'll need a plan fast. If they've really poisoned the stream, that means anyone or anything who drinks from it is at risk. We gotta find where they're contaminating it, because anything downstream is in danger until it clears out."

Travis's jaw tightened, his eyes narrowing back to the creek once more. Every single instinct inside of him told him to protect everyone by hunting down the source. To confront Kane and Sharpe with two bullets. One between each of their eyes.

But he couldn't. Not yet.

He thought of Evelyn and Mason, too. Kane's malicious greed could put them at risk, too, if they didn't find the source of the poison soon enough. Something strong enough to take down a horse could certainly take them all down, too.

Buck stomped at the frost-covered ground. "Let's get to lookin'," he said. "We'll look for anything in the stream. Every part of it."

If anyone thought they would take what was his, they had another think coming.

Lawson nodded, then clicked his tongue at his horse. "Ya!" he yelled out, slapping his reins to ride further upstream.

They had to find the source. Luckily, he was beginning to have a pretty good idea where to start. Only horses in specific stables and pastures had been affected.

The cold gnawed at his bones as he rode, but once again, Travis barely felt it over the anger heating his blood near boiling, pounding in his temples, as he narrowed his eyes and continued on. He had to find it. He had to.

Every time he shut his eyes, he saw those poor horses labored breathing. Saw that some of the horses went quicker than others. That some suffered more.

Duke, though, he still held on—and all Travis could think about was his labored breathing. The sores around his mouth. Whatever it was, maybe Duke hadn't taken as much as the others.

Not like Sweetheart. The way her mouth had started to foam, and her eyes had rolled back, right before Royce had to put her down. He swallowed hard. He'd seen animals die before, but never like this. Never so many at once.

They'd been busy burying them, struggling to get holes dug in the bitter cold with the hardened ground. He had to stop it from happening, or he'd be down to no stock and no manpower. Everyone was tired.

Cold.

Blistered.

He swallowed hard, gripping the reins until his gloves creaked. If the horses continued to die, the ranch died with them. And if the ranch died…what was he? What future did he have left? And what about Royce? He wasn't fit enough to go to another ranch.

The wind shifted again, cutting sideways across his face, and Buck tossed his head, snorting uneasily. Travis leaned forward to pat the horse's neck. "Easy, boy. I know. I don't like it either."

Lawson hopped down off his own horse and crouched down at the bank again, for what felt like the hundredth time. He cracked a thin sheet of ice with his boot heel and scooped it into his glove, sniffing it. Grimacing immediately. "Somethin's off," he muttered. "Smells wrong. Like oil mixed with—hell, I don't know what."

Travis hopped down from Buck and knelt, dipping his fingers into the blackened slush at the water's edge. The back of his neck prickled, and he felt his hair stand on end.

He looked down the winding stream. Most of it was hidden under ice by now, but in a few places, the water still gurgled through gaps. Any one of those places could be the source.

He rubbed his face with both hands, exhaustion setting in. If Kane wanted war, why not just come out and say it? Why kill innocent animals? Why destroy what generations had built?

Then the answer hit him.

Because cattle and horses couldn't shoot back. Because poisoning a man's livelihood was easier than facing him at dawn with pistols.

Because at his core, Kane was a yellow-bellied coward.

Chapter Eighteen

Travis had been locked in his bedroom for hours, which wasn't like him. He was always busy doing something. She'd even heard him pacing earlier, his steps sounding heavy. Panicked, almost. But she didn't dare bother him.

She made coffee, closing her eyes and taking a breath at the smell. There was something about it that always calmed her nerves. She only hoped the same was true for Travis.

Carefully, she poured it into a cup to carry it toward his door, but went a couple of steps further toward her door first, to peek in on Mason. He was asleep in his cradle, his small hands tucked close to his chest in little fists, his breaths causing his chest to lift and fall softly.

She smiled and walked in, noticing his blanket had slipped off. Gently, she pulled the small baby quilt back to cover him, kissing the top of his head before walking back to Travis's room.

When she got to the door, though, she paused. She could hear the sound of papers rustling inside, followed by a sharp scrape that she assumed was a chair sliding across the wood floor.

"Travis," she called softly. "I brought you some coffee."

At first, he didn't say anything. But then, she heard a heavy sigh followed. "Come in".

She pushed the door open.

He sat at his desk, his hair mussed, likely from running his hands through it too many times. His eyes were red, bags underneath them, papers were stacked up high on the surface of his desk. She took a few steps closer. His face was drawn, pale around the mouth. He was tired.

Whatever the trouble was, he'd been at it too long.

There was a letter in his hand, the paper creased and stained from where his fingers had gripped it. She couldn't say who it was from, but by the way he was clutching it, she didn't think it to be good news.

She set the cup down carefully. "You've been in here all morning. I thought you could use something warm."

He didn't look at her right away. His eyes stayed fixed on the letter, although it was practically crumpled in his fist.

"The bank," he said simply. "They're foreclosing."

Evelyn took a step back, "Foreclosing?"

He nodded. "I've missed too many payments. I had a plan to sell off some of the horses to local ranches. But four of them have been killed now. With that, I won't be able to pay the debt. If I don't come up with the money before Christmas, I'll lose the ranch."

"Oh, Travis…" Her breath caught. "Killed…how?"

"Lye. In the stream."

Evelyn's eyes widened in horror. "Our water?"

He shook his head. "I worried about that at first, but we found it. It was downstream from the house. Upstream from one of the horses' grazing areas. We found it and closed off that pasture 'til we're sure it's cleared up."

He saw her eyes well up. "Oh, Travis. I'm so sorry."

He let out a rough laugh, bitter and empty. "You can save your sympathy. I know exactly who's behind it." He slammed the letter down with a fury she'd not seen before. "Fletcher Kane. He's been trying to buy me out for months. The bank manager's one of his cronies. They play cards at the saloon together every week. And I know that he's in Kane's pocket. Kane's poisoned my horses, and the bank can't give me an interest accruing extension 'til spring, even though he does it for everyone else."

Evelyn's hands twisted in her skirt. "You really think this man poisoned the stream?"

He looked up at her. "I don't think it. I know it."

She stepped a bit closer, unsure what to say. He looked... broken. Angry, yes, but underneath that, like there was something deeper. She wondered if he was afraid. She knew she would be.

Before she could say anything, though, a thin wail drifted into the room.

Mason.

Evelyn turned, but Travis was already on his feet, the scrape of his chair loud against the floor. "I'll get him," he said abruptly, striding off past her.

She followed him to Mason's cradle. He was fussing, face scrunched, small fists waving in protest. Travis leaned over him, his large hands gentle as he lifted the child onto his arm and cradled him with a tenderness that almost startled her.

"Hey there," Travis said softly, softer than she'd ever heard him. "None of that, little man. You're all right."

Mason hiccupped once, blinked up at him, and then, as though recognizing something in the man's voice, gave a wide, toothless grin.

Travis froze.

The corners of his mouth lifted, slowly. An uncertain smile, but for a moment, the hardness of his face completely disappeared. He looked younger all of a sudden. Happy, maybe.

Her breath caught in her throat. This mean, unyielding rancher was smiling at Mason in a way that made her heart lurch like it never had before.

But just as quickly, the moment broke. He blinked, as if realizing he had let her see too much, cleared his throat, and awkwardly handed Mason to her. "He's... fine now," he said gruffly.

She took the baby, still smiling. "He seems to like you."

Travis shook his head, looking away. "Doesn't matter." He hesitated, then added, quieter, "I'm sorry, Evelyn. But I don't know if you can stay here 'til Christmas, like I said."

She stared at him, stunned. "What?"

He met her eyes, his own filled with something she couldn't place. Exhaustion, regret... she wasn't sure. He just sighed heavily.

"I'm losing the ranch. There's nothing left. This was only ever meant to be temporary until things settled. But there's no future here. There never was, but it looks like I won't even have 'til Christmas to figure my own stuff out. So I'll need you and Mason to get on and find somethin' else before..." he trailed off, sighing. "Before Christmas."

She stood there for a moment, clutching Mason, as he turned away from her. "Go on, now, I got to try and finish up in here."

Finish up what?

From the sound of it, he was already giving up. She had half a mind to tell him that, but she shook it off. She would have been quite out of line. At the end of the day, this man didn't owe her a thing.

He wanted her out, and that meant that she should—and *would* leave.

She turned and stepped out into the hall, closing the door behind her, her mind spinning. But how could she leave? After everything? After she had worked so hard to make this place feel alive again for the holidays?

To make a home for her and Mason for Christmas time…?

Mason stirred against her bosom as she forced back tears and continued toward the kitchen. She wouldn't let herself cry. Not now.

When she finally gathered herself, she went to the kitchen, her footsteps sinking into the rug, and saw Royce sitting by the stove, nursing a cup of coffee, not looking at her. They hadn't really spoken since the incident between them, but seeing him now, his weathered face looking down at the table—it stirred something inside her.

"Well." She spoke more harshly than she'd intended, but she couldn't stop it. "Your wishes have come true."

He looked up, startled. "What?"

"Travis told me to leave," she replied bitterly. "Before Christmas. Out in the cold again."

Royce's brow furrowed, and for a moment, he looked... hurt. "That isn't what I wanted," he said quietly.

Evelyn scoffed. "Of course, it's not."

"No. I mean it." He shook his head slowly. "I was angry. Foolish, too. Every time I saw you... doing the things my wife used to do, the way you cared for Mason the way my daughter once cared for her boy..." His voice faltered a bit. "It hurt. It reminded me of what I'd lost. And I reckon I took it out on you."

Evelyn swallowed hard, her anger softening. Maybe this man wasn't cruel. Not truly. Just wounded, as they all were. She hadn't even thought about the fact that there wasn't a missus. Which meant that he had to have lost his wife, too.

"I understand," she said softly.

It was Christmas, after all, and it would do no one any good holding a grudge on a broken man.

Royce looked up at her, eyes wide. "You'd forgive an old fool like me?"

She gave a small smile, weary but sincere. "Yes. But it doesn't change the fact that I have to go."

He shook his head firmly. "You can't. Not now. Not in this weather, and not before Christmas. You were told when the weather stills, and you were told after Christmas. And Travis Baldwin is a man of his word, the same as I am."

"I don't have a choice," she said quietly. "Travis made it clear."

Royce set his cup down, his bottom lip trembling slightly. "Then I'll talk to him. You've done nothing but good for this house, and I think it's only right."

"You'd do that? For me?"

He nodded, looking almost like the man he must have been before grief had made him something else entirely. "That baby deserves to be here, with people who can look out for him. And so do you. You work hard here, and you've made something of this place."

Her throat tightened. She wanted to thank him, but the words stuck in her throat, tangled there as emotion swelled inside of her. All she could manage was a quiet, "Thank you."

Royce stood up slowly. She could hear his joints crack after a long day of work. "Go ahead and finish up supper," he said gently. "I'll handle Travis."

Chapter Nineteen

The sizzle of the cast-iron pan was one of the best ways to wake up. Mason and Royce had already had breakfast, and she'd ended up eating Travis's portion, since he hadn't been to the kitchen yet. She was making another batch of eggs, hopeful he'd be in the kitchen soon enough. The brittle December light that turned everything silver and white caused her eyes to squint as the morning brightened. It was beautiful, truly, but Evelyn's mind plagued her.

A thin mist hung in the distance, but the snow had nearly quit altogether. There was nothing but a few little dust flurries swirling about in front of the window. Nothing else.

She had sat awake by the dying fire for hours the night before, Mason sleeping peacefully in her arms, her heart aching with uncertainty. She had known from the beginning that her time at the ranch was only temporary. But the thought of leaving—of taking Mason away from what had been a steady home for weeks, just before Christmas—weighed on her.

By morning, she decided that she couldn't sit idle any longer. She would do something, anything, to help. She'd gotten up early that morning, swept the hearth, set the coffee on the stove, and made breakfast—nearly twice, now that she was making more eggs.

Suddenly, a sharp knock came at the side door by the kitchen.

She jumped. She hadn't been expecting anyone that early in the morning.

When she opened it, she found Sheriff McCrae standing on the porch, brushing snow from his hat, his badge glinting faintly in the gray light of the day. His face was ruddy from the cold, his eyes kind as he looked at her.

"Morning, Miss Rhodes," he said with a polite nod. "Is Travis around?" He craned his neck around her.

"He's not made it out of his room just yet," she replied, stepping back to let him in.

"He ain't up and workin' yet?" McCrae asked, his brows furrowing.

Evelyn shrugged. It wasn't anyone's business what he'd been doing the last couple days. And something told her that he especially didn't want the sheriff in his business. "He should be in the kitchen soon for breakfast. Would you like a cup of coffee while you wait?"

Cade smiled, taking his hat off. "If you're offering, ma'am, I won't say no. It's a cold ride up from town."

Evelyn motioned him toward the kitchen, quickly pouring him a cup. He sat down at the table just as she finished pouring and turned to face him. "Here. I imagine you've had a long morning."

Town was easily a half-hour's ride from the ranch, but he looked like he'd been outside a lot longer than a half hour.

"Thank you kindly," Sheriff McCrae said, sighing as he took a sip. "You sure make good coffee."

Evelyn laughed. "I'm sure you were just ready for something warm!" She paused. "Sheriff… you said you came to see Travis. Is it about the bank?"

He looked up, brow furrowing. "The bank?"

She hesitated again. She wasn't the type to gossip. But still, hearing about the bank foreclosure worried her. And if anyone knew what they could do, it would surely be the sheriff of the town. "He got a letter yesterday. They're foreclosing. If he doesn't pay before Christmas, he'll lose the ranch."

McCrae's expression darkened. He set his cup down slowly. "So it's come to that," he muttered, looking down at his coffee cup. "I was afraid it would."

"You knew?" Evelyn asked softly.

"I knew he was behind on his payments," the sheriff admitted. "But I didn't think the bank would move this quick, not right before Christmas." He sighed, rubbing his chin. "But then again, if Fletcher Kane had anything to do with it…"

"You think he does?"

He gave her a look. "Miss Evelyn, Fletcher Kane has had his eye on this ranch for a long time. Ever since a speculator found traces of gold in the hills north of here, he's been itching to get his hands on it. The man's got half the town in his pocket. The banker. The freightmen. Even some of my deputies. As far as he's concerned, Travis is holdin' him back from a fortune."

Evelyn's fingers tightened around her own cup nervously. "He said as much yesterday. He told me Kane poisoned the stream, killed his horses."

He nodded weakly. "I'm here to talk to him about that," he said. "Royce and Lawson came and told me. Travis should have."

Evelyn's stomach churned. "And the bank?" she repeated.

She wasn't going to get into his business too much today. She agreed he should have gone to the sheriff, but she also knew that Travis Baldwin had his reasons for everything he did. Right or wrong or indifferent. It was his land, his choice on how to handle it. At least, as far as she was concerned.

"The bank manager's one of Kane's oldest friends," McCrae said. "The two of them are thick as thieves. If Kane says the word, the bank moves. That's how it works in this town."

Evelyn swallowed hard. "Then Travis doesn't stand a chance," she said. "Is that what you're saying, Sheriff?"

McCrae flashed a half smile. "Don't count him out yet. Travis Baldwin's as stubborn as they come. This ranch… it's not just land to him. It's all he's got left."

Evelyn felt her throat tighten and looked out the window. "I can see why," she murmured. "It's a beautiful place. I can't imagine it gone."

"You care for him," McCrae said slowly. "As all right as this ranch is, I don't see a woman being as set on it if she didn't care about the men runnin' the place."

She flushed, looking down quickly. She wasn't sure she'd ever thought about it before. "He's been kind to me. To Mason."

The sheriff gave a small, knowing smile. "Travis Baldwin's a hard man, but not an unkind one. His father was my best friend and taught him to be a good man. And I'd say you did exactly what I wanted you to do here."

"What's that?" she asked.

"You've brought something back into this house that's been missing for a long time."

"Christmas decorations?" She laughed, and he joined in.

"You know," he said. "Speaking of Christmas, did you hear that Mrs. Cobb had to cancel the Christmas fair this year?"

"Christmas fair?" She didn't even know there was a Christmas fair.

"Yeah, we do it every year. It's a big to-do. She's come down with an illness..." He clicked his tongue. "No one else has the space or the time it takes to take on the responsibility. It's such a big event most people can't get it done."

Before she could respond, the door opened behind them, and Travis stepped in. He paused when he saw Sheriff McCrae.

"Cade," he said shortly. "Didn't expect you here so early."

"Morning," McCrae said, standing. "Heard about your horses. Think we should talk."

The men clasped hands together in a brief shake before Travis sat down.

"Come on, then," Travis muttered, groggily.

Evelyn handed him some bread. "Please eat this, at least," she said. He nodded, grabbing the slice, and flashed a small, sad smile.

"Thanks," he whispered, then gestured for McCrae to follow him.

Evelyn watched them both disappear down the hall. Anxiously, she stood up and started cleaning up, her hands twisting in her apron. She cleaned the cups, fed the fire in the sitting room, and tried not to think about their meeting and what was being said. The same thing she'd tried to do when Royce went in to talk to him before supper the night before.

She had seen Royce shrug and shake his head before heading to his own bedroom. He'd whispered a small, "Give me a little time," over his shoulder before going to bed.

She only hoped that McCrae's conversation with him would be more...fruitful.

Not for her, but for him. She wanted nothing more than for Travis Baldwin to have everything he deserved. His ranch, his home. And whatever semblance of a life he thought he could have from this day forward.

She just wished there was something she could do, something she could do to stop the bank. Or at the very least stall them until everyone could come up with a better plan...

But after half an hour, when McCrae finally emerged, his face was grave. He nodded to her politely, but left without a word. Travis lingered by his door, staring at the floor, his face red, his tongue pressed firmly in his cheek.

Evelyn hesitated, then stepped into the hall. "Travis?"

He looked up, his eyes weary. "What is it?"

"I need to talk to you."

He looked like he wanted to refuse for a second, but he didn't. He just sighed and motioned toward the sitting room. "All right," he said.

Evelyn followed him, taking deep breaths in hopes that she could settle her nerves. Stop trembling, and simply present an idea that had just occurred to her.

"I've been thinking," she began carefully. "There might be a way to get the bank off your back."

Travis frowned. "What are you talking about?"

She took a steadying breath. "Sheriff McCrae said that the town's Christmas fair is going to be canceled, all because the person organizing it fell ill and no one else can take it on."

He shrugged. "So?"

"So..." She clasped her hands together, her pulse racing. "What if I take it over? We could hold it here on the ranch."

Travis blinked. "Here?"

She nodded quickly. "If we host it all here, the whole town will come. It'll be good for the community, and the bank wouldn't dare foreclose before Christmas if a major event was being held here on your land. It would ruin their reputation with everyone in town. Plus, I think it would be mighty fun!"

Travis stared at her, dumbstruck. "You mean... use the fair to stall the bank?"

"Yes," she said, her enthusiasm growing. "At least until after Christmas. And maybe even longer if I can come up with something." She winked at him, without even meaning to. "I've organized things like this before. Now most of that was with my mother before my parents passed away, but I can definitely do it!"

For a moment, there was only silence. Then Travis gave a low, incredulous laugh. "I'll be doggoned," he said. "That might actually work."

Evelyn's heart leapt. "You think so?"

A slow smile spread out across his face. The first one she'd seen in days. "I think so," he said. "You really are a clever woman, Evelyn."

She felt the heat rise up in her cheeks. She wondered if they were as red as they felt. "I just thought it might help."

He studied her for a moment longer, his expression softening. "Clever and beautiful rarely go together, but you're both, Evelyn Rhodes."

The words stole the breath right from her.

"You're—being kind," she stammered.

Travis shook his head. "No. Just honest."

She couldn't meet his eyes. She felt her entire body begin to tremble, butterflies fluttering in her stomach, her knees getting weak. She cleared her throat, adjusted the folds of her skirt, pretending that took more attention than it did.

She dreaded what it was that she thought she might be feeling.

The man was handsome. That was clear as day. Strong, masculine. A hard worker. But there was something else, too. Something underneath. Something she found herself desperate to see more and more of.

And she knew that she was approaching dangerous territory. The territory that included falling for Travis Baldwin.

But she knew better. He was still bound to his wife, even after her passing. And she knew, from experience, that this moment of warmth from him would soon be gone. But still, she looked into his dark eyes and felt her chest ache. The man in front of her was strong, proud, and smiling at her with a softness she wished would stay forever. And although she knew it wouldn't, she couldn't help wanting it anyway.

Chapter Twenty

"I'll get the horses settled," Travis said as they pulled up next to Marigold's storefront.

Evelyn smiled widely and launched herself and Mason off the wagon.

The snow had all but stopped, although the morning air was still sharp enough to cut the lungs. But Evelyn hardly felt it now. She was far too excited. Instead, she simply clutched Mason close beneath her cloak and pressed on as his fists tucked under his chin.

The streets were bustling. With the weather settling down, more townspeople were clearly coming out into town.

The bell above the store jingled when she went inside.

Warmth and the scent of cloves greeted her. It always smelled so nice in there.

Clara spotted her first. The young woman's curls bounced as she hurried around a stack of fabric bolts.

"Evelyn! Is it true? You're taking over the Christmas fair?"

"Yes," she replied, smoothing Mason's cap. "It will be at the ranch."

Clara's eyes got bright. "We needed someone to do it! It's a tradition no one wanted to give up!"

Marigold poked her head up from behind the counter, spectacles perched low on her nose. "A blessing indeed, and about time Travis and Royce have company! The whole town isn't exactly what I expected, but it'll be good for them."

"And this place has felt like a funeral since Mrs. Cobb had to cancel."

Evelyn flushed, grinning. "I just hope I can do it justice."

"You can," Clara said. "What do you need?"

Evelyn opened her notebook. "Booths and tables. Lanterns for evening. Fresh pine garlands, baked goods, quilts for raffle, music...Anything anyone in town is willing to lend."

Marigold thumped a heavy sewing table with her palm. "You'll have this for anything you need! Me and Clara and this ol' thing. And I'll bake sweet buns enough to feed half of Wyoming Territory."

Clara pushed a bolt of cream-and-green cloth toward her. "Skirting for the tables. And Mama's lace tablecloths. And we'll hang paper stars. I have the best shears for it. All I need is one quiet afternoon."

***

Together, they skipped to stores, one by one, telling the townsfolk about the change of plans. The rumors had been true. She was going to have it at the Baldwin ranch.

Mrs. Abernathy, the bakery owner, said she would bring pies. Mrs. Loudman, the schoolteacher, said she would send the children to sing carols, which Evelyn was especially excited for. The blacksmith in town, a man by the name of Jonathan Duly, happened to be an old apprentice of Travis's, so she asked if he would be so kind to bring lanterns. He'd wiped soot from his brow and smiled right away. He told her he would do anything she—or Travis—needed.

With each errand and each promise and each and every nod of support, something really took hold in Evelyn. Hope. Real and true hope.

She carried Mason from shop to shop with Clara hot on her heels. Mason was asleep, which was quite perfect given that she had to get through everyone she could before Travis got tired of waiting.

"Look at that precious baby," a woman cooed over him as her husband tipped her hat to her. She smiled, and Clara pulled her toward a group of men standing near the general store. "Any of you men want to donate to the fair?" she asked, batting her lashes.

Evelyn giggled.

"Anything you need, Miss Clara," one of the men said. And then the store door swung wide open. The man that Evelyn recognized from the last time she'd gone to the store—Mr. Dawson—smiled. "I heard y'all are planning a fair!"

"We'll be needing some of your famous ginger biscuits for planning fuel!" Clara laughed.

"You ladies help yourselves," he said. "Take some to Mr. Baldwin, too."

Evelyn's heart pinched at the name. "He'll appreciate it," she said.

"He used to look half-starved when he rode through town," a woman from behind the counter said, with a sniff. "A man grieving forgets to eat. But I tell ya what, looking at him now, he looks like he's had to loosen that belt a bit!" Evelyn looked to where the woman's gaze was. It was right past her. She turned, and sure enough, there he was. Kicking at the rocks near the wagon.

She smiled, blushing, before turning back to look at the store owner and his wife. "I try to keep him fed," she said shyly.

"Looks like you've been doing a mighty fine job," the store owner said.

Clara nudged her a bit with her elbow. "I'll continue to ask people for some help," she said. "Go on out there and tend to whatever it is he's waiting for."

Evelyn smiled gratefully. They had one more thing to do while they were here.

Probably the most important thing.

Her breath rose in white puffs. This... this could save them. Not forever, perhaps, but long enough to breathe. Long enough to fight. She walked back where Travis waited with the wagon. He stood beside the horses, pacing now.

"Ready?" he asked.

"Yes," she said. "I got what I needed from the people in town, for the most part."

And so they went toward the bank, with Mason's tiny breaths warm against her neck. She felt her stomach tighten with Nerves. But she lifted her chin despite herself. This is what they all needed.

As soon as they walked in, there was one desk off to the side and one at the center. The one in the center held a man, a middle-aged man, with a tidy mustache and slicked back here. Crow's feet pulled at the corners of his eyes, and he looked up almost meekly. Not at all what she had expected of the banker colluding with a criminal like Fletcher Kane, or from someone trying at Christmastime to steal the ranch Travis's family had owned for years.

He looked up from behind his polished desk. His spectacles glinted in the light.

"Mr. Baldwin," he said, in a bland tone. "Do you have my payment?"

Travis cleared his throat.

"Mr. Presley, I just wanted to let you know that the town's Christmas fair will be held on my land," he said. "The entire community is involved in the event. If you seize the property before Christmas, you'll destroy the town's celebration. You definitely don't want to be to blame for no one getting a fair."

Mr. Presley's mouth opened, then closed again. His throat bobbed.

"You surely—you don't expect the bank to—"

"Yes," Travis said flatly. "We surely do."

Evelyn almost snickered at the condescension in his voice.

"Give us until after Christmas, Mr. Presley," she chimed in. "Show goodwill. That's all we ask."

The man held his pen tightly and sighed. "Very well. The bank will delay proceedings until after Christmas."

"Put it in writing," Travis said.

It was clear he didn't trust the man. Evelyn could have told that from the next town over.

Presley scribbled, stamped, signed. When he handed over the paper, Evelyn released a breath she hadn't realized she'd been holding. *They had bought time.*

That was what mattered.

Travis and Royce could keep their house just a bit longer, at the very least. And she and Mason would be able to stay until at least then.

Then, before she could speak—before she could even turn—Travis caught her at the waist and swung her up off her feet.

The world spun, flurried snowflakes blurred into a white curtain, and she laughed. Boy, did she laugh. It spilled out completely unbidden—alive. And he laughed, too. Deep, rough, and completely unguarded. Mason squealed, kicking in excitement as they were twirled.

Then, Travis lowered her slowly, his strong hands still firm on her waist, and their laughter faded into breathless stillness. They stood too close. Far too close.

She could hear her heart beating in her ears.

His eyes seemed to search hers, and when she searched his, she could see something there. Something unspoken, frightening...sweet.

He opened his mouth to speak, but a voice slithered in from behind them, cold and sleazy. "Well, now. Ain't this cozy."

Evelyn stiffened. Travis's hand dropped instantly from her waist, like he'd been caught doing something wrong. He stiffened, too.

The man that spoke approached them slowly, a malicious smirk on his face.

He was tall, broad-shouldered, but slender. He wore a nice black coat and a white hat, cleaner than any she'd ever seen. His boots were white, too. Spotless.

The other man was far less spotless. In fact, he wore grime on every stitch. He was also much shorter than the other man.

"Miss Rhodes, I presume," the taller man drawled, tipping his hat.

She wanted to scoff. But that wasn't the ladylike thing to do, so she kept silent.

"My name's Fletcher Kane, proprietor of Kane Mining. I am sure you've heard of me. This here," he said, pointing to the shorter man, "is Mr. Sharpe."

Evelyn shook her head. "I've not heard of you," she said pertly. "But I appreciate the introduction."

His gaze dragged over her, as if he was somehow sizing her up. But then he turned back to Travis. "How are the horses holding up, Baldwin? Shame what's happened to them."

Evelyn herself wanted to launch at the man's throat.

Kane smiled wickedly.

Evelyn felt Travis go taut beside her. He was just a moment away from drawing his gun. She could feel it, and she didn't even know the man that long. She couldn't understand how this Fletcher Kane was as comfortable walking the fine line between life and death.

A man who threatened another man's property and livelihood usually didn't make it very long. The fact that this man could do it, and still be so callously calm, made Evelyn curious.

"Kane," he muttered the man's name like it was a curse word.

She shivered. Not from any winter cold, though. From Travis's facial expression, hard as shale.

***

They climbed into the wagon, and Travis gathered the reins. The last person he wanted to run into in town was Fletcher Kane. When he'd looked at Evelyn, he had seen nothing but red. And he knew right then and there that if he didn't grab her by the arm and get out of there, there'd be a showdown in the middle of town.

The horses stamped, breath pluming, and Travis wondered just how far Fletcher Kane intended to push him. Because he wasn't the type of man that took too kindly to being poked and prodded, especially not in front of someone he cared about—

"We bought time today," she whispered, shaking him out of his thoughts, ignoring the entire thing between them and Fletcher Kane. He wasn't sure if she was telling it to herself or to him, but his jaw eased, and he smiled a half-smile anyway.

He wished he could be like Evelyn in some ways. She was so hopeful. So positive. He wasn't sure how that was possible, being that she had clearly had a difficult road. Although, admittedly, he hadn't asked her nearly as much as he wished he had. He didn't know her entire story. But from what he did know, she had suffered plenty of loss, too. She would have had to have, to not have any friends or family at all to turn to, and to need to stay with an old grump like himself.

"Buying time matters..." she went on. "Aye," he said. "It does."

It was true. No matter what happened now, they had at the very least won a day.

As they rode back, though, he couldn't get the scowl off his face. The sun was starting to lower behind the pine trees, and he wondered if it would melt the snow, but that chill—it was harsh.

"So pretty..." Evelyn whispered, and he nodded, but his mind was elsewhere, not on the glimmering snow on the ground.

Mason poked a hand out from her cloak, gripping at her chin and giggling.

It was enough to make him crack a smile, but he couldn't. Not now. Not when he was so mad. Not when he couldn't stop picturing Fletcher Kane's smug face.

He just stared straight ahead, the reins loose in his hands despite the storm raging inside his mind.

One minute, he was on top of the world. Proud of Evelyn Rhodes and her idea. Lifting her up, twirling her around, looking into her gorgeous eyes—feeling his chest do something it hadn't done in years.

Immediately feeling guilty for it.

And then, having Fletcher Kane come in to make the moment even worse.

He stole a glance at her, feeling a sudden shame he couldn't explain. He'd been foolish. Snow dusted her lashes, just like it had when he'd twirled her around in excitement earlier.

He hadn't been able to help himself earlier, but he should have. Because Fletcher Kane had seen it. He had noticed. A man that would poison a stream would do anything. Travis knew the longer he stayed on the ranch, the more desperate the man would become. And the more desperate he would become, the more ruthless.

He would not let Kane touch her. He would not let him near Mason. And he would not let him take the ranch. Not while he still lived and breathed.

The ranch roof came into view. From the looks of things, Royce had kept the fire going nice and cozy as smoke curled steadily from the chimney.

He heard Evelyn sigh. A content sigh, one that sounded peaceful. Something tightened in his throat, like it was choking him. He wished he could be that content. But with a man like Fletcher Kane on the move, he wasn't sure he could.

"You did good today," he said.

She blinked, then offered him a small, warm smile. "So did you."

It hit him square in the chest, ridiculous as it was—that smile. He looked away sharply, once more almost ashamed of himself. How could he be losing control like this? How could she make him feel things like this?

They rolled into the yard. "Whoa there!" he yelled out, tugging on the reins when they pulled right next to the porch. Quickly, he hopped down to help her and Mason alight. And again, as if by some sort of instinct that he wished he could stop, his hand closed around her waist.

She steadied herself by grabbing hold of the lapel of his coat, and for a moment, everything stilled.

"I…" he began.

She looked up at him, eyes wide, expectant, almost. But he stammered and let go, taking a step back as if distance could undo whatever had just passed between them.

"Go on inside," he said. "It's cold."

She hesitated, then nodded and carried Mason toward the porch, her skirts whispering in the snow. She didn't look back; he watched her go until the door closed behind her and tried to remember how to breathe.

What in tarnation has gotten into me?

Chapter Twenty-One

Wind whipped across the high pasture, strong enough to feel like a grown man had just slapped him in the face, and he felt himself growl as it rattled through the fence rails and ripped at his coat. With icy grit flying against his cheek, he braced a post upright and drove a nail home with sharp strikes. The hammer beat hard and fast.

He'd always liked manual labor. And this almost reminded him of his blacksmithing days.

He'd been out here since sunrise, tending to small chores that needed doing. Repairs that winter storms would only make worse if he left them to wait any longer. But mostly he worked because work steadied a man. When his hands were busy, his mind had less room to wander.

Today, that was harder. No matter how much and how hard he willed himself into working, Evelyn still crept into his thoughts.

He set the hammer down, breath steaming. It should have brought him some bit of peace. Hard land, harsh weather, and simple duty. *Put your head down and work.* Those things used to quiet him. They had steadied and calmed him for years. Until her.

He shifted the fence plank, leaning into the post to test its hold. Solid. Good.

But still, he couldn't get her face off his mind.

The way she'd looked inside the bank. The way she'd stood in front of Presley like she was ready to battle a giant. The way she felt in his arms and the way she laughed when he'd spun her in the street.

He squeezed his eyes shut.

She'd had courage, that was for sure. More than a lot of cattlemen he'd met. More than a lot of ranch hands. All with a baby in her arms.

She had literally walked into his home carrying nothing but that little boy and still managed to change everything about the way the place felt. Even after he and Royce had been so sour to her.

His hands tightened around the hammer. "Amazing woman," he muttered under his breath.

He was fascinated by her. She had dealt with her fair share of hurt, too, it seemed. He only wished he could work through his own hurt half as good as she could hers.

It scalded him to admit it, even alone.

He had sworn there would be no more tenderness, no more trust. Tenderness made a man stupid, blind, after all. He had lost too much already to ever gamble with his heart again.

Yet there she stood in his thoughts..

He reached for the next plank, jaw clenched tight. "Fool," he told himself. "Doggone fool."

The memory of Bonnie and Troy flooded in, too. Pain pierced him sharp like a knife, tearing a wound right through his flesh. Remembering love—the smell of Bonnie's hair, the sound of Troy's laugh—tormented him.

Which was proof enough that loving someone didn't save you.

It hadn't saved him, and it surely didn't save him now. He gritted his teeth and drove another nail in, the wood practically splintering.

He only wished it could.

Evelyn's plan had worked, though. Her courage had bought them time. Saved them for a little bit. Given him a little ground to stand on for now.

He respected her for that. More than he knew how to say.

More than he should.

He hung the hammer back at his belt, wind tugging harder at his coat now as it scattered straw from the fence into the air. Clouds thickened above his head.

Time to head back.

His gaze swept the yard and stopped cold

There, near the woodpile by the side porch right off the kitchen, she stood. Her shawl was gathered up close, and she lifted logs into her basket as snow clung to the hem of her dress. The baby's cry could be heard faintly from inside the house, muffled enough to tell Travis he was in the bedroom. Must have woken from a nap. Evelyn paused and turned instinctively toward the sound before hastily grabbing pieces of wood.

She hadn't seen him there watching her.

And she also hadn't seen the man sitting on his horse just beyond the edge of the yard, tucked behind trees.

But Travis had seen him. And his blood boiled.

Amos Sharpe.

His eyes were fixed right on her. Travis's stomach turned. He was watching her. Like he was marking her as a target.

Something inside Travis snapped. He didn't feel the cold anymore. Didn't hear the wind. Didn't think of anything except his rage, hot and rising fast, burning through his ribs.

He ran fast, the snow under his feet crunching as he pounded toward the intruder.

Sharpe looked away from Evelyn at the last second before Travis made it to a skidding halt in front of his horse. He smirked, as if the entire thing amused him.

"Afternoon," Sharpe drawled casually. But this was far from casual to Travis.

Travis's breath drew ragged. "Get off my land."

Sharpe lifted one brow. "Just passing through. Didn't see a sign saying I couldn't admire the scenery."

"You so much as *look* at her again," he retorted, "and I will put you in the ground."

Sharpe's grin widened. "Touchy subject, is she? Kane said you'd gone and gotten sentimental."

The man spit at Travis's boot.

Travis saw red. "Last warning."

Sharpe shrugged. "No harm done. *Yet.*" Sharpe shifted his horse to the side and leaned down, closer, eyes glinting. "Might wanna tell your woman not to wander far alone. Rough country, after all."

It was a threat. Clear as day.

Rage snarled inside Travis like a trapped animal, but he didn't move. Didn't blink. Refused to give Sharpe the satisfaction.

"Ride," he told him flatly. "*Now.*"

Sharpe held his stare a moment longer. Then he snorted, feral and mean, before turning away.

"See you soon, Baldwin," he said over his shoulder as he and the horse trotted away at a pace meant to infuriate Travis. Slow, unafraid, cocky.

Travis watched him until he was nothing more than a speck fading out against the gray sky, over the hills. And that was when he was able to draw a breath.

His hands shook. Knees quaked.. He felt almost sick remembering how closely Sharpe had just been watching Evelyn.

He looked at the house, thinking about all that he'd lost. Evelyn had gone back inside, clearly taking care of Mason. He thought of the boy and how soothed he must have been by her. By this woman giving up her entire life to become his mother.

He thought about her, how amazing she was. How clever she was

He wasn't going to let anything happen to her or to Mason.

He strode toward the porch and stopped on the steps, gripping the railing hard. He wouldn't be able to survive it if something happened to her and that baby because of him.

If Kane touched her — or that baby — *No.* He would see Kane dead before he ever got the chance. And Sharpe, along with him.

He opened the door, and there she was, next to the hearth, Mason in her arms, her cheeks flushed. She turned to him and blinked in what looked to be surprise.

"Travis? You're shaking!"

She ran over to him, all at once shifting Mason with one hand and pushing him toward the fire with the other.

He swallowed the truth. Sure, it was cold outside, but the reason he was shaking was pure, unadulterated fury.

"Wind," he managed to lie, and moved closer to the fire.

She stepped closer, and Mason gurgled happily. Something inside his chest lurched.

It was clear as day that the baby trusted him, and so did she. That almost made everything worse. Because that meant they also believed this ranch was safe. That he was safe. And he was going to make sure that was true. Whatever it cost.

Travis pulled his hat brim low. "Stay near the house. Don't go out alone." His voice was gravelly with emotion.

Her brows lifted. "Why? Did something happen?"

He shook his head. "I just need you to make sure you stay inside. I'll deal with the rest. Keep planning the fair, and stick to the house. If you need anything outside, you call on me or Lawson or Royce."

She nodded. "All right."

He turned away, because he knew that if he stayed one more second, he might admit that he was afraid. That he—

No. Not yet. Not now.

He looked once more at the line of trees, fists knotting. Kane had just done something he shouldn't have. He'd just drawn first blood as far as Travis was concerned, and he'd done it without even lifting a hand.

Travis was done waiting.

He would defend them all, no matter what it meant for him. Because, some losses, a man could survive only once.

Then it hit him.

What was he *really* feeling for Evelyn Rhodes...that she would be a loss of that magnitude to him?

"Oh, Travis," Evelyn said, causing him to turn back around. "There's some dried meat and a bit of bread in there if you'd like something to eat. Royce already had some."

He swallowed hard, the fire's glow blurring as moisture pricked the corners of his eyes. He dragged a hand roughly down his face, forcing his throat clear before he spoke again.

"Where's Royce, anyway?"

"Upstairs," she said softly, shifting Mason. "He hasn't been down since breakfast."

Travis nodded, relieved in some small way. Better for the old man to stay put if Sharpe was sniffing around. Better for all of them. His pulse still thudded in his ears.

Evelyn studied him, her brows pinched with concern. "You sure you're all right?"

"Yeah," he lied through his teeth. "Just cold."

But he wasn't cold. He was afraid. And he hated that fear more than he hated Kane himself. But he wasn't afraid for himself. Not by a long shot. He could easily shoot Kane down and not think twice. Even if Kane got the upper hand, at least he'd be killed knowing he wasn't a coward.

No, he wasn't scared for himself.

He was afraid for her. For the boy. And for the little slice of life building itself inside the walls of this house. Something he had started to look forward to without even realizing it. He cleared his throat harder, hoping to clear out the thick muck that was starting to rise up.

He'd already lived through the worst of it once, and it had broken him so completely he hadn't thought he'd survive. He didn't want to go through it again.

Sharpe's words echoed in his head. *Might wanna tell your woman not to wander far alone.*

His woman. She might not have been his woman, but he was not going to let that snake lay a single finger on her. Not now. Not ever.

"Remember what I said," Travis said firmly. Just stay inside."

He turned away before she could ask any more questions.

Before he admitted to himself that he wasn't just protecting her because she was a woman and Mason was a baby.

Before he could confess that the thought of losing her did something unthinkable to him.

Before he could worry about what that all even meant and just how dangerous it was.

Chapter Twenty-Two

A knock sounded at the door— a lively, cheerful sound.

Evelyn opened the door, winter air rushing in. She'd been busy by the fire, planning the fair, and the cool air was a huge contrast to the heat from the hearth. Travis had come in earlier and asked her to stay inside, and although it seemed a strange request, it gave her more opportunity to work on these details.

"There she is!" Clara declared, her plum-colored skirt ruffling as she rushed inside. "Our brilliant festival mistress!"

Marigold stomped snow from her boots on the porch. "You look bright as spring, Evelyn. After Christmas, I'll be sure counting the days to spring. This has been the harshest winter we've had."

Evelyn smiled at her, closing the door from the draft behind them. "We brought what we promised you," Marigold went on, gesturing to a large sack over her shoulder. "And more than that, too."

"You two are too good to me." Evelyn laughed, ushering them into the sitting room.

"Nonsense," Clara said, unpinning her cloak. "You're doing a service for the whole town."

"Besides," Marigold added, "You're also dragging this ranch into Christmas by its ears. It needed it."

"Let's go to the kitchen and get you ladies some coffee." Evelyn gestured toward the back.

"Coffee sounds great," Marigold breathed, her cheeks still pinked and chapped. As much as these women had been out in this cold, she was surprised they'd not become permanent icicles yet.

Women's boots clanked against hardwood floors toward the kitchen, and Clara and Marigold sat at the table while Evelyn fetched coffee from the stove. She smiled, realizing Royce and Travis hadn't eaten the full bread loaf she'd made that morning, too. What a great snack for company.

"I'm going to grab that precious boy!" Marigold declared before disappearing quickly, only to bring him in a basket she'd clearly taken from the corner of the room. A laundry basket. Inside, he laughed and rattled his toy. "He wants to be with company, too." Evelyn just shook her head. It was a nice change of pace, though, everyone loving on the boy so much. When she'd first arrived, she wondered if she'd be ostracized for her entire life because she was unwed with a child. Just like Arabella was destined to be—which was why she'd arranged to be a mail-order bride in the first place.

Mason's basket sat between them, and Clara leaned over to brush her finger along his cheek. He cooed, delighted.

"Oh, look at him," Clara whispered. "You'd think he owned the ranch already."

"He owns my heart," Evelyn said softly. Marigold reached across and squeezed her hand. "You're a good mother, Evelyn."

Evelyn bit her lip to keep emotion at bay. She'd never thought of herself as a mother. Not really. But there was something in the praise that made her feel that the words were true.

***

They worked for hours.

Ink stained all of their fingers from writing flyers for the fair, and letters thanking business owners for their help in making it all happen. Clara, a beautiful artist by any account, sketched holly leaves on the edges of the flyers.

Every so often, they paused to warm hands, to sip coffee, to coo at Mason when he burbled or kicked his little feet. But what Evelyn noticed the most was how the women talked so easily together.

As friends.

As if they'd been friends for a long time.

Evelyn felt, for the first time in a long time, like she truly belonged. She hadn't let herself become part of a community before Arabella, and after, the community wanted nothing to do with either of them because of how scandalous it was to be an unwed mother.

Maybe I can be part of something again.

They'd been so wrapped up in everything they were doing, they hardly noticed the front door opening. It wasn't until the blast of cold air came in that Evelyn looked up, hearing boots thud, and there Travis was in the doorway.

Travis stood in the entry, shoulders squared, his hat low over his eyes, but from what she could see, they were drawn tight with something. He didn't take off his gloves, and he didn't even greet any of the women. Instead, he kept his jaw locked and moved toward the hall and walked off to his bedroom.

The women all shared a look. "Is he hungry for supper already?" Clara asked. "Isn't it awfully early?"

Marigold sniffed. "He needs a good meal, sure, but he also needs a better temperament."

Evelyn forced a gentle laugh, but unease prickled her bones. There was something different in his face from earlier. He'd looked fearful earlier, but now, just purely angry.

"Well, we should get on and make supper, and let you make supper, too," Marigold said. "It's getting a bit later than we meant it to be."

Rising, the older woman kissed her cheek. "We'll be back tomorrow. And the next. Christmas waits for no man."

Evelyn hardly had time to say goodbyes before the door closed behind them, and silence returned so abruptly it almost startled her.

She smoothed her skirt, gathering courage. She wasn't sure what had gotten into him again, so suddenly, she felt like she was getting whiplash from his mood swings. She walked the hall.

His door stood partly open.

"Travis?" Her voice was soft, careful. "Are you well?" It was early to be in his bedroom, and when she opened the door a creak, he was on his bed. It was definitely too early for rest.

He didn't look up. Not immediately.

His brooding was something she should have been used to by now, but every time she felt they were getting closer and closer, he seemed to engage in a different sort of brooding than the one before. That was the part that seemed to get to her the most.

And this time, he looked... haunted.

"What's wrong?" she asked gently.

He straightened. "I told you the other day," he said, voice hard, "that you needed to leave, so after the fair, you'll need to leave. You and the child."

Her fingers trembled where they clutched the doorway.

"I—pardon?" she asked, blinking fast. "What if we come up with a way to prolong the bank again?"

"You heard me." He didn't meet her eyes now. That hurt more than the sentence itself.

Her throat tightened. "I thought… after the bank… after everything…"

"It changes nothing." His voice was thick with an emotion she couldn't quite name. "You can't stay. Not after Christmas."

She stared at him, vision blurring. She wasn't sure what she expected. The entire plan was just to stay until the storm, and then after Christmas. Her doing this fair was to ensure she could have a Christmas with Mason at this home without having to uproot.

She'd known it would happen, that she would have to go. Had told herself she did not belong. And yet—when she made herself believe that, he did something to pull her back into wishing whatever arrangement they had was more permanent.

"You know, it seems every time something goes wrong in your day," she said quietly, "you decide my fate in a single breath." His jaw clenched. "One moment, we're welcome. The next, you cast us out all over again. I can't live under the mercy of your moods!"

His eyes snapped up to meet hers. "It ain't a mood. It's out of necessity!"

"Then explain it." Her voice broke. "You've got to do something if the bank ends up taking this place! So where are you going to go? What are you going to do? Wouldn't you still need someone around to help you get settled?"

"That ain't your worry!" He sprang up from the bed.

"It might not be," she snipped, pointing her finger at him. "But just answer me. Once and for all. Do you want us here, or do you not?"

He flinched. Actually flinched. "Want has nothing to do with it."

"Then what does?" He turned away, fists tightening. His shoulders rose with a shuddering breath. "You can't see that you're in danger here? You don't see that I have men tryin' to sabotage me in any way they can? Kane will not stop. If you stay here, you will both be targets. The same as me, and the same as them horses out there. He's already sent one of his dogs out here to watch you, and I ain't gonna watch you get hurt."

She opened her mouth to speak, but he shook his head. "You're goin' to leave after Christmas. That's it. Don't send Royce in here, or Lawson, or Cade, or anyone. Just know that's what's been decided."

Her heart broke.

"I have nowhere," she whispered. "No one."

Silence. He stared at the wall. Said nothing.

Tears stung her eyes. "I thought—I thought perhaps we'd grown closer."

His expression hardened. Humiliation blistered inside of her like a physical pain.

"Very well," she said hoarsely. "I will not trouble you further. Mason and I will be gone the day after Christmas."

She turned before he could see her break. Her vision blurred, warping the hallway as she stormed out of his room. When she reached the kitchen to start supper, her hand clapped over her mouth to smother the sobs threatening to spill. Just when she felt like the two of them were getting close enough to combat this together, he ripped the rug right out from under her.

She sank to the kitchen chair, letting a few sobs break loose. Not loud. Not enough for anyone to hear. But deep and shaking.

She bowed her head. And she prayed. But not for herself. For Travis Baldwin. *May he find peace. Whatever that means for him.*

Chapter Twenty-Three

"Easy, now," Lawson muttered as he braced a hand against the mare's flank. Sweat slicked the animal's coat despite the cold, and she fought the contractions with a wild-eyed sort of fear. "Come on, girl. You can do it."

Travis knelt down in the straw, sleeves rolled, hands at the ready, his teeth gritted. He had assisted dozens of births in his life, but it never got easier when there were complications like this.

The mare trembled, her muscles shuddering. He pressed firmly and tried to guide her as gently as he could. They'd seen way too much death already over the last week. They didn't want to lose another.

They had been lucky to find the source of the poisoning, and now they had one job: keep it from happening again, or worse.

Royce hired men who would work for some food and a place to sleep, so they were all shacking up with Lawson in the bunk house. In exchange, he had extra men to work and watch out for Fletcher Kane

He had to hand it to Lawson.

He'd been the only one inside that bunkhouse for a while, and to know he was fine giving up his privacy for the extra help to watch out meant a lot to Travis. And he also had to hand it to Evelyn. She was cooking for a lot of extra men the last couple of days, and honestly, it probably did him some good, considering she was still sore at him.

"Lawson," Travis muttered. "That leg's just not right.."

"I know," the ranch foreman replied. "She's trying to turn him wrong-way. Hold on."

The mare kicked, dangerously close to Lawson's ribs. "Woo-ee!" he yelled out, a slight smile curving at his lips.

Travis shook his head. "Easy!" He wasn't sure if he was talking to the mare or to Lawson, but the last thing he needed was his foreman getting kicked in the sternum. "Come on," he whispered to the mare. "You've got strength. I know you do."

With one final painful groan of effort and one last desperate push, life slid into the straw in a slick, trembling heap. The foal lay still, only a breath too long, and dread clawed at him. "No..." he muttered, but then it shook, weak limbs scrabbling, finding breath.

Lawson let out a long exhale. "Well, I'll be doggoned."

Travis wiped his brow with his sleeve, heart pounding.

Relief.

It hit him so hard that his knees nearly buckled. He took a step back, giving the mare some space as she turned to nuzzle her new colt.

Lawson clapped a hand on his shoulder. "Still got your touch."

Travis huffed what sounded like a laugh, but he couldn't manage a smile. "Luck. That's all."

Lawson looked at him with his head tilted, brow furrowed. "You look worse'n that mare did giving birth."

"Long last couple of nights." He slicked his hair back with his fingertips, stood up fully, and grabbed his hat off the railing. "You ain't slept proper in days. And you've been wound tighter than a fence."

Travis sighed. "Sharpe was on the property the other day."

Lawson swore under his breath. "Why didn't you tell me? He don't ride anywhere without reason."

Travis sighed. "He was watchin' Evelyn." His neck ached. He craned it and stared at the wall past Lawson. There were a few rickety boards rattling from the wind outside. He sighed. "I didn't like the way he was lookin' at her."

Lawson spit at the ground. "So that's why you been spittin' nails."

Travis didn't deny it. Couldn't.

Lawson sighed. "What'd you do? I didn't have to bury any bodies, so I take it you didn't shoot him where he stood."

"Told him to get."

Lawson shook his head. "I don't reckon that'll be enough."

"Think you're right there."

"And Evelyn?"

Travis's chest tightened at the thought. Her eyes were wide, her tears were there–in her eyes. He felt like the worst man in the world, but that'd been the plan all along, Hadn't it?

He swallowed hard. "Told her to leave after Christmas."

Lawson stared at him. "You fool."

Travis stiffened. "Don't," he warned. He already felt bad enough. He'd heard her crying for almost an hour and head off to her room for the evening with Mason. Food was left in the kitchen for supper, and she'd made breakfast early that morning, too, but he hadn't seen her. She must have gotten up even earlier to feed Mason and get breakfast cooked just so she could avoid him.

He couldn't blame her.

"Does she know?" Lawson asked. "Know why you're tellin' her to do that?"

"She knows the bank is gonna take this place." He wiped his hands again, though they were clean.

"And what about the fact that Kane and his men are making it hell around here, and you're taking everything as a threat now after they clearly poisoned the water?"

Travis sighed again. "She knows they poisoned the water."

"She know he was lookin' at her, and that's why you feel threatened?"

"She doesn't need to know that," Travis said firmly. "She does," he said. "I didn't want to tell her. I wanted her to be able to enjoy with her friends and Mason and then go on, but she wouldn't let it go. I know that Marigold and Clara will hire her at the dress shop, and I know they'll find boarding for her. I have no doubt she'll be all right."

Lawson groaned. "You can't protect a woman from danger by tossin' her out."

"Better toss her out for the wind to carry her than to leave her here for a wolf," Travis snapped.

"She ain't your wife—but I can tell, and so can everyone else, that you care about her," he said. "Don't let them scare you into sending her out!"

"I ain't scared!" he snapped, gripping the stall rail hard. "I just can't do all that again."

Lawson wasted no time in his response. "You can't stand to lose what you love? That's human. But pushing her away won't save you from that."

"She deserves better than me anyhow!"

"She deserves someone who'll fight for her," Lawson replied, as calmly as anything Travis had ever heard. "Not shove her out the door."

"You don't understand."

"No, I think it's you that don't understand. Bonnie wouldn't want this for you." Lawson turned but looked over his shoulder "She wouldn't want you punishing yourself. It ain't betrayal to live again, or love again."

Wind slammed through in a sudden gust as Lawson pushed the door open. The lantern flickered next to Travis. Love again? Evelyn? Was he even capable of loving anyone?

He could barely breathe. "I can't—I don't—"

No one was even there to try and convince. Just himself.

Bonnie, forgive me.

He didn't say it out loud, but the thought was there. He did wonder if he cared about Evelyn Rhodes more than he should. He did feel like he was betraying Bonnie, although he knew Lawson was right. Bonnie would have wanted nothing but good things for him after her absence. She would have wanted a woman in the house to help him.

Only he didn't want to lose what he already had all over again.

But then... Evelyn's face came into his mind. She was so beautiful. Fierce. Smart. Soft and passionate in the same breath.

"Boy." He heard the word as if out of thin air.

Royce?

He hadn't even noticed anyone else come into the stable. But sure enough, there he was. The older man walked toward him slow, shoulders hunched so far Travis wasn't sure how he was still upright. His body was going downhill fast.

That was a lifetime's worth of ranching.

His heavy coat flapped all around him. He'd lost weight over the last couple years, and it was obvious just how much when he wore that coat. His face bore deep lines. It wasn't going to be long before he couldn't work this place anymore. And then what would Travis do? Even if he could somehow get some of these horses sold in the next couple weeks and get the bank off his back, what was he going to do?

He couldn't afford extra help forever.

Not to watch over the land and the creek, and definitely not to work it.

He could give housing, but he wouldn't be able to afford to feed men for long. And besides that, eventually, they'd want a little pay. Things for themselves.

He had no idea what his next steps were; he only wished his father was around to talk to him about it all.

"What'd you quarrel about with that woman?" Royce asked.

That woman.

Travis didn't answer. He just shook his head and looked down over the railing, clutching it hard.

"I know you did," he grumbled. "You know, I was cruel to that girl. I lied. I said things I had no right saying and had her get rid of things I had no business gettin' rid of because I was angry. Because grief makes fools of men," he said. "She forgave me anyway."

Travis's jaw twitched. "She forgives everyone."

"Maybe," he said. "But you know, that says something about someone. That woman… she has endured more than most men could. And she can still find grace. I wronged her. I didn't have grace. She showed me that grace that I needed to learn. And you see, I don't reckon I could forgive myself if I let her slip away now. Not after seein' what she's brought back to this house."

Travis's chest constricted. "She's safer gone."

"No!" Royce shot back. "She's safe where she is protected. And she has *you*." He grabbed Travis by the shoulders and looked him square in the face. "Don't be a fool!"

Travis's throat closed. "I—"

"She loves you, too," Royce huffed. "Don't think I don't see it. The way she watches the door for you. The way her face changes when your boots sound in the hall. Women don't look at men like that unless their heart's already given."

Travis stared at him, feeling numb.

Royce's voice broke, but he continued to speak. "We have lost enough in this life, and it seems to be that she has, too. Don't make that poor girl walk away thinkin' she isn't wanted anywhere in this world."

Lawson was right. Royce was right. Bonnie wouldn't want him to wallow in this forever. She wouldn't want him alone. And Evelyn… Evelyn was no replacement. She was her own woman. And he had his own love for her…

God help him, he loved her and that child.

But how could he protect them?

Chapter Twenty-Four

Evelyn had been planning for the fair all morning, but knew that housework needed to be done. More than anything, though, she needed to keep herself busy. Not only was there a lot to do, but the house being so quiet—it made it easy to think about things.

Things she didn't want to think about.

Things regarding Mr. Travis Baldwin.

A sigh slipped out before she could stop it. It was absurd how easily he seemed to infiltrate her thoughts now—a man who barely let her get a full sentence out some days. A man who looked at her like she was a problem he didn't really want to be bothered with fixing.

But then there were the other moments, softer ones, that she couldn't quite stop herself from thinking about. The way he looked at Mason. The way he'd rushed home with milk in a storm. The way he'd stood up for her with Royce, and the fact that he'd let her decorate for Christmas even though he no longer celebrated. The man had been kind. Far too kind at times than he wanted to be.

Those moments stayed with her as she wiped harder at the dresser surface, trying to polish away feelings along with dust. "This is ridiculous," she muttered under her breath. *You're just here to help in exchange for a temporary place to stay. Keep your head on straight.*

But even admonishing herself didn't quite get rid of the sensation swirling around and tightening inside her chest. She didn't know if it was just simple admiration, gratefulness, or if it was something deeper entirely. But whatever it was terrified her.

Caring for Travis Baldwin might well be a waste of time.

He was distant, guarded, and carrying the kind of grief that could swallow a person whole. Grief she'd experienced, but never the same kind as losing a spouse—or a child. She couldn't imagine the toll it had taken on him.

She shook her head. No. She couldn't care for Travis Baldwin in any more ways than keeping his house clean and being grateful to him for sheltering her. That was the extent. She couldn't get wrapped up in any more than that.

She carried a rag from room to room, working on the dust, trying to still her mind. Trying to force herself to stop thinking about him. Only it was impossible.

No place in this house now didn't carry his scent. No place didn't carry *him*.

No place where she didn't think about him.

His boots by the door, his hat on the peg next to it. Hearing his voice as if he was here, although he was outside working. Like there was no distance at all, except what he forced between them every time he decided to. And yet, somehow, she still wanted to do everything she could for this household.

As she worked, she hummed softly, while Mason lay in his cradle, kicking his feet so his blanket popped up in the air, and batting at the rattle. That simple toy made her chest constrict every time she saw it. Travis was such a talented man. A woodworker, a rancher, and a blacksmith to boot? She wasn't sure there was anything he couldn't do.

She moved through the sitting room, down the hall, wiping woodwork, freshening linen, brightening every surface she came across. When she reached his bedroom door, though, she didn't go in. She hadn't ever looked in his bedroom. Not really.

For a moment, she wondered if she should go in. It was his sanctuary, the place where he shut out the rest of the world. A place from which she knew she needed to keep her distance. But it was a place where dust surely gathered, too.

Her hand trembled as she pushed the door open.

She lingered on the threshold for a full breath, almost expecting her conscience to shout at her to turn around. This room was different from the rest of the house. Quieter. Still. Almost sacred. A room which she probably had no business entering.

Inside, she could detect the scents of cedar, leather, and him. The curtains were drawn halfway, letting just a bit of the winter light inside. His bed was made, and everything seemed tidy. Tidier than the rest of the house had been, by a long shot.

She swallowed hard.

With careful steps, she moved further in and started wiping down the nightstand. She polished the lamp's base and then stopped, seeing a portrait resting near the lamp.

Without even thinking, she lifted it.

Travis was younger by some years, face free of all the grief carved into it now. He stood in the portrait, holding a baby boy, with a woman sitting beside him. She was absolutely beautiful. Dark hair, kind eyes, a soft smile. The way she leaned against Travis as though she belonged next to him made Evelyn feel weak, and tears sting at the brim of her eyes.

Bonnie. And little Troy.

Evelyn stared, throat thick, as her fingers brushed over the image and pain unfurled within her. Not of jealousy, only sorrow. Like she was mourning someone she had never met.

She whispered to the portrait, "You were loved. So loved..."

Small wonder the man was so lost; he was afraid to open himself up to the possibility of love again. She couldn't imagine losing someone you were promised to be with for the rest of your life, then for that person's life to end so soon. She couldn't imagine losing Mason, and the grief that would follow. She wasn't sure she would have been able to look at another baby, either.

Life was cruel sometimes.

So, so cruel.

She would give anything for him to have both of them back. As long as he were to take Mason, too. And suddenly she understood, with devastating clarity, the depth of what Travis had lost, and her fingers began to tremble.

Footsteps sounded behind her. Startled, she turned to see him standing in the doorway, eyes wide. His face changed the moment he saw the photograph in her hands.

"Put that down," he snapped. Not loudly, but sharply just the same.

She flinched. He was right. She shouldn't have touched it. He was lucky to even have something like that left after the fire.

She put it down gently.

"I'm sorry," she said, voice shaking. "I didn't mean—I was only dusting. I didn't—" Her cheeks burned, and she hurried toward the door. "I'm sorry. Truly. I shouldn't have—" She tried to bypass him, but he stopped her, grabbing her by the forearm.

"No, I'm sorry." He sighed.

Tears welled in her eyes as she looked at him.

"I lost them," he whispered. "Bonnie and Troy. I couldn't protect them."

"T–Travis—"

"I told you to leave because I don't want to fail again."

"No." Her voice tore out before she could stop it. She took one step toward him, then another. "The fire was not your fault."

A bitter laugh ripped from him. "I left them alone. If I had been home, maybe—"

"You would have died with them," she said fiercely. His eyes widened, but she continued. "Or maybe you would have saved them, and maybe the roof would have fallen on all three of you. You don't know what would have happened! Torturing yourself won't change the past, but it will change your future!" "I wasn't there," he said with a shaky breath. "I did nothing. I deserve—"

"You deserve happiness." She took a half-step toward him. "You deserve peace. You deserve a life."

He looked at her like she'd spoken in a foreign tongue. Like the words didn't belong to him. Like he had no business hearing them at all. And, for a moment, something wavered in his eyes.

"I want to stay," she whispered. "I want to stay here with you. Even if it means we're homeless next month, and we start the year over. I want to do that with you, Mr. Baldwin. Lord help me."

Silence followed. Stunned, aching silence.

"If you'll have us," she finished.

His chest rose sharply, his breath coming out ragged and hard.

"You are a good man," she finished haltingly. "And you would be a good father to Mason. I know it."

His face crumpled.

"I ain't never thought… after everything…" he spoke slowly. "…that anyone would look at me the way you're lookin' at me right now."

She felt tears threatening. "And how am I looking at you?"

He tried to turn away, let out a small broken laugh. It was an honest sound. "Like I ain't a lost cause."

"You aren't."

He averted his eyes as if he'd just been burned. His hand slipped from her cheek, and she immediately missed the contact, but he didn't move away. Didn't retreat like he normally would have. Instead, he nodded shakily, his Adam's apple bobbing.

She felt so unbelievably close to him in that moment—and then, he stepped a bit closer. She held her breath.

He wasn't touching her, but it felt as if he were. Her whole body warmed, suddenly aware of just how close together they were.

His eyes dropped to her lips, then away instantly, and his jaw clenched hard, as if he was somehow scolding himself. But the damage was already done. She'd already seen him do it. If she reached out just a little, if he leaned in just an inch—

"Evelyn…" he breathed, and the sound of her name on his tongue made her weak in the knees. Before she knew what was happening, and before she realized her legs would even hold her, she moved another half step closer. His hand lifted, and for a moment she wondered if he would touch her face.

She wanted him to.

God help her, she wanted him to.

Then—just as he opened his mouth to speak—

CRASH!

Followed by a sharp cry from her bedroom.

Mason.

Evelyn gasped, clutching her chest, and Travis jerked backward. Together, they bolted down the hallway.

Chapter Twenty-Five

The sound wasn't loud, not like a gunshot, but it was loud enough to shake them both to their core. The panicked sound of the baby was even worse. They skidded to a halt, using the frame of the door to brace themselves.

The cradle was pushed away from the wall, all the way to the middle of the room, with the vase on the bedside table next to it shattered. Bits of it were scattered all over the floorboard. And Mason—he was on the floor.

Screaming.

For a moment, Travis felt like his soul had left his body. Like the world around him had utterly exploded.

This child. This beautiful, perfect child. Crying, helpless, on the floor. Travis scooped him up almost without thinking. Memories of his own son flashed into his mind all over again. The smell of charred wood. The loss of an innocent life. Mason's cry scraped that scar clean open.

With a strangled sob, Evelyn looked into his arms and checked every inch of the boy.

"Is he hurt? Is he hurt? My goodness! Travis, what was that! Goodness!"

Her hands trembled as he handed the boy over to her. She gathered him to her chest, rocking him, pressing frantic kisses to his temple. His cries muffled against her as she pulled him close, hugging him like she could just love him back to safety.

Travis couldn't breathe. Couldn't think. He bolted to the window, frantic, yanking the curtain to the side. The cold wind came in, and the latch of the window hung loose. Something had left the sill dirty. A smudge of dirt. Like a handprint.

And fresh tracks of men's boots just outside of it. Fresh. *That son of a—!*

Someone had been here, inside his house, beside this child, tormenting him, and the only person who had brought life back to these walls. It had to be Fletcher Kane.

Something feral awoke inside him. For a second, all Travis could hear was the sound of his own pulse pounding in his ears. It roared like a flooded river and drowned out everything except the sight of Mason on the floor.

A tiny, helpless child.

A child who had trusted him to keep him safe.

A child he had already, without meaning or wanting to, started to care for.

His fingers curled into fists. He was so angry he didn't even trust himself to speak. If he opened his mouth, then he might bark words so harsh that they'd frighten Evelyn more than she already was. Might frighten Mason more than he already was.

He looked again at the overturned crib. These men had done a lot more than trespass. They had threatened his home and his peace.

Well, he had failed before. But he wouldn't this time.

Not if it killed him.

When he turned around, Evelyn was shaking, looking at him wide-eyed, fearful. Thankfully, Mason had finally settled a bit, clinging to her dress, but tears streamed down her face. He moved toward her but stopped halfway. If he reached out, if he touched her, he might break. So instead, he spoke. Feeling raw. Rough.

"This is why you have to leave."

She gasped. "What?"

"This." His voice cracked. He pointed to the crib, the vase, and the window all at once. "They got in here. They touched him! They laid a hand on him! I have men all over this ranch on the lookout, but they still got in my house!"

Her lip trembled. Mason whimpered in her arms, burying his face against her neck.

"They wanted me to know they could do it," he forced out. "Kane and Sharpe. They wanted to make a point that they can take anything I...anything here."

He'd nearly said *anything I love.* He barely bit it back in time, so hard that it tasted like copper filled his mouth.

Evelyn whispered, "Travis, please..."

But he was already halfway gone. He couldn't help but imagine walking into the room and finding not a crying, scared child, but a completely silent one. He imagined Evelyn's scream. He imagined reliving the fire.

He couldn't do it.

He shook his head.

"I should never have let you stay this long," he rasped. "After the fair, you go."

Her breath choked. "And where do you suggest?"

"I don't know."

"Of course, you don't." She let out a breath. "But, yes. All right. I'll find another place after Christmas. You've said this before, and I've accepted it by now. I've been thinking about what we'll do. But don't you worry, I'll figure it out!"

Every instinct inside him screamed to take the words back, to ask her to stay, to tell her he would die before letting anything happen to her or Mason—but he couldn't promise their safety.

And fear made men cruel.

He couldn't look at her, because he knew if he did, he might lose every bit of resolve he had left. He didn't deserve peace. Not after he wasn't able to save his family before.

Evelyn might have looked at him like he was worth everything, like she saw more of him than he thought he had left—but he didn't deserve it.

Pushing her away was the only thing he had left to do. The idea of her out there having to try to 'figure things out" got to him, but the idea of her getting hurt while there at his ranch was worse.

His chest squeezed so tight he thought he might collapse. He wanted to say, *Don't go.* He wanted to say, *I need you.* He wanted to say, *I love you. I just can't lose you.*

Instead, he said nothing. Maybe it was a yellow-bellied silence, but it was the best he could do. Telling her what he really felt would just make things worse, especially if Royce was right and she did feel the same way.

He turned and walked out, because if he stayed, he knew his resolve would break and he would tell her he didn't mean it. Instead, he headed to his room and went straight for his rifle.

Grabbing that weapon with one hand, he checked his holstered gun with the other.

This was it.

He marched through the house and outside, ignoring the cold air. He bent down at Evelyn and Mason's window and looked at the tracks. They were a broad tread, a heavy stride. Heavier than Kane.

They'd been from Amos Sharpe.

They had to be.

"Coward," Travis yelled into the wind. "Show yourself. Face me like a man!"

Nothing answered but the wind. He looked at the tracks and where they led, scowling. He was going to end this. Once and for all. He ran out to his barn to get Buck.

He'd given them enough warnings. It was time to face them both.

***

Just as he finished saddling Buck, his senses flooded back in. He couldn't go in slinging his gun without any real plan. That was a way to get himself killed. He needed backup.

His first stop was the sheriff. When he hit town, he didn't even bother to tie Buck up. He just hopped down and stormed into Cade's office. So violently that when he blasted the door open, it slammed into the wall.

Cade stood quickly, chair scraping. "Goodness, Travis, what—"

"They got into my house." His breath was strangled and raw from the cold. "It was Fletcher Kane and Amos Sharpe. They picked up the baby, kicked over the crib, broke a vase, and left the boy in the middle of my floor!"

Cade looked at him, eyes wide, every bit of color draining from his face. "You're sure it was Kane?"

"I saw the tracks," he roared. "Window open, cradle moved, vase smashed. They wanted me to know they could take him. That they could do whatever they wanted to do!"

Cade stood up quickly from his desk, grabbing his coat and gun belt. "That's beyond threat. That's attempted kidnapping if you ask me. You stay here, I'll—"

"I'm coming."

"You can't go in breathing fire," Cade warned. "They want you riled up and makin' mistakes. Kane will twist it into trespass or somethin' else, and he'll demand a duel. I need you to think."

"I'm done thinking. He touched that baby!" Travis's breathing was ragged. "And I don't give a gosh darn if he wants a duel! I'll give it to him!"

Cade shook his head. "If you do this wrong," he said steadily, "Evelyn loses you, and the baby loses the only protection he's got right now."

Those words stopped him cold.

"Cade, I can't—" He scrubbed a hand across his face. "I can't lose anyone else—" The rest died in his throat.

"I know." The sheriff rested a hand on his shoulder. "I'll talk to Kane. You go home. Get all the ranch hands on high alert. Keep watch."

Travis nodded once, rigid, then stumbled toward the door. He paused at the threshold. "If something happens to her or that child—"

"It won't," Cade promised. "Not on my watch."

Travis walked outside, into the wind again. He didn't know why he was trying to be civilized. If he just killed them, they'd never hurt anyone else. But he didn't want to resort to that. Killing a man wasn't something he ever wanted on his conscience.

Even if it was a man like Fletcher Kane.

He mounted Buck again, who stood still just outside of the Sheriff's office.

I won't fail them.

Not again.

He didn't know how, but he knew one thing for certain: he would rather die than see Evelyn and Mason harmed in any way.

And if Kane thought fear would drive him off his land… he had another think coming.

Chapter Twenty-Six

The wind came bitter off the high ridges, and the gray sky pressed low over the plains as Travis rode toward Kane's land with Sheriff Cade McCrae. Neither man spoke, letting Travis stew, brooding and angry. He preferred it that way. More ammunition to do damage—and he knew he'd have to deal out damage sooner or later. Because nothing was going to stop someone like Fletcher Kane; someone that had never heard *no* a day in his life.

Yes, Travis knew right then and there, this would end in bloodshed.

One way or another.

A man didn't threaten what belonged to another man without getting shot.

Kane wouldn't be an exception to that.

Not that Evelyn and Mason are mine...

With no sound but the crunch of snow and soft clanking of bridles, Travis felt a bone-deep weariness. He hadn't slept. No way he could, until this was finished. The thought of that cradle being knocked around, the baby on the floor wailing—it was too much. Evelyn had clutched Mason in her arms, distraught, the way a mother only could. That image was burned hot in his mind.

There was no question that had been Kane's doing. It had to be him. Him and his *dog*, Sharpe. He thought about what he might do when they finally got to the Kane property, and he finally saw Fletcher Kane's face. He thought about what he'd say. Every scenario ended the same—Fletcher Kane on the ground.

Cade broke the silence. "You're not going to help matters by losing your temper."

"I won't lose it," Travis said tightly.

Cade let out a small grunt. "You always say that right before you do. Just like your pa did."

Travis didn't reply. He just gripped his reins tighter, envisioning Kane's throat in his hands.

When they reached the long dirt drive, the sound of the horses drew attention from two men in heavy coats who stepped from the porch, rifles slung over their shoulders, their narrowed eyes barely visible under the rims of their hats. They watched, scowling, as Travis and Cade approached. Travis wondered if they knew why he and McCrae were there or if it was just that they weren't too keen on visitors of any kind.

"Sheriff McCrae," Cade called, tipping his hat. "Here on business."

The taller guard nodded, motioning toward the house. "Mr. Kane's inside."

They rode over close to the porch, at the nearest hitching post up front, and dismounted. Still angry, Travis hitched his horse a little harder than necessary. And pushed himself off to round up the steps, his boots striking heavy and hard, with purpose.

One of the men opened the door, and Travis held back a sneer. The devil's lair, as far as he was concerned. A fire roared in the hearth, which was at least three sizes larger than his. It made him sick, just how wealthy this man was. Ill-gotten gains, made off the backs of other men. Hard-working men.

Kane's house was an ostentatious dwelling designed to show just how much money he had. It didn't even look lived in—

overly polished, like its interior had never seen a speck of dust. Travis slid his boots over the rug in the center of the room, purposely, just to make it dirty.

Much of this had to have been imported—God only knew from where—down to the paintings of horses on the walls as if the owner was some kind of rancher, too. It was all unreal. All a façade. Nothing that had anything to do with the man's real life.

Then, Fletcher Kane came out from one of the rooms down the hall, glass of brandy in hand, smiling like a man greeting old friends instead of enemies. He raked fingers through hair that was always trimmed neatly and hidden away under his expensive hat—even if inside his own home, the hat was not on his head. His waistcoat was blue, expensive, unwrinkled. If he'd been out anywhere earlier, he would have had to have freshened up quick.

He must have sent Sharpe to do his dirty work.

He usually did.

Travis scowled, wanting to jump on him already.

"Well, gentlemen," Kane drawled, "to what do I owe this pleasant surprise? A social call, I hope."

Travis grimaced, but before he could open his mouth to speak, Cade did. Calmly. Professionally. Like the lawman he was, through and through.

"There's been an incident at Baldwin's ranch. We're just here to ask a few questions."

Kane's brows lifted just slightly. "An incident? I do hope no one was hurt."

Travis's jaw flexed. He wanted to tear Kane's throat out. As if the sheriff could read his thoughts, Cade shot him a warning glance.

"There was an intruder," Cade continued. "Window forced open. A child's cradle moved. Travis here believes someone's been trespassing a lot lately. Someone from your outfit."

Kane gave a soft, sympathetic whistle that Travis knew was fake as they came. "My word. That's dreadful."

"Where were you today?" Cade asked, still calmly.

"I've been home all day." Kane took a slow sip of his drink. "Plenty around here can vouch for that."

Travis felt his blood spike. "And Sharpe?" he bit out harshly. "Where's your hired snake been?"

Kane's smile didn't waver. "Sharpe? He's here, too."

Cade stepped forward before Travis could. "Mr. Kane, this isn't an accusation," he said. Travis's fists tightened at his side. *The heck it ain't!* "It's all just procedure. Travis's here stock was poisoned not long ago, and—"

"Tragic business," Kane interrupted smoothly. "But as I told you before, Sheriff, I had nothing to do with that, either. I'm a businessman, not a monster."

Travis's fists curled. *Liar.*

Even as Kane spoke, the front door opened behind them. Cold air swept through, along with the sound of boots striking wood. Travis turned. And there he was. Amos Sharpe.

He wore the same smirk he'd had before at the ranch when he was watching Evelyn, the same black hat pulled low, the same insolence that made Travis's vision pulse red-hot.

He looked at Travis like a trapped but lazy animal, struggling only half-heartedly against its cage, lazy amusement plastered all over his face.

Travis was about to show him what a trapped animal really could feel like.

"Mr. Kane," Sharpe spoke to his boss without looking at him, his gaze still fixed on Travis with a smirk. "What's all this?"

Kane chuckled, a sound that made Travis's jaw tense. "The sheriff was just asking if you'd been out today."

"Me?" Sharpe grinned. "Been right here."

The lie came so casual, so slick, it nearly sounded true. His brown pant legs were still wet with snow, his eyes red from the wind. "Been out workin' the fields," he went on, sniffling.

Something inside Travis snapped. In less than two full strides, he was across the room. His fist hit Sharpe's jaw with a crack so loud it may as well had been a gunshot, though Travis wished it had been. The man stumbled and caught himself on the table, but managed to knock the brandy from Kane's hand. The glass shattered against the floor.

Travis lunged again. "You touched that baby, you son of a—"

"Travis!" Cade grabbed him, pulling him back hard.

Sharpe wiped his mouth with the back of his hand, a smear of red there now, but his grin never wavered. "You sure hit harder than I thought," he sneered. "I mean, for a weak man who can't even take care of his own horses."

"You son of a—!"

Travis would have lunged again but for the sheriff's hold on him.

"Enough!" Cade barked, dragging Travis back another half step. "You want me to arrest you? Because that's what'll happen next if you don't stop."

Travis knew he couldn't go attacking people on their own property. He knew Cade wouldn't let that happen, but he also didn't care.

"Get him out of my house." Kane had dropped all pretense of civility then. Clearly, he no longer wanted to entertain them.

"We're leavin'," Cade snapped. "Get on your doggone horse," he muttered to Travis, "before I have to take you to jail."

Travis scoffed. "Take me to jail!" With all he had, he wanted to flip back around and break a lot more than a glass. But the sheriff's hold was firm, and he kept moving.

"You step foot on my property again, Baldwin, and I'll have you shot." Kane spat out the door behind them. "That's the law, isn't it, Sheriff? That I shoot someone I deem a threat to me?"

The two of them halted at the bottom of the porch steps. "It is." Cade let out a breath. "If you're really in danger."

"Then I suggest he remember it," Kane finished.

Travis simply glared back at him, his breath ragged and hard. "One day you'll slip, Kane. And I'll be there to witness it."

Kane's lips curved again, mocking. "We'll see."

Cade hauled Travis further out to the hitching post, holding him tightly by the collar. He didn't let go until Kane was back inside and they'd reached the horses.

No sooner had Travis snapped Buck's leather rein loose from the post, though, than the lawman turned on him.

"You out of your mind?" he rasped. "Are you?"

Travis wiped a hand across his mouth, still shaking. "He's lying. Both of 'em. You can see it in their eyes. You just stood there and let them get away with it!"

"I saw you throw a punch," Cade snapped. "You gave him what he wanted, and that's an excuse to shoot you dead. He could have. You would have if it was him in your house accusing you, attackin' Lawson out of nowhere."

"He wouldn't get a chance. I'd take care of him first." Travis bit back. "To come on my property, poison my stream and my horses, and terrorize a baby? That deserves a whole lot worse than a bullet between the eyes!"

On that, his voice broke, and Cade sighed.

"I know. But if you keep swinging before thinking, I can't protect you."

"I don't want protecting," Travis muttered. "I want justice."

"Justice doesn't come by way of your fists," Cade persisted. "You think Kane's stupid? He's rich, connected. Men like him buy their innocence by the barrel. If we can't prove he was there, I can't do anything about it."

"Then what do you suggest I do?" Travis demanded. "Wait? Let them try again? Til next time and it goes further and they hurt him? Or her? Or both of 'em?"

Cade stepped closer, his eyes narrowed. "We'll catch him," he said quietly. "But we have to do it right."

Travis's laugh came bitter. He wanted to turn around and set fire to the place and watch it burn. But he didn't. Only because Evelyn's face came to mind. He didn't have anything to lose, but he didn't want to risk not being around if Kane tried something else.

"You find out how to arrest him, Cade," he said at last. "Or I will take care of it myself."

Cade shook his head. "You'll get yourself hanged."

Maybe he would. But he'd make sure if he did, Fletcher Kane and all his men were dead first.

Chapter Twenty-Seven

The house suddenly felt wrong—off—now. And the feeling got even worse when Travis and Sheriff McCrae brought more ranch hands and deputies out to patrol.

A prison, yes. That would have been the closest word Evelyn could have used to describe it. A prison implied bars and stone walls, and this didn't have that, but it had guards. A lot of them. And the rooms felt smaller with all of them coming in and out.

She told herself over and over that she was safe, that Mason was safe, that the men patrolling the grounds were there to protect her...but that didn't mean her heart believed it.

She wasn't allowed to go outside.

She wasn't allowed to get fresh air.

She couldn't even do her chores properly. She had to ask for help from all of them—which in turn made her feel like even more of a burden than before. At least before all this nonsense, she'd been able to properly earn her keep. Now, she felt even more like she was imposing on Travis. Like she was more of a headache than she was worth.

Evelyn moved slowly through the house that morning, tired from making all the men breakfast. At least twenty of them, at any given time. And, of course, she had to feed them.

She tried to make herself feel better about it. At least she was providing for them.

But she knew that was a strain on Travis, too. He wouldn't be able to afford feeding an army for very long. He couldn't even afford the roof over their heads, for heaven's sake.

She could only stay until the fair was over.

She blew out a large, steadying breath and gripped her teacup harder. She couldn't shake a chill that seemed to go through her, despite a warm cup and a fire that burned high and steady.

Dawn had barely crept across the sky, but faint winter light seeped through the windows in silvery beams. Mason slept in the sitting room, in a basket lined with quilts she'd sewn during those first days she'd been on the ranch, when her greatest worry had been whether she'd brought too few winter clothes from her house in Green River. She bent to adjust his blanket, a pointless move when she'd already made sure it was on top of him. But she had to do something with her hands, with her nerves. Any woman would be on edge after all they'd already had happen.

The stream.

The horses.

The cradle knocked over.

At least Mason was sleeping now. He hadn't slept well in days—not a surprise, when she hadn't, either.

She couldn't forget that awful, sickening image, the memory that seemed to be right in front of her every time she closed her eyes. Mason on the floor, his tiny fists clenched, his cries so sharp, his face so contorted. She still hadn't recovered from that sight. She wasn't sure she ever would.

Her throat tightened, and tears tugged harshly at her eyes. She sniffled, dabbing the corner of them. *Deep breaths, now. Deep breaths.*

Bad enough, it was, to be confined to the house, with each hour seeming to stretch out endlessly. Torturously

But worse? Travis barely spoke to her now. Barely looked at her. Barely seemed to breathe easily in her presence.

She knew it wasn't because he hated her. There had been fear behind his eyes when Mason was on the floor crying like that. If anything was obvious, it was that Travis was trying to protect Mason—both of them, really. And that was another reason she hurt so much.

She lifted her hand and let her thumb brush one of the snow-etched windowpanes. "I don't want to leave," she whispered to no one. "But he doesn't want me here."

Of course, he didn't. Even if the threats had never happened, he'd said it from the beginning. She and Mason were only a temporary arrangement. But she had been foolish enough to forget that, for a few days at least. Foolish enough to feel safe here. Foolish enough to imagine belonging.

The sound of the front porch boards creaking jerked her to look back, startled. Even after three days, every unexpected noise rattled her badly. But then came a sharp knock—not threatening but familiar. Probably something she should have expected, with so many men coming and going from outside.

Giving herself a stern talking-to, she drew a shaky breath and moved to the door—to a gust of cold wind, snowflakes, and a sight that cheered her soul.

Clara!

"Oh, thank heaven!" Clara swept quickly into the house. "Evelyn, I've been trying to get out here since dawn. I didn't care what all those men had to say—I needed to see if you were okay!"

Evelyn let out a breath that trembled. "Clara…"

Clara took one look at her and shook her head, reaching out to cup Evelyn's face. Her hand was cool to the touch, but it still warmed Evelyn inside.

"Come sit," she said to Evelyn, with a no-nonsense authority. "You look like you've been wrung over a washboard."

Evelyn tried to laugh, but the sound cracked as Clara moved her to a rocking chair. She closed her eyes and sighed.

"Smells good in here," Clara went on curiously, craning her neck toward the back of the kitchen.

Evelyn swiped at her face, brushing tears away, and nodded. "Thank you, I'm making bread."

"With everything going on, you're making bread?" Clara gave a soft laugh.

Evelyn sniffled and cleared her throat once more. "It's been hectic doing breakfast for everyone since Travis had all these men come here." She pulled herself straighter. "I figured some loaves of bread for tomorrow would be a lifesaver. That way I can prepare for the fair, and they can still have something to eat."

Clara nodded, her lips moving into a tight line. Then she moved to kneel before Evelyn and took hold of her hands.

"Tell me what happened," she whispered, eyes glistening. "The whole town has been talkin'. Something about an intruder? Please tell me that's exaggerated—"

"It's not."

Clara's face drained of color.

Evelyn drew in a breath, but it shuddered, and before she could stop herself, tears spilled out all over again.

"Someone came in and touched Mason..." she managed, through sobs.

"Oh, Evelyn..." Clara pulled her close.

She tried to say more. Lord help her, she tried. But the words tangled in her throat, and she only sobbed harder. She pressed both hands over her face, ashamed of falling apart.

"Dear God," Clara whispered. "Someone really came in and touched the baby?"

Evelyn nodded. "Picked him right up and put him on the floor. Knocked things over. And left, like it was nothing."

Clara covered her mouth. "I'm going to be sick. You didn't see them?"

Evelyn shook her head. "I was so stupid," she said haltingly. "I know to always check the window latch, I should have—"

"No." Clara gripped her shoulders tightly and met her eyes. "That is not your fault. Do you hear me? Someone broke in. *You* didn't cause that."

Evelyn closed her eyes. The memory burned. The way Mason's blanket had twisted on the floor, the cold draft rolling through the window. The fact that someone had touched him. Had gotten to him like that—without either her or Travis knowing...

"Listen to me," Clara went on deliberately. "Listen. You and Mason can come stay with me and Mama. Tonight, if you want. We have a spare room. You'll be safer there. We even have a little room above the shop in town. There are lanterns lit all night over there, and neighbors close, and—"

Evelyn shook her head. "Travis has men posted outside and everywhere. You saw them."

"I know that. But, still, you don't have to stay here if you're scared."

Evelyn looked at Mason, still asleep. "I'm terrified. But—" She paused, then blurted it out. "I don't want to leave."

Clara's expression softened. "Because of Travis?"

Because of a lot of things.

Because she wasn't ready to start over.

And yes, because of Travis. S

he trusted him. To keep them safe. To do everything he could to protect them. And despite herself, she'd started to imagine—maybe foolishly, but that couldn't be helped—that she might build something here. But she couldn't say so, not out loud. Not yet. Not with all this danger around them.

"He's asked me to leave after the fair, so that's what I'm going to do." She lowered her eyes. "See this all through, then go."

Clara inhaled sharply. "Evelyn…?"

Evelyn shook her head. "That's what's going to happen. That's what we've agreed to. I'm not going back on my word."

"Well, all right." Clara sighed softly. "But just know…you have options. Mama said you could work in town at our shop, stay in the little room above. But I know another seamstress in Fort Bridger. She would take you, too. She would have boarding as part of your salary."

Evelyn blinked. *Options.* She really, truly, had them. She hadn't imagined that far ahead. Hadn't dared to hope. But maybe there was a path for her here, after all.

"I don't want you to go," Clara reassured her. "But I want you alive, and happy, and safe. If you don't feel safe here, then

I would understand if you wanted to leave town. The choice should be yours."

Evelyn stared at her for a moment, still stunned.

Options.

She hadn't had options in what felt like forever. Life had always just happened; nothing really felt like a choice.

This? It was a gift. She knew that. She looked at the woman she now considered her dearest friend, aside from Marigold, and smiled. "I'll think about it. I will. I promise."

Clara pulled her into a hug again and kissed her cheek. "Then, I'll see you tomorrow at the fair. Do you need me to do anything else?"

Evelyn shook her head, going over the details quickly in her mind. They had it pretty well covered. All the merchants were bringing things. She had worked on decorations; so had Marigold and Clara. All that remained was putting it all together the next day.

"I'll see you tomorrow, then," Clara said.

Evelyn rose, still smiling. "I'll see you tomorrow. Tell your mother I'm looking forward to her company, too."

Clara grinned and hugged her once more, then took her leave. As soon as the door shut behind her and the room warmed up again, Evelyn found herself all but falling back onto the rocking chair beneath her.

She stayed there, sitting. Thinking. For a long time.

She listened to Mason's soft breaths, to the sound of her own heartbeat thudding in her ears—until she heard boots shuffle across the floor. Abruptly, she turned to find Royce standing in the doorway, hat in hand, his expression unusually gentle.

His weatherworn face carried something tender now. Something sensitive, something empathetic. Something like sympathy…or even sadness.

She couldn't help wondering why.

"Miss Evelyn," he said softly. "Mind if I join you?"

She straightened up, brushing her tears away. "Of course not. Please. Do."

He lowered himself into the chair across from her with a slow groan, and it occurred to her that maybe his old bones were finally catching up to him. It really was past time that Royce stopped working on the ranch. She wasn't sure why he still did; Travis and Lawson seemed to have most of it handled.

Perhaps he loved it. Or perhaps he simply didn't know any other life. But still, it was obvious that his body was aging faster than he wanted it to.

He waited what seemed like minutes before he finally spoke.

"I heard you were still thinkin' of leavin'."

Evelyn's throat tightened. "It's what Travis thinks is best."

He nodded slowly. "Maybe. But sometimes what seems best ain't what's right."

She swallowed the lump forming in her throat. "Travis wants us gone. That's all I know. If he wants it, then it's the right thing to do."

"It ain't that he wants you to leave." Royce shook his head. "Travis just wants you to be safe."

"But—" She hesitated. "It was always the plan for me to be here only temporarily. I was always going to leave."

"Maybe so," Royce said. "But now I think he's just letting it happen because he's scared. I think the boy is more afraid than he's been since the night we lost his Bonnie and little Troy." He leaned forward. "Travis... he don't let people in. Not since Bonnie. And he didn't want to let you in, but he started to. That much I've seen. He's hurtin' now because he thinks he's not protectin' you. Just like he feels he didn't protect them."

Evelyn looked down at her hands. "I don't know if staying is right anymore," she said. "For him or for me. I don't want to make it any harder for him. He has to figure out how to pay the bank and keep this ranch. He doesn't need to worry about us, too. We've caused enough headaches, and I really do think at this point it's best to go, whether I want to or not."

Royce studied her for a long moment. Then he nodded toward the cradle. "You got a strong spirit, miss. And that baby boy, well, he's got a better chance in this world with someone like you lookin' after him."

She blinked back tears.

Royce's voice cracked. "I just want you to know that you ain't alone here. Not anymore. And—" His throat worked. "And I was wrong about you. I know that now."

She looked up, startled.

Royce nodded. "I should've said it sooner. But us old men are stuck in our ways."

Evelyn swallowed hard, sadness swelling so high she had to breathe around it. She wasn't sure what to say, but fortunately, he didn't seem to need an answer. Royce just stood up slowly, placed his rough hand on her shoulder, and gave it a light squeeze. "Whatever you decide, just know...you'll have a friend in this house."

He walked away, and she leaned back in the chair, still feeling weak

The fair was tomorrow.

Tomorrow, she would see Clara again, the townsfolk, the children, she would see lanterns and music. Christmas would be right there in front of her face. Although, suddenly, it didn't feel like Christmas any longer.

Chapter Twenty-Eight

It was the kind of winter day that felt almost like an apology for all the harsh weather coming before it. After days of nothing but iron-gray skies and wind that cut through you like it was out for revenge, everything seemed to soften. Sunlight spilled over the ranch, setting against the snow and making it look like glitter. The sky was blue, with not a cloud in sight.

It was still cool, but the sunshine was warm through the window. and Evelyn was warmer than she'd been any morning since she'd gotten to the ranch. Sighing contentedly, she stood up and walked over to the window, taking it in for just a moment.

She couldn't believe it.

She'd slept in until daylight.

Her hand rested against the warming window sill and watched as all the men moved across the yard. For a moment she panicked, wondering what they'd eat for breakfast—but then she'd remembered she'd purposely made loaves of bread the day before and laid out dried meats. Something easy for the morning of a very busy day.

For the first time in three days, her first thought upon waking had not been the window or the floor or Mason's cry. It had been *The fair is today*. Then the weather.

Now, the rest came crashing back.

Those men. All those men.

And Travis asking her to leave right after it was over. She would have to leave tomorrow, and she still had no idea where she was going. Clara's offers were the only ones she had. But would she choose to stay with her and Marigold, in the little apartment in town above their shop, or would she go further out to another town?

She had options. Marigold and Clara had practically offered her a job three weeks before, and Clara had solidified it. She could work with them. But she could also go—make a whole new start somewhere else. Should she go to Fort Bridger and meet with the seamstress there, instead of staying in Evanston?

She looked outside sadly, taking in the ranch under the fresh light of day.

The garland and lanterns she'd hung out there would be the last she would ever hang on this ranch. But that didn't matter. It couldn't. Not now. Not when there was so much to do.

What mattered was the day was finally here. A blessing. A fair. A community event. A celebration. Something warm and bright that people were looking forward to. That *she* was looking forward to. Christmas was next week, and this would be the town's last chance to celebrate together before holing up with their own families for the holiday.

And the day was beautiful. The sun perfect. The sky without a single cloud.

God is being kind.

Behind her, Mason stirred in his little crib, letting out a soft, fussy sound that was all complaint and no real distress. She laughed. At least he had slept. They both had. She turned from the window and crossed the room to him, immediately lifting him up into her arms. He couldn't take part in the dried meats and bread, so he was surely hungry.

She smiled and nuzzled him. "Good morning, my darling," she said, kissing his warm cheek as he peered closely at her. "It's a big day. Your first Christmas fair."

He blinked up at her, then rewarded her with one of the lopsided, gummy smiles that never failed to cheer her up no matter what. His chubby hand patted her chin, gripping it and digging his little nails into her skin.

She needed to get Mason changed, fed, burped, and dressed in his absolute best for the festivities. And of course, she also had to make herself presentable for all the people already outside setting things up.

***

Evelyn dressed Mason in the little woolen outfit that Clara and Marigold had brought. It was adorable. Dark blue, with tiny brass buttons and a matching cap. Something that would surely look great for the fair tonight.

She smiled, then laid him back in his crib so that she could ready herself—thankful that she wasn't very worse for wear. The men had already started working. Not on the ranch, but on her decorations. By the time she had changed Mason, banners of evergreen and red ribbon hung from poles—some that had been there for feed and lanterns along the horse path, but others that had clearly been dug and placed into the cold, hard ground just this morning. She couldn't even imagine how hard that had been. Long planks were laid over barrels to make tables. Lanterns hung up on hooks where they usually were, but holly and garland accompanied them.

She quickly braided her hair and pinned it up, straightened the skirt of the green gown she'd chosen, scooped up Mason, and hurried to the front porch.

When she stepped out, she gasped at the sight. It was even more beautiful up close. It was like the entire place had been transformed into a marvelous Christmas village. Garland everywhere, ribbon, holly—and lanterns galore.

"I had them go ahead and get started," Travis murmured, stepping out onto the porch with a piping hot cup of coffee. The steam rose almost ferociously, and she looked at him, stunned.

This was the first time he'd said more than two words to her in what seemed forever.

"Thank you," she said sincerely.

He nodded, taking a sip. "I thought you'd be glad to not have to rush yourself getting ready when there were plenty of men out here to do it."

"You're going to enjoy it tonight, right?"

He shrugged. "Christmas really isn't somethin' I enjoy anymore. But I'll be glad if it's everything you hoped it would be."

She blushed and watched as he made his way down the steps, her gaze not leaving him the full length of his walk to the barn. She really couldn't quite put her finger on what it was that Travis Baldwin really felt about anything, but she knew without a shadow of a doubt that there was something between them she wished she could ignore.

***

Once the festivities got underway, it didn't take long for joy to find its way into her heart. She was surrounded by so many happy voices, especially of children. Their laughter rang out, a sound that always warmed her soul through and through. Despite cheeks flushed rose-colored from the cold, their smiles were bright and exuberant.

Merchants had their tables set up, some with toys, some with sweets, but all beautifully done and accompanied by eager people ready to enjoy the company.

The general store had gingersnap cookies and toys abounding, where children quickly crowded to take a peek. The butcher had a large kettle set up, too, atop one of the barrel tables, and her stomach growled at the aroma of stew drifting through the air. Then, a lively tune came from a man with a fiddle near the barn, and her breath caught.

Everyone had come together. She'd asked, and the town had answered. It made her chest ache with something that she hadn't felt in a long time.

True hope.

Marigold and Clara arrived not long after, both completely laden with parcels.

"There she is!" Clara hurried over, skirts swishing, curls peeking from beneath her bonnet as she gripped hold of a bundle she held for dear life.

Marigold was right behind, practically jogging over to her. "The Lord surely smiled on you with this weather!" she exclaimed, with a wide smile.

Evelyn smiled back, shifting Mason in her arms so she could grab a few things from each woman. "It's more than I hoped for."

"You deserve it," Clara said simply, exhaling as if the couple of things Evelyn had taken was the brunt of her load. "And then some!"

She blushed and moved to place their things on their own free table so that Marigold could set up. Then, she continued on, checking on all the merchants, making sure every one of them had everything that they needed.

She wanted this all to go without a single hitch!

She answered questions, directed people who needed directing, and even reassured the general store owner's wife, Mrs. Dawson, that yes, there would be someone to mind her stall if she wanted to take a turn listening to the music and dancing later on in the evening.

Wagons seemed to roll in and out unceasingly as the day drew on, with families pouring out, laughing and stomping their boots to the music almost immediately. Everyone was dressed in their Sunday best, and Evelyn reveled in every moment and every new face. Children tugged their parents over to see the candy table, while men drifted toward the hot cider barrel.

"Miss Rhodes!" a bald man with a fine brown suit called out to her, waving. She smiled brightly as he approached. "I'm Reverend Ellis."

"Pleasure to meet you," she said, curtseying. She was sad that she hadn't had the pleasure of attending services, with all the winter storms isolating them so thoroughly over the two weeks since she'd arrived.

"You as well," he said. "I've heard quite a bit about you from Miss Clara in the few times she's managed to make it out to town with all of this weather. I must say you've really stepped up to do something precious here."

"Oh, I'm not so sure about that." She waved a dismissive hand.

"Well, I am," he said. "This town really loves this fair. It brings a lot of families together, some that don't see each other practically all year."

Evelyn flushed again, muttering a small "thanks." Whether she stayed in this town or not, her efforts had hopefully counted for something.

Throughout the day and into the night, more than once, people told her how lovely it all was, how she should stay, how she should attend church. Each time, she felt a fresh crack through her heart. She wasn't sure. She wasn't sure of so much…

If someone was really trying to hurt them to get back at Travis for some slight or grudge, maybe her absence would solve that problem. But then, an even sadder thought occurred to her: even if she could feel safe without him, would she be able to run into him in town and not think of what she wished had been?

Whether she liked it or not, Evelyn had to admit she'd begun feeling things for the man.

She watched as Travis dismounted his horse and handed off the reins to one of the new ranch hands. He wore a good coat, one that Evelyn hadn't seen him wear yet. It was deep black, clean, and made his shoulders look even broader.

She watched as he walked through the crowd, his eyes on everything, and yet, she wasn't sure if he was looking at the fair in full swing or not. He almost looked through it, rather than at it. She wondered if he was proud that something like this was taking place on his property, proud of her…or if he was merely scanning everything, searching for any sign of a threat.

She watched him as his gaze fell on Cade, who was over by the barn, his badge visible. They nodded to one another, and Cade set off into the crowd, too, half-smiling, appearing for all the world as if he were a man at leisure as he greeted people.

It would've been a lie to say that she wasn't tense. Nervous. Anxious. Knowing, deep down, that they couldn't completely relax set her on edge. She tried to ease her own twisting shoulders, to tell herself that everything was going to be all right. There were too many people around for anyone to start something now.

But fear never seemed to answer to logic. It hadn't, either, when she was just a girl, and her father would tell her there was nothing under her bed. She very much knew that, but it didn't stop her imagination from running wild at every creak of the floorboards. Part of her still expected the tall tales to come alive there in the darkness and threaten to gobble her up.

Even as she watched, she noticed Travis didn't approach her. Their small interaction earlier that day had been the only one she'd had in days, and the only one she would likely have the rest of the day, if his demeanor now was any indication. Then, again, honestly compelled her to acknowledge that he didn't really interact with anyone…but she always knew where he was. Her awareness of him had become another sense of sorts.

Meanwhile, the fair bloomed around them. Children ran with sticky fingers from candy, their eyes bright, their arms full of little toys and sacks of roasted nuts. Women shared gossip and recipe talk. Men had their own jokes about God-knew-what, clapping each other on the back, razzing one another.

"Miss Rhodes!" a little girl cried, tugging on her skirt. "Mama says to tell you thank you for makin' Christmas happen this year!"

Evelyn crouched to be level with her. "I believe Christmas would have come anyway, dear," she said. "Remember, Christmas is right here." She poked the girl lightly on her chest. And with a wink, the girl laughed and skipped away.

Each and every praise, though, was a gift. But, unfortunately, one like a two-edged sword, making everything much more difficult. She smiled, thanked everyone, even laughed at times—while all the while, inside, she felt like she was slowly bleeding to death. *If only they knew I'm already half gone.*

As dusk deepened, the lanterns grew brighter. The fiddler and his companions moved into a livelier set of tunes, merchants started to close up their tables, and the crowd remaining clearly intended to enjoy the festivities a bit more

She had really wanted this. For the town. For herself. For Travis. Not just the fair. Just a simple reminder that joy still had a place in the world, even when it seemed like it had all withered away

But looking at him now, scowling off in the corner, his eyes narrowed as they scanned the crowd, she felt a sinking defeat about making any difference where he was concerned. Even if she couldn't worry about that now.

You have built a celebration you may not ever get to see again.

Yes, she did. And she needed to have the sense to enjoy it.

She kissed the top of Mason's head and heard laughter. Someone called for a reel; someone else for a waltz. And she laughed along, even if that laughter was half-sadness, and even if it sent unwanted tears down her cheeks—

"You should be out there, too," Marigold said, sidling up to her and nodding at the dancers. "You're the reason they're all stompin' holes in Travis's yard. You've been doin' nothing but checkin' in on everyone else and not enjoying the festivities for yourself."

Evelyn managed a small smile. "I'm quite content here."

Marigold's gaze softened. "You look tired, child."

"I am," Evelyn admitted. "But it's a good tired."

Lawson waved as he passed by with Clara, both of them laughing at something, and tears filled her eyes afresh. There was definitely something budding between those two. She'd seen it for a couple of weeks now. And although she was happy for it, she couldn't help but feel her own heart ache.

She found herself scanning the grounds for Travis, suddenly realizing she no longer felt that extra sense of knowing where he was. Trying not to let herself get upset, she swept her eyes over the crowd of people, zeroing in on first one group, then another. The ones dancing next to the barn, the ones at the merchant tables, and even the food tables.

She looked under each lantern. She looked even back toward the house. Nothing.

Until he was right in front of her.

And her breath caught in her throat.

"Evenin'," he said, without preamble. He shifted awkwardly, uncomfortably even, hat in hand. "They're startin' a couples dance," he went on, nodding toward the dancers. "Royce told me just a second ago, you ain't danced all night."

She found herself looking over at Royce, a mere few feet away, and she watched as his eyes did everything to avoid her as he sipped on—likely spiked—cider. Holding her breath, she turned back to Travis.

"I was wonderin' if it might help you loosen up, if I—" he stammered a bit. "What I'm sayin' is, it's been a long time since I took part in a dance."

Her heart gave a painful little leap. "You should, then," she said kindly.

He swallowed once. "I...was wonderin' if *you'd* dance it with me."

"You...want to dance with me?"

A faint, self-conscious line crossed his brow. "I asked that poorly, I suppose." His voice rumbled, deeper with nerves. "Would you...do me the honor of a dance, Miss Rhodes?"

Marigold let out a little hum of approval and elbowed her a bit roughly in the ribs. "Go on," she whispered, already plucking Mason from Evelyn's arms. "I'll hold this fella. I've raised enough young 'uns in my time to mind one more for a few minutes."

Evelyn's arms felt strangely light without Mason's weight. She smoothed her skirt to keep her hands from shaking, then nodded.

"Yes," she said. "I'd like that."

He offered his arm. She laid her hand on top of it gently. Even through layers of coat and sleeve, she could feel the heat of him, the strength. He led her out toward the cleared space where couples were already lining up. The fiddler called out a few instructions, and the music shifted into something lilting and sweet.

They faced one another, and for a moment, neither of them moved. His hand hovered, hesitant, above her waist. She inhaled, then stepped closer to him. She watched as he swallowed hard, his hand lightly brushing her back. The contact was careful, but it caused a flutter of emotion in her belly. Her own hand settled in his callused palm.

And then they were moving.

Slowly at first. Awkwardly.

His steps were sure enough, but her senses were on fire, and her stomach was doing flips. She was hyperaware of each and every touch. The curve of his palm on her back, the steady grip of his other hand, the warmth of him so close. Her heart was practically beating out of her chest, her mouth gone dry.

The lanterns swung above their head softly, casting golden light over the glittery snow. She knew there were other couples around them, but for a moment, it felt like it was just the two of them.

How had it come to this?

She had completely intruded on him in the middle of a winter storm just weeks before Christmas, with a baby and nowhere else to go. And now she was dancing in his arms? Caring about a man she was never meant to care for?

If only things were different...

"Thank you," she heard herself say. "For today. For letting the fair be held here. I know it wasn't...easy."

His gaze held hers for a moment. "It was the right thing," he said. "And you stalled the bank. You made somethin' good happen on this land. Haven't seen that in a long time."

Her throat thickened. "I'm glad you're at least getting one dance in tonight," she said softly. "And it'll be a good send-off." When he didn't answer, she surged on. "I really am sorry for all the trouble, Travis. But I'll be gone soon enough."

"I wish it was different," he muttered.

She swallowed. "It's foolish to wish for things like that. I was a fool for it myself."

"You're not foolish," he said a bit roughly. "Not for wantin' more than just survival."

She wasn't sure whether to laugh or cry. Or both. "You don't know all the things I've wanted."

"I know some," he answered.

Half-afraid to breathe, she dared to look up at him. His eyes held a heat, an intensity, that made breathing even more difficult. The music was there in earshot, but suddenly there was nothing in this place but the two of them. For one brief, fleeting moment. That was all she would allow herself. She thought of Clara's offer. Of a room in town, or even a job with another seamstress in another town.

The promise of a new start... again...

She knew what she was going to do.

Tomorrow, she would ask Clara to write a letter to her friend. She wouldn't be able to stay at the ranch now, or even in Evanston. Wouldn't be able to see him in town and pretend she didn't feel something for him. Because, Evelyn knew on sinking certainty, she couldn't.

Their bodies were even closer now than they had been at the beginning of the dance. So, so close. His hand was firmer at her back, her fingers resting more willingly against his shoulder. Her chest rose and fell in shallow, quickened breaths, brushing against his body. She felt like she might float away, being so close to him. She couldn't stop herself from looking up at his lips, wishing more than anything that he would kiss her.

"Evelyn," he said quietly. She shuddered, hearing her name spoken so low as he looked down at her.

She lifted her face, lips parting, every part of her aching for him.

And then—

A crash. Loud, brutal. Someone screamed. And then more.

They jerked apart in a jolt.

HANNAH LEE DAVIS

What has happened now?

Chapter Twenty-Nine

Fear had a sound.

It wasn't one noise but all of them at once: banging—not gunshots, but loud enough to be; shouting; boots pounding hurriedly against frozen ground, horses panicking and stampeding all around. Women screaming out for their children. Babies crying. Travis tried to look through the crowd, still holding Evelyn's hand firmly.

Where was Marigold? Where was Mason?

He had felt kept on a tight coil all day, wound so hard he thought he might snap. He had tried to hide it and let down his guard just a little bit to dance with Evelyn, because to his mind, she hadn't been enjoying the fruits of her labor nearly enough. But he had known something was coming. He had felt it in his bones, the same way he sensed a storm hours before it broke across the plains. He couldn't believe he'd let down his guard.

She'd just looked so lovely that he couldn't help himself from going up to her to tell her she'd done well. But he'd been foolish. He knew it now, with a clawing intensity. He shouldn't have left the watch.

People flew in every direction, scattering as their horses fidgeted and wagons groaned and shook. Lanterns swung wildly on their hooks. Barrels were overturned, rolling downhill toward a fence line.

"Mason!" Evelyn screamed as she fell down beside him. But he couldn't let her stay there. Roughly, he pulled her to her feet once more. They had to get to Mason—

They found him, face red and scrunched, crying. Marigold panted, holding him close.

"He's all right," she breathed out. "Don't worry, honey. He's all right."

Relief shot through Travis so sharply it nearly took him down.

He forced his eyes from Evelyn and turned back into the screaming crowd.

"Get back to the house with him!" he barked over his shoulder to her. "Now! Move!"

His boots skidded on a patch of snow-slick earth, toward Cade. Faces flashed past him as horses continued to pound at the dirt all around them, still spooked, still showing no signs of settling.

Cade stood at the far side of the barn near a table completely overturned and a man lying on the ground, with a heavy, gaping wound on his head. Mr. Dawson. The general store owner. Barrels of apples rolled across the snow, and Travis crunched a couple with his boots as he crouched down next to the man.

"What happened?" he demanded.

Mr. Dawson looked shaken, his breath coming in ragged puffs. "Men," he rasped. "Four of 'em. Maybe five. Came over here, hit me in the head, flipped my table, and lit a match right on the backside of my horse!"

"You recognize them?" Cade barked.

Dawson shook his head. "I didn't recognize any. They just… they came out of nowhere. "They grabbed the whole table, and I don't know what they hit me with—"

Travis felt a cold shiver travel up his spine. "Which way did they go?"

Dawson pointed toward the far edge of the ranch, toward the road leading north. "That's toward Kane's property," Travis ground out.

Of course, Kane would pull something during the fair.

"Doggone it." Cade rubbed a hand over his jaw, scanning the panicked crowd. "They knew what they were doin'. Hit fast, hit hard, create absolute chaos, and hightail it out."

"Of course they knew," Travis seethed. "This has Kane written all over it."

Cade shot him a look. "We don't know that yet."

Travis laughed outright, without humor. "Who else would send a pack of thugs onto my land during a Christmas fair? Everything's not always just a coincidence, Cade."

"What if you're wrong, Travis?" the other man retorted, in the most official-sounding voice Travis had ever heard.

He laughed again, this time in scorn. "I ain't wrong."

And then he couldn't stand around talking any more.

"Where you goin'?" Cade called out, even as he turned to go.

"Where do you think?" he retorted. "I'm goin' after him."

"No." Cade jerked Travis around by his forearm. "You're goin' home." The sheriff pointed to the house where Evelyn and Mason were supposed to be waiting.

"The heck I am," Travis snapped. "He's the one behind this, and you know it."

"You can't prove it," Cade shot back. "And if you storm his property right now, all you'll do is give him exactly what he wants, a reason to claim you're the threat and shoot you!"

Travis took another step toward the road, but Cade caught his arm hard again.

"Don't," he warned, and Travis stopped. If he ran off now, he'd have little but a sore arm to show for his temper and far worse consequences. "Cool off. I'll deal with Kane. Because if you ride out there half-cocked, you'll ruin any chance I have of pinning this to him."

"What are you waiting for?" Travis sputtered. "I'm not sittin' around while he targets my home."

"I said I'll deal with him," Cade repeated evenly. "Now go on home! Git!"

Travis tore his arm free, teeth grinding. "Fine. This time. But I tell you, Cade, if he touches anyone else—"

"I know," Cade said, more calmly this time. "Get home. Protect what's yours."

Travis didn't say another word. He just stalked back toward his horse, tearing through all the people finally getting hold of their horses and restoring order bit by bit. As far as he was concerned, Cade better deal with Fletcher Kane, because he wasn't going to give him another opportunity.

That much was for certain.

***

But when he went into the house, he found trouble of a whole different sort.

Evelyn was in her bedroom, with belongings she'd brought laid out on top of her bed. He watched from the doorway as she threw a few more items on top.

Then, she became aware he was there...and froze.

Travis forced himself to speak. "What are you doin'?" he asked.

She didn't look at him, but he saw tears on her face. "Packing."

The word cut him clean in two.

"Packing," he echoed, stepping fully inside. "Evelyn, I—"

"You told me to leave," she whispered, still not looking up. Her voice trembled. "After the fair. The fair's over, and so, I'm leaving."

He felt the floor wobble underneath him. He had said that, yes. And he knew it was what was for the best, but seeing her actually doing it... it gutted him.

She placed a quilt gently in the carpet bag she'd brought and smoothed it with shaking hands. "Clara told me about a seamstress position in Fort Bridger. Board and lodging included. I'm going to write them first thing tomorrow."

His mouth opened. Closed. It felt like something was lodged in his throat. "You're not staying in Evanston?"

She still didn't meet his eyes.

"But even if the position doesn't work out..." Her voice cracked. "I'm leaving anyway. I can't risk Mason's safety. I—I won't."

Finally, she lifted her gaze. Tears glazed her eyes. Her lashes trembled with them, and her cheeks were flushed. Even as he watched, her throat moved convulsively. As if she were trying to swallow something that wouldn't go down.

He knew the feeling. But it didn't hit him in the throat.

The pain came over him like nothing else he'd ever felt, slammed through his chest. So violently, he wasn't sure he would be able to steady himself.

This was exactly what he'd been afraid of.

Not only had he started caring for her, when he had no business caring about anyone. But he'd cared about someone again, knowing he wouldn't be able to protect them.

He wanted to stop her. He wanted to beg her to stay. He wanted to grab her shoulders and say *Don't go. Don't take him away. I'll protect you. I'll protect him.* But as much as he wanted to believe it, he couldn't.

Travis hadn't protected anyone from anything.

He hadn't been able to protect his own wife. Hadn't protected his own son. Hadn't even been able to protect those horses that died last week.

What right did he have to ask her to stay?

None.

He had to face it. And deal with it.

"Well." He forced words out. "I guess it's for the best."

As soon as he said it, something broke behind her eyes. Just like it broke inside of him.

"For the best," she repeated, her voice suddenly cold. "You really believe that?"

He swallowed hard. "I can't protect you. I can't protect Mason. I've already failed too many people. I ain't going to do it again."

It felt like he'd been shot in the chest, admitting that to her. As if she felt the shaft of pain, too, her breath shuddered.

"Travis..." She paused, shaking her head. "You need to forgive yourself for the past. What happened with Bonnie and Troy was not your fault, and you will never be all right if you don't find a way to forgive yourself."

He closed his eyes briefly, a low ache rolling through him, threatening to make tears fall. He wouldn't let them, though. He couldn't.

"Evelyn—"

"I tried," she said, tears spilling over her cheeks. "I tried to help you. I tried to show you that you aren't alone. I failed in that, myself." She was crying in labored sobs now. "You don't want us here. You want us to go, and I think you're right. It's time to go."

Lord, the sound of those tears...it nearly ripped him in two. He wanted nothing more than to walk the length of the room and wrap his arms around her.

But he didn't move. He couldn't. Because everything she said was true. He had asked for this. Had insisted on it. Had told himself again and again that having her there was dangerous.

But now...now, she was leaving.

He stared at her for a long, painful moment. Her hair had come loose from its pins and was now frazzled at the top of her head. Her gown was creased, her eyes were red, her lips trembling, her hands twisting uselessly at the fabric of her skirt. Anxiously. Nervously. Maybe even fearfully.

She looked like heartbreak itself.

He couldn't bear it.

He turned away sharply and stomped out of the room before he could betray himself. His boots were heavy against the floor, through the house, out the front door to the porch. He slammed the door behind him, as if by doing so he could somehow keep the pain at bay, and gazed almost unseeingly at what was left of the town fair. The celebration. The happiness and joy.

It was almost completely gone, as were most of the people by now.

What a perfect day, ended by such a perfect disaster. He hated it for Evelyn. She'd worked so hard. He gripped the porch railing so fiercely it groaned under his hands.

He'd always known he'd wind up alone. He'd told himself it was better this way. Safer. Cleaner cut. Easier. But now that he was going to be alone again, he wasn't sure what to make out of it.

He was losing them...

For the first time since he'd lost Bonnie and Troy, being alone no longer seemed like a comfort. Now, it felt more like a curse.

Chapter Thirty

Evelyn sat at the kitchen table with a sheet of paper in front of her and a pen in her hand, and tried to will her fingers to move.

The words were simple. They should have been simple, at least. She had already written them once, and although it felt like her heart had been completely pulled from her chest, she had folded it, sealed it, addressed it.

Only to tear it open again, her hands shaking...

She'd burned it.

It had felt too real. Too final. Too much like a door closing that she knew could never be opened again. Even if every shred of common sense told her it was time to shut that door...she couldn't bring herself to do it.

Her small carpetbag already waited by the door, completely packed. Her trunk stood in the little bedroom off the hall, holding all that remained of her life: a few dresses, Mason's blankets, her sewing kit, the tiny handful of mementos she had from before, and received since, coming to Travis's ranch.

Things that she would want to remember once she finally had a home of her own.

Home?

She wasn't sure what that word meant anymore.

She would be staying above Clara and Marigold's shop in town until she heard back from the position in Fort Bridger. Marigold said there was a cot. A warm stove.

They were kind. Generous. And she was so grateful. But she was ready to settle somewhere, not spend time in another way station.

She stood abruptly and paced nervously.

As she moved from room to room, the house felt smaller than ever.

Down the short hall was the bedroom she and Mason shared, bleakly stripped back now. The tidy little nest she had made for them was reduced to nothing more than the bare bones it was just a few weeks ago. The small homey touches from Marigold, or that she herself had made, were now packed up in the corner, waiting to be carried out.

If it wasn't for that small pile, she might never have been there at all.

She swallowed the tightness in her throat and nervously straightened the already-straight blanket on the little cot beside the wall, for something to do with her hands rather than anything else.

Clara was due to arrive before midday with the wagon. They would ride into town together. Marigold had insisted she come, too, to help with Mason and the bags and to get her settled.

Another gust of wind rumbled the house as she crossed to the front window and peered outside. The world had shrugged on one more layer of white since the night before.

The decorations were still up, and she hoped Travis would leave them up until at least after Christmas. Everyone had worked so hard on them, after all. Snow was really coming down at this point, in a way that made it difficult to see to the edge of the property.

"Oh, Clara…" she whispered worriedly. She couldn't help but wonder if Clara's horses would be able to make it through. She knew they had strong horses, but still….

On a jolt of dismay, it occurred to her that she might not be going anywhere today. It might be too dangerous with the way the storm was picking back up again. Her stomach fluttered, in an untenable mix of relief and dread. Relief that maybe she wouldn't have to climb aboard that wagon leaving the ranch just yet, dread that staying at the ranch even a second longer meant more time trapped in an in-between.

Her eyes fell on the letter again on the kitchen table. The black ink scrawled across the page seemed to stare back at her. Proof of a decision made. Or at least trying to be made.

Behind her, a sound broke the hush. A bubbled, gurgling chuckle that lifted through the air with startling brightness.

Mason.

Before her mind even had the chance to catch up, her feet carried her toward the bedroom where she'd laid him down—only to stop, frozen, in the doorway. On the braided rug near the crib, stretched out on his back, was Mason, fat little arms waving.

And Travis was right there on the floor beside him.

He had shrugged off his heavy coat and tossed it over to the bed. His blue shirtsleeves were rolled to the forearms, the muscles there flexing as he wiggled his fingers with exaggerated slowness over Mason's round belly.

"Gonna get you," he said, his voice low and playful, the likes of which she'd never heard before. "Gonna get you…"

His fingers darted about, tickling Mason's side.

The baby squealed with laughter, kicking his legs in glee.

She gripped her chest, feeling her heart throb painfully. She watched as Travis stopped, and a sigh escaped her before she could hold it back. Then, slowly, the corners of his mouth curved into a smile.

"Love that little laugh, buddy…" he said quietly.

Evelyn stood very still, hoping to remain unseen for a second longer.

Travis ducked his head closer, his dark hair falling a little over his brow. She bit her lip as she watched. "You think that's funny, though, do you?" he asked. "You like it when I get your belly?"

He repeated the slow, teasing motion. Mason shrieked again, hands batting at Travis's wrists, trying to grab hold with his clumsy fingers. An expression crossed Travis's face that stole her breath completely. Wonder. Awe. Something painfully close to joy. Something completely unguarded. It took ten years off him, at least. Made him look like the man in the portrait she'd seen with Bonnie and Troy.

And her heart cracked, silently… but he seemed to sense it and looked up.

"I didn't know you were there." He cleared his throat.

"I heard him laughing," she replied.

He looked back down at Mason, who had discovered one of his own feet and was now attempting to haul it toward his mouth, cooing with his little eyes fixated in complete concentration. Then he leaned back, resting his hands on the rug.

"I'm sorry," he said, looking up at her.

"For what?" she asked.

"For all of it," he said simply. "For not being the kind of man who can keep you safe. For askin' you to go when…when I don't want you to. For…" He swallowed, eyes dropping briefly to Mason. "For not bein' enough, I guess."

"You *are* enough," she whispered, the words escaping before she could even think them through. "You are a much better man than you think or that you seem to give yourself credit for."

His mouth twisted, but he didn't say anything. Instead, he reached out and let the back of one knuckle brush gently along Mason's arm and up to his cheek. The baby grabbed at his finger, curling his small hand around it.

"I'll miss him," he said. "More than I can rightly say." A pause. "I'll miss you, too."

She couldn't breathe all over again.

This was perhaps the closest he had come to admitting anything clearly, and it only made it harder, not easier. She swallowed, her eyes burning so much she could barely see.

"I'll miss you as well," she choked out.

He looked up again at that, and something edged with pain moved behind his eyes. And then, there didn't seem to be anything else left to say.

"Storm's pickin' up." He stood up and gestured toward the window.

She nodded with a sigh.

"You shouldn't go in weather like this," he went on. "Road'll be bad. Won't be able to see much ahead of you. The horses could stumble, hit a drift. You'd be better off stayin' till it calms. 'Sides, I doubt Kane would be too keen to be out this way with weather like this."

"I—I can't," she stammered. "If I don't go now, I—I might never work up the courage again."

He stared at her, and she thought, fleetingly, that he might say *Then don't*. That he might tell her to unpack, to stay, to let him figure the rest out. That he might finally admit that what she was feeling wasn't one-sided.

But his mouth pressed into a thin line instead. And he merely gave a tight nod.

"Storm's still a risk."

She had no argument there. It was clear he cared about her safety, but through the window, she could see a faint dark shape come into view through the white fog of snow falling.

Clara's wagon.

"She made it," Evelyn breathed.

Travis followed her out, grabbing Mason up in his arms, and together, they went into the sitting room.

"She shouldn't have tried that in this weather," he said, now sounding bitter. But again, he didn't go further. Didn't order her not to even think about it—much as she wished he would.

When the wagon pulled up closer to the house, the horses' heads were bent low, plowing through the snow as it clung to their manes and harness. Clara climbed down, nearly disappearing to the knee in a snowbank just off the porch, and stomped her way up onto the step.

Evelyn bit back a laugh when she heard Clara curse.

She pulled away from the window and made way to the door, hesitating on the handle. She looked back at Travis, then, for a moment. Just a moment. She couldn't bear not to.

"You have done...more than you know, taking us in. I will always be grateful for that."

"You don't owe me thanks," he said roughly. "Especially if it ends with you out in a storm because I couldn't keep you safe here. I let you stay this long to ride out the winter blizzard coming in. Now it's right back again, and I feel like I'm sendin' you out in it."

Before she could untangle the emotions inside herself—or Mason from Travis's arms—a brisk knock sounded at the door, followed by Clara's voice. "Evelyn? It's me."

Evelyn swallowed, lips suddenly dry. She reached for Mason, watching closely as Travis hesitated.

"Goodbye, little man," he barely whispered. "You be good for your mama, you hear?"

Hearing the word *mama* applied to herself still seemed foreign. But she smiled, letting one tear fall down her cheek before turning back to the door and opening it.

Clara's cheeks were flushed pink from the cold. "We need to go quick," she gasped, her teeth clattering as she pushed her scarf down from her mouth and hurried in. "The road's passable now, but it won't be soon enough. And I don't want to be caught after dark. Mama headed down to town already to get everything set up for you so we could save time and ride back together."

Evelyn nodded, though her legs felt strange beneath her, as if they might forget how to carry her at any moment. Clara took the carpetbag from her, despite it being just as big as she was. As if she could feel Evelyn's hesitancy, she looped her free arm around her shoulders, drawing her out the door into the storm, toward the wagon.

"I'll get the rest of your things," Travis said quickly, moving back into the house.

No time at all seemed to pass before she settled into the wagon, wrapped herself in blankets, and Travis came back out—with the crib he'd let her use. The one he'd carved for his own son.

"Travis, no—" she started as he loaded it up.

He shook his head and held up his hand. "It's Mason's now," he said simply.

The cold grabbed her lungs almost as hard as the emotion did.

"Y'all be safe," he said firmly, his gaze locked onto Clara's as she steadied herself in the front wagon bench and slapped the reins.

"We will!" Clara called behind them, and they lurched forward. It was clear she was determined to get to town before the storm got much worse.

Evelyn found herself looking back as they lumbered down the snow-covered road. Through the blur of white, she could still make him out.

He stood on the top step, his shirt collar upturned in the wind, one hand resting on the post, watching them leave. She bundled Mason closer underneath her cloak, bit back tears, and shivered.

She couldn't understand how he was outside without a coat. But he was. And they held each other's gazes for a long moment as the wagon moved away.

Her chest ached fiercely as she thought of the ranch. Of the sound of Travis's boots coming inside from a long day of work. Of Royce's grumbling. Of Barrett Lawson's kindness.

She thought of the way Mason quieted when Travis spoke near him. Like he'd grown familiar to the man, just as much as she had.

And then she thought of Bonnie's portrait and the baby in her arms.

He will never truly be mine. I was never meant to stay.

The words echoed in her heart for what felt like the hundredth time in her life. First, she'd lost her parents. Second, she'd lost Arabella. And now the third... she was losing Travis Baldwin, his ranch, and all the lovely people who helped her feel at home at Christmastime.

She knew one thing for certain: she would never make herself another burden. Not to anyone. Especially not a man already drowning in grief and obligation.

She lifted her chin in a small, helpless gesture, part farewell, part thank you, part *I'm so sorry.*

He didn't move as they continued down the road. He just stood there, watching her leave. The smaller he got, the more white flakes that fluttered between him and her—the more her heart crumbled.

Chapter Thirty-One

"You fool," Travis hissed to himself, his hands gripping tightly into fists as he paced inside the front sitting room.

Thirteen minutes.

They'd been gone thirteen minutes, but the storm had already worsened, as wind slammed against the windows and seeped into the house. He wasn't even sure how Clara had made it to them the way it was, and now it was even worse than when they'd left.

He felt guilty that he was inside with a fire.

His boots stomped heatedly. He couldn't stop. Couldn't sit. Couldn't ignore the fact that he'd just let her leave—her and Miss Clara both—into a storm like that. With Mason!

The moment Evelyn and Mason had climbed up into Clara's wagon, something went all wrong inside him. The kind of wrongness that started in the pit of his stomach and climbed steadily upward until it pressed against his ribs, causing him to gasp. His heart raced. His throat clenched so tight it felt like he was swallowing glass.

He had stood on the porch as the wagon lurched forward and watched as it disappeared behind a blanket of white. He'd tried to tell himself—lie to himself, more like it—that it was for the best. That she and Clara would make it to town soon enough. But how would he know she made it? He should have accompanied her. He should have taken her himself!

He raked a shaky hand through his hair and gripped the back of his neck, squeezing hard.

What if the wagon tipped?

Clara was a good driver, capable. Her parents had taught her well. He knew that. But the road to town cut through uneven ground. In a storm, drifts hid dips and holes that a wheel could catch just the right way and leave them tipped—or worse. A wagon wheel could slip, catch, wrench sideways, overturn. Anything.

His stomach lurched.

The room felt too small. He couldn't pace anymore. He couldn't stand waiting. He wasn't even sure what he was waiting on. He would have no idea if they'd made it or not. "They won't have made it to town by now," he muttered under his breath, turning away from the window again. He should just go. Now.

Ride out fast and meet them. Accompany them the whole way.

Insist that Clara stay put with her and ride out the storm completely before heading back home. Marigold, too. Insist that they all just stay put.

Lawson had gone out ten minutes ago to check the outbuildings. Royce was in the kitchen sharpening the blade of an axe, scowling with every scrape of stone against steel, clearly doing nothing but wasting time. Truth was, they were all three anxious. Nervous. Thinking the same exact thing.

No one should be traveling in this weather.

Let alone three women and a baby.

That's it!

He turned sharply toward the door, grabbing his coat from the peg and hauling it on with frantic, clumsy motions. He tugged the front door open. Wind blasted inward, chilling him to the bone. Lawson was rounding up the steps, stomping snow from his boots.

Travis barely heard him. "I'm goin' after them."

Lawson blinked, breath coming out in visible bursts. He nodded. "I'm comin' too," he said. "They shouldn't have gone out in this!"

"This storm… it wasn't this bad when they left," Travis said. He wasn't sure if he was trying to convince Lawson or himself that he hadn't acted as foolish as he felt.

Lawson scowled. "You told her to go."

Travis froze in his tracks. Even through the roar of wind rattling his teeth and the trees around them, the words were loud.

He was right.

It was his fault. He'd told her to go. And he hadn't demanded she stay, even knowing the weather was getting up like it was.

Lawson shook his head. "Come on," he yelled out over the wind as Travis shut the door. "I was comin' to tell you the same thing; that I was goin' after them. I got two horses saddled."

Travis whirled. "You *what*—?"

"I figured if you didn't mention it first, you'd want to at least go with me. Either one of us would need another set of eyes out there with as thick as this is, and I've got more than one reason to go after them."

"What reasons do you have?" Travis asked over his shoulder as he pounded down the steps toward the barn.

"I love Clara!" Lawson yelled behind him.

Travis whipped around to look at his foreman and best friend, stunned. Not by the fact that the man was smitten with her, but that he was admitting it.

"And you," Lawson said, brushing past him to the bar, "love Miss Rhodes."

"I don't—"

"Save it."

Travis bristled. "I'm not—"

"You love her. You've been fightin' it since the moment you set eyes on that woman. I seen it. Royce seen it. And you gotta be blind if Royce sees it before you do. I'm pretty sure you're the only fool who doesn't see it."

Travis shook his head sharply. "It ain't that simple."

"The heck it ain't."

"We gotta go," Travis said, ignoring his friend. "Now."

Lawson nodded once as he tugged open the barn door. "Horses are bridled and waiting."

The horses stamped agitatedly, sensing the danger. Lawson's gelding snorted, tossing its head, eyes rolling white. Travis moved to Buck and laid a gloved hand over the animal's neck. The horse shivered under his touch, but leaned into him, trusting him.

"Easy, boy," Travis said softly. "We're goin' after them, and you gotta help me."

He swung into the saddle. Lawson did the same. They exchanged a look.

Lawson lifted his chin. "Ready?"

Travis drew in a breath so cold it burned his lungs. "Yeah," he practically gasped out.

And then, with a kick of their heels, they raced out into the storm. Into the blizzard. Into the unknown. After the women they loved, and the baby that made him believe he might need to have a second chance of being a protector, after all.

He saw her face in his mind as she'd turned to look back at him from the wagon. Her fragile smile. Her trembling chin. Mason beneath her cloak, surely bundled snugly against her chest. The snow whipping around her, making her look like something from a dream. He thought of her laughing at the fair. How beautiful she looked. He thought of her cooking in the kitchen. Smiling down at Mason every chance she got. He saw her standing in the doorway of his house as he stood torn between letting her leave and making her stay, and then he thought of how much of a fool he was to choose the former.

Lawson's voice was in his head. "You love her."

It wasn't an accusation. It was truth. The God's honest truth.

And suddenly he knew it.

He loved her. Travis Baldwin loved Evelyn Rhodes.

It wasn't the quiet fondness he'd pretended it was. It wasn't just admiration of her mothering. It wasn't the protective instinct he insisted was just ordinary responsibility of a man's protectiveness towards a woman and a child.

It was love. Pure and simple.

He loved her gentleness, her stubbornness, her courage. Loved the devotion she had for that baby and her cousin to take on such a responsibility. Loved her outlook on life, even while facing her own crushing losses. Loved the way she faced the world despite everything she'd lost.

He loved her. The way she came into his life so unexpectedly, looked at him like he wasn't a lost cause, reminded him of how wonderful life could be.

He truly and endlessly loved her.

Chapter Thirty-Two

The storm had gotten much worse in no time at all.

Mason fussed in her arms, restless, and she knew why. The whirling of the wind was almost as loud as the whistle on a train. It was clear that the boy was frightened.

"It's all right," she whispered, although she was a little panicked herself/ "Mama's here. We're almost there. Just a little longer, sweetheart."

"I can't see anything!" Clara yelled out, tugging the reins to go a bit slower.

Evelyn bit her lip nervously. They were numb. Going slower meant it would take even longer to get to town, and that frightened her. Not only were they cold, but the thought of the storm getting even worse was terrifying.

Mason burrowed closer to her, and she tucked the blanket tighter around her, snuggling him under the cloak as much as she could as she cupped his head with her trembling hand. She wished more than anything that she could shield him entirely from the ferocity of the storm...

...and so much more.

The wagon rolled over something, a buried rut, a half-frozen clump, something—causing them all to jolt and the wagon to shake and tilt to the left heavily.

"Clara?" she called, raising her voice to be heard over the storm. "Are you all right up there?"

Clara muttered something Evelyn couldn't hear and climbed down from the bench, boots landing with a dull thud in the snow. "Wheel feels off," she called back. "I'm going to check it!"

It surprised Evelyn just how capable Clara was.

She was a lady if she'd ever seen one. Beautiful. Poised. Well-spoken. But she was just as capable as any man Evelyn had ever met, as well. Within seconds, though, the storm swallowed her fully, and she could no longer see her, not even the few feet down and toward the wheel.

She tried not to think of the ranch, of the house already gone behind her. In that moment, there was nowhere she would rather be. Especially right next to the fire. But it didn't matter. She had made her choice.

Another hard gust slammed into the wagon.

"Clara?" she called again, louder this time. "Maybe we should find a house nearby—"

The wind continued to tear at them, and Clara still hadn't come back from the wheel.

"Clara?" Evelyn called, shifting to look over the side, her voice sharper now. "Is everything all right?"

No answer.

"Clara!" she tried again, louder, more desperately. "Are you alright?"

Still nothing. No shout back over the wind. No familiar "Just a moment!" No string of curses to say that the wheel was damaged too much to continue on. Just the storm and silence.

She shifted to one knee, tucking Mason's head under her chin, and inched herself forward to look over the side of the wagon.

"Clara?" she called again, as close as she could get to the front. "Answer me! What's happening?"

The wagon dipped, just slightly, but enough to make the boards creak beneath her.

Evelyn's breath hitched, and she whipped her head around. "Clara, why didn't you answer me—" she started, but instead of Clara, there was a man next to her. And a man's face inches from hers.

"Afternoon, miss," he drawled, voice rough as gravel. "Going somewhere?"

Her heart seemed to stop dead.

She knew the man. She'd seen him before. In town.

Mason wailed, terrified by the cold and the sudden intrusion. Evelyn clutched him so tightly she feared she might hurt him. In an instant, she saw that afternoon in town again, the day she and Travis had gone to the bank. The way Travis had stiffened, fingers tightening around her arm right after he'd spun her around. He was the dirtier man that had stood next to Fletcher Kane.

She jerked back instinctively, pressing herself against the far side of the wagon, trying to shield the baby with her body. Her boots slid on the boards.

"Don't touch me!" she cried. "Stay away!"

"Now, now," he said, still grinning as his fingers closed around her upper arm. "No call for rudeness. Mr. Kane just wants a word."

"I'm not going anywhere with you!" she snapped. She knew how on edge Travis had been. These were the men terrorizing him, causing problems at his ranch. The men that had touched Mason while he was in his crib.

He squeezed her arm hard enough to make her wince. "I really don't think you're in any position to make demands."

Mason's cries grew louder, shrill and panicked. Evelyn tried to twist away, but there was nowhere to go. The wagon bed was small. Her back hit the rail. His grip tightened.

"Come on now," he said. "You and the brat both. Mr. Kane's waitin'."

She didn't have a chance to ask what Kane possibly wanted with her before the man dragged her out of the wagon, brute strength yanking her up.

"No!" she screamed. "Stop! You'll drop him—"

Her heel caught the edge of the wagon, and she stumbled forward, but the man's grip shifted, hauling her downward, not letting her fall. At least not completely. Her knees still slammed into hard-packed snow. Pain shot up her legs.

Mason wailed.

She swayed when she stood, her vision blurry. She was dizzy. Disoriented. Freezing.

Evelyn gathered him tighter, trying to wrap her cloak and her body around him, to block at least some of the wind and hopefully drown out some of the harsh sounds of the man's voice. "It's all right, darling," she choked out, though she was anything but sure. "I've got you. I've got you..."

She turned her head toward where she was getting dragged, and standing just a few feet away, just beyond the horses, was Clara, her shoulders heaving.

Her bonnet hung crooked. Her scarf had slipped, exposing her pale white throat, her eyes full of terror as another man held a gun to her temple.

"Don't move," the man with the gun said in a low, almost bored voice. "Don't even think about it, girl."

The road—if they were even still on the road—had completely disappeared. The horses stamped, snorting clouds of steam, where a man looped around toward them all.

Even bundled in a thick coat, he looked more put-together than any man had a right to in such weather.

"Miss Rhodes," he said, tipping his hat as if they were meeting at a church social instead of in the middle of a storm, where his men held guns on them. "We meet at last, properly."

Her mouth was dry. There was nothing proper about this. Her tongue felt thick, heavy all of a sudden. All she could manage was, "Please—"

He looked almost amused. "You remember who I am, I trust?"

Her throat worked. "Fletcher... Kane."

His eyes flicked down to Mason, who was still wailing, beneath her cloak.

"He's noisier than I expected," he said, taking a few steps closer, reaching out toward the cloak.

Evelyn tightened her grip instinctively. "Don't you dare touch him."

Kane's smile didn't change, but something in his eyes went colder. "You're in no position to make demands, my dear."

She swallowed back her fear and tried to stand up a bit straighter.

"What do you want?" she asked, forcing the words out. "Why are you doing this?"

He gave a small, almost pitying sigh. "Because Mr. Baldwin has been dreadfully uncooperative. What a wonderful coincidence that we were headed out to pay him a little visit after last night's warning, knowing he would be cooped up inside, and here you are, out in the middle of the road, stuck on some roots. You know, he's lucky I've not set fire to the rest of his property..."

The rest of—?

Her blood froze. Did he have something to do with the fire that killed Bonnie and Troy?

"I made him a generous offer for his land after tragedy struck his home. He refused. Time and time again. I applied pressure by other means. He still refused. I am a patient man, Miss Rhodes ...but my patience has limits. And this is the only way. He'll either relent, or he'll come after me, try and kill me once he finds out what I've done, and I'll have him killed. Then take his land at auction."

He took another step closer. She could feel heat radiating off of him now.

"Travis Baldwin is going to learn that everything can be taken from him," Kane said, "His home. His animals. His...attachments. And they'll keep being taken, as long as he doesn't do what I want."

Horror washed over her.

"You're going to—" Her voice failed. She tried again. "You're going to hurt us just to get him to sell you *land*?"

He shrugged one shoulder beneath his coat. "Hurt is such a vague word. I intend to make a point. A very clear one."

Tears stung her eyes. "This baby's done nothing. He doesn't even know why he's cold or scared. He's just a child. I'll go wherever you say, I'll do whatever you want, just don't—don't hurt him, don't hurt Clara—"

Clara made a tiny, broken, and gasping sound, tears freezing on her cheeks as they fell. The man with the gun pressed harder against her skin.

Evelyn felt Kane's eyes on her.

"I gave Baldwin time," he said. "Warned him. Poisoned a stream, killed a few horses. That was mercy, Miss Rhodes. Truly. It could have been worse, even then. But he did not listen." He got so close she could smell the whiskey on his breath. "It is far too late for mercy now."

Her knees nearly buckled.

Think. Think. There has to be something. Say the right thing. Offer the right thing.

But what could she offer? What did she have that could outweigh a man's hatred and greed?

"I'm begging you," she choked out. "For his sake." She looked down at Mason, his face blotchy and damp, lashes spiky with melted snow and tears, face beet red. "If you have any piece of a heart at all, don't do this to a child."

Kane looked at her as if he was regarding her and what she was saying, for a moment. One, long, heavy moment. He sighed and then shook his head, slowly, almost regretfully.

"I'm afraid it's far too late for that," he said. "Whatever happens now... will happen. And Baldwin will live to see the consequences."

She thought of Travis. Of how he would be after all of this was over...

Please. Please forgive yourself. Please forgive me for not knowing what to do to save us all.

Wind screamed around them, drowning even her thoughts.

And Evelyn closed her eyes, bracing herself for whatever would come next.

***

Travis gritted his teeth as the winter wind tore at his face, pulling tears right out of his eyes. He couldn't see anything. Snow ripped sideways across an obliterated trail. And he could see no signs of them being ahead of him, either. The snow was too heavy. Too thick. It had completely covered up any tracks they'd left behind.

But he and Lawson had to be close. They were traveling faster than the wagon would have been able to, out in this—

"This storm!" Lawson yelled out. "I can't see my doggone hand!"

It didn't matter, though. They had to keep pushing. If they were struggling like this on horseback, Travis couldn't imagine what the women and Mason were experiencing in a wagon. His jaw was clenched so tight it ached. It all made his stomach lurch so violently he thought he might be sick. Clara's wagon had been out in this for too long. Evelyn... Mason...they'd all been out too long.

He should never have let them leave.

He should never have let her climb into that wagon. He should've listened to the part of him that had screamed *no*. But he'd been a coward. A man still chained to his past. A fool who thought pushing a woman away was the same thing as protecting her.

"Wait," Lawson hollered out. "Look there!"

Travis jerked his head to where Lawson was pointing, his eyes squinting to look through the wall of snow. There was something there in the distance, something dark.

A wagon. Clara's wagon. Stopped. Half buried in blown snow.

The horses were still hitched, stamping anxiously, whinnying. And there was movement off to the side. Figures. Shapes. It looked like more than just Clara and Evelyn.

"There!" Lawson shouted, pointing to something closer.

A group of horses.

Three horses, to be exact.

"Is that...?" Lawson started, tugging at the reins of his horse to come to a halt.

Travis did the same, biting the inside of his cheek so hard it bled.

That was Fletcher Kane's horse—right alongside Amos Sharpe's.

Snapping his head back up, he could see it now. He could make it out.

Sharpe was behind Evelyn, holding her. A gun pointed right at her head. Another man held Clara. He could hear Mason's cries through the wind; in fact, the wind carried them. Travis's breath left him all at once.

"That bastard!" Lawson pointed his gun to shoot, then shook his head and lowered it almost immediately. "I don't have a good shot from here, not with this wind."

"We circle up there." He pointed to a low rise of snow-covered brush to the right. "They can't see us through the storm. We'll come down on them from behind those trees."

Lawson cursed softly but nodded. "You lead."

They pulled their horses off to the far left, behind the tree-covered hill, and dismounted, tying the reins low on branches nearby.

The snow was knee-deep at the wood line, and dragged their legs down, but Travis wasn't about to stop now. He knew one thing: he wasn't going to let her get hurt. He was going to make sure she and Mason both survived.

Clara, too.

He refused to fail them. Now and forever.

He'd also warned Cade. Fletcher Kane would not live to tell this tale.

They climbed down to a short rise, on hands and knees, ignoring the blistering cold that ripped at their hands. Every breath was like a knife right to the lungs, but they didn't have time to slow down. Not for a second.

Kane was talking, his face twisted with cruel amusement. Evelyn was pleading—Travis could see it in the way her shoulders shook, the way she curled around the baby. Clara was sobbing openly now.

"They're gonna kill 'em," Lawson whispered.

Not if Travis had breath left. He motioned to Lawson and mouthed his count. *One... two... three....* And then, without holding back, they stormed down on the men.

Travis grabbed Sharpe from behind, wrenching the gun from his grip and slamming him down into the snow while Lawson lunged at the man holding Clara and tackled him. Evelyn gasped. Clara shrieked. Mason cried out in confusion in Kane's arms. Kane spun around, firing immediately—right at Travis.

Pain ripped through Travis's leg like fire, his knee buckled, and snow rushed up to meet him as he hit the ground hard.

"Travis!" Evelyn's scream tore through the evening.

Lawson roared, scrambling with his own pistol, but Travis yelled out to stop him. "No!"

Kane had Mason, and they couldn't risk him being hit. Sharpe scrambled up, too, using the distraction of the baby to his advantage as he reached for his fallen gun. But before his hand closed around it, another shot cracked out. And then another, at their feet as a stampede of hooves pounded around them.

Men approaching. A lot of them.

Travis was losing blood. Fast. But he could see men surrounding Kane and his two henchmen—led by Sheriff Cade McCrae.

Cade's deputies yanked guns away, shoved each of them face-first into the snow—and Cade grabbed Mason right out of Kane's hands.

"You're done, Kane," Cade said, snapping cuffs around his hands. Travis blinked, the world spinning. His blood was warm against the snow, and the red puddle steamed through the winter mist. Before he knew it, Evelyn was crouched down beside him, tears in her eyes. She shoved snow away frantically as hair plastered to her cheeks.

"Oh God—Travis—Travis—" Her hands trembled as she reached for him, touching his face, his shoulders, not knowing where to touch first. "Don't move, you're bleeding—Cade, someone help him—Travis, don't you dare—don't you—!"

He reached up, fingers brushing her cheek as she sobbed.

"You're safe," he whispered. "You... and Mason... safe..."

That was all that mattered to him. That, and one more thing.

Lawson was right. It was there all along. He loved her. He really loved her. And he knew one thing was for certain: if he never woke up, at least she deserved to know.

"I—I love you..." he whispered.

And then, everything went black.

Chapter Thirty-Three

"Get him up!" Cade McCrae barked, grabbing Travis's arms. "Lawson, take his legs…Easy now, easy!"

The world tilted in on itself as Evelyn stumbled after them through the downpour of snow. Her skirts dragged through the drifts. She didn't see anyone except the three of them, although there were plenty of men all around—and Marigold and Clara, too. Deputies had dragged Sharpe and Kane off, but she wasn't concerned about them anymore.

Travis had lost a lot of blood.

It was freezing out.

She worried they wouldn't get him somewhere fast enough. Her breath came in gasps, each one icy enough to burn. A dark red trail ran across the white ground, dripping despite Lawson trying to put pressure on the bullet wound.

"Please—please—Travis—" she kept repeating over and over again, even though she knew for sure he wouldn't have been able to hear her.

He didn't respond. His head just lolled against McCrae's shoulder, his face completely drained of color, his mouth slack. They threw him over McCrae's horse, and without wasting a second, the sheriff mounted behind him, one arm locked around Travis's body to hold him steady. "Meet us at the ranch!" he yelled out to two men. "Out of the way!"

"Clara, you all right?" Lawson yelled. Evelyn had been so distraught she'd barely noticed her standing off with two deputies.

"I'm fine!" she replied loudly, finally coming into Evelyn's view. "Just get her out of here!" She ran over to take Mason from Evelyn's arms. "I have him, Evelyn!" she reassured her. "We'll head with these deputies to the ranch! You can't go as fast with a baby!"

She nodded to her friend, thankful to have her.

"Clara!" she heard Marigold wrench out from behind her. "Thank God!"

"Come on, Evelyn!" Lawson hollered to her, mounting his own horse. She didn't have time to worry about everyone else. She had to go.

Now.

She ran. She ran hard, grabbing his arm as he slung her up. Clinging to the man's coat, she hung on for dear life, and they charged toward Travis's ranch.

Snow stung her eyes, and the cold had nipped so hard her cheeks were numb. Lawson was driving his horse hard and fast. It was clear he was just as concerned. Sadness welled up in her throat so hard she started to choke. She pressed her face to his back and sobbed.

He's going to die.

That's all she could think.

Oh, Lord, no. Please, please, don't take him, too.

By the time they reached the ranch, her hands were frozen, and her legs shook so hard she nearly toppled when Lawson helped her down. McCrae didn't wait, though; he had already carried Travis straight inside, two deputies he'd hollered to trailing behind with Marigold hot on their tails.

"I knew you and Clara had to have run into some trouble!" Marigold stripped off her wet gloves and hurried inside with them, pushing past the deputies. "Cade!" she yelled. "Lay him flat on that bed! Lawson, get me a basin! And Evelyn, dear, you need to breathe!" She didn't realize she'd been holding her breath until Marigold had said it. "He's alive."

Evelyn's knees buckled, and Marigold caught her by the shoulders. "Sit, honey. He's strong. He'll be all right."

***

He was alive. And stable, from what Marigold had said. She hadn't left his side for even a moment. Some of the deputies had gone off to town to take Sharpe and Kane in to the jail. McCrae wanted to make sure that they'd all made it safely, and Sharpe and Kane were locked up behind steel bars. So he'd ventured into the storm—well before it calmed—while a couple of deputies stayed behind to keep an eye on everyone at the ranch.

Royce had moved quickly inside, angry that no one had asked him to go with them. Angry that he'd missed it all.

"It's a good thing," one of the deputies said. "You're gettin' too old."

Royce had merely scowled and sat next to his son-in-law. Almost as long as Evelyn had.

"So how the hell is everyone involved in all this?" he demanded.

"Marigold rushed into the sheriff's office," one of the deputies replied, leaning against the door frame. "Bust through the door like a bat outta hell. Said they were out in this weather and something had to be wrong because Clara would have never taken so long."

Marigold huffed from the desk chair in the corner of the room. She folded her arms in front of herself. "Well, I couldn't just sit and wait for these two young women to make it through a blizzard with a baby!"

Evelyn smiled. "I'm sure glad you were in town."

The deputy's jaw flexed. "So we rode out. Started where the tracks bent east. Didn't expect to find trouble but... we did."

Evelyn felt her stomach drop. If Marigold hadn't gone to get help, what would have happened? She shuddered. She didn't want to think about it.

"Ain't that the biggest bit of luck I've ever heard of..." Royce muttered, eyeing Lawson as he stood in the corner with Clara. "You two are goin' to get yourselves killed."

Lawson opened his mouth to speak, but Travis groaned, his eyes fluttering open. Evelyn's eyes widened as she gripped his hands tighter.

"Where am I?" he groaned. Then, his eyes fell on Evelyn, and a smile spread over his face.

"You're home," she said, blushing slightly. "Thank God, and you're okay."

"We'll give you two some time," Marigold whispered, then scooted her chair over the wood floor. She gestured for everyone else to filter out of the bedroom, and Evelyn sighed. The time she had both been looking forward to and dreading had come. She was happy he was awake—but being awake meant one thing.

She had to tell him about the fire.

"Travis..." Evelyn said softly. "I need to tell you something."

"What is it?" he asked, and immediately her gut rolled anxiously. He was so unsuspecting. She hated to do it. But she couldn't keep it a secret, either.

"About the fire…" she whispered, the words painful.

McCrae cleared his throat from the door. She hadn't known it, but he'd clearly come back to the ranch as soon as the weather calmed down. "Maybe I oughta tell him." He walked toward the bedside and set his hat on the table. "Sharpe talked."

Travis didn't flinch. Evelyn did. "About what? You already know what they were up to, terrorizing those women."

"That's not all there is to what they did," Cade went on deliberately. "The fire… your fire? It wasn't an accident. They planned it. Kane and Sharpe both. Picked a time they knew you'd be gone. Thought Bonnie and Troy were at Royce's house. Didn't mean for it to happen like it did—but it was still their doing."

Evelyn felt Travis's entire body go stone-still—until he tried to push himself upright.

"Travis—" Evelyn moved to stop him.

He shook her off—not harshly, but enough.

"I'll kill him." The words came out gravel and fire. "I'll kill Kane with my bare hands."

"Travis," McCrae warned, standing over him.

"He burned my family." Travis's voice cracked. "My wife. My boy."

Evelyn's heart ached. Tears spilled down her cheeks before she even knew she was crying. Travis had already swung his legs off the bed. The moment his boots hit the floor, he nearly collapsed, but he caught himself on the bedpost, trembling, and Evelyn wasn't sure if it was from fury or grief.

McCrae grabbed his shoulders before he could take another step. "Travis, stop."

"Move," Travis snarled through clenched teeth. "He took everything from me. *Everything.*"

"Save your damn strength," the sheriff snapped back. You can't even stand!"

Travis faltered immediately, and Evelyn reached for him again. This time, he didn't pull away.

"I'll make sure he pays!" McCrae continued. "You hear me, Baldwin? Kane will never see the light of day again. Not one sunrise. Not one breath of free air. I swear it on my badge and my life. He'll pay."

Travis's face finally broke. Not anger. Not fury. Grief. Devastating, silent grief. He crumpled back onto the bed, burying his face in his hands. A raw sound tore from him—half sob, half roar, a sound that was pure and utter devastation.

She sank down beside him, wrapping him tightly in her arms.

"I'm here," she whispered, pressing her forehead against his. "I'm here. You're not alone." His fingers clutched her arm like she was the only thing left in the world. "I love you, Travis Baldwin. And I'm here."

***

"Ow, ow, ow!" Travis yelled as Evelyn tried to put another pillow under his injured leg.

"Stop being such a big baby," she countered, swatting at his uninjured leg.

"Tell me again why I love you?" he grumbled.

She smirked, moving around the side of the bed to place a soft kiss on his lips. "Because I'm probably the only one willing to take care of a grumpy ol' complainer like you!"

He chuckled, and a blush rose up on her cheeks at the way he stared at her.

"Merry Christmas!" Royce said from the doorway, knocking on the frame.

"Merry Christmas!" Evelyn called out to the older man, but all that did was remind her of everything she had to do to get ready for the day. She ran quickly to the kitchen, throwing her flour-dusted apron on.

It was time for a feast!

The roast goose rested now, with its perfectly crisp skin. Potatoes were finished to accompany it, with a beautiful-smelling herb butter Marigold had brought over. Green beans that had been canned from the warmer months steamed atop the stove.

She wiped her hands on her apron and smiled widely.

She'd done it.

While she inspected the preparations, Royce got Travis to the kitchen, helping him sit down on a chair. They propped his injured leg on a stool instead of pillows, at which she half-expected to hear him gripe, but no complaints fell from his lips.

Then, Royce hovered near the stove. "It smells so good," he groaned, practically drooling as he held Mason in his arms.

A knock sounded at the door.

"They're here." Evelyn wiped her hands again, though they were already clean. "Royce, go get the door."

And then the crowd came in.

Marigold charged into the kitchen first, her cheeks flushed from the cold, carrying a basket wrapped in a red cloth. "Merry Christmas!" she sang, crossing the kitchen to peck Evelyn's cheeks. "Mr. Price is tending to the horses and will be in soon."

Evelyn chuckled.

She still hadn't formally met Mr. Price. After all his family had done for her, she knew she had to thank him properly. *What better way than a meal like this...*

Behind her came Clara, holding a tin of cookies, cheeks red and eyes bright. Sheriff McCrae behind her, tall and—and then, bringing up the rear, like he didn't live on the ranch, was Barrett Lawson. He hung back, his hat in his hands, looking shy and helpless all of a sudden.

Evelyn looked at him curiously, then to Clara, who blushed and busied herself at the counter. *Well, well, well...*

"Merry Christmas," she greeted everyone with a grin, then gathered their cloaks, coats, hats, and scarves. It was nice, having the house fill up so quickly, especially with people as wonderful as these.

"Merry Christmas, Travis." McCrae crossed the kitchen to sit next to him. "How's the leg?"

"I've had worse," Travis replied dryly.

"How's the rest of you?" McCrae asked, his brow raised.

"He's been tolerable today," Lawson piped up from the corner of the room, his hands stuffing into his pockets. "Might be the holiday spirit."

"Might be the company," Travis muttered, and she immediately felt his eyes fall on her. She pretended not to notice, but her face warmed at his attention.

Soon, the table was set, and they all squeezed around it; some on dining chairs, some on rocking chairs from the sitting room. But all huddled perfectly together like one big family.

McCrae gave Travis a steady look. "Your father would be proud of you," he said.

Travis nodded, looking down at his plate.

"He'd be proud of you, too," Travis muttered. "Thanks for all that you do, Cade."

"You're like a son to me, boy," he said. "I hope you know that."

Travis nodded and Evelyn couldn't help but watch his Adam's apple bob as he grunted. She rolled her eyes. *Men.* They never could admit it when they were moved emotionally.

But she didn't need to dwell on that. With a heartfelt prayer said by all, the meal began.

"This is a darn good goose," Lawson said.

"Yeah, we can see that," Clara teased. "Yours is gone."

Marigold laughed. "Get the boy seconds!" Then, seeing Clara blush, she chuckled again. "Come on, dear, we all know the two of you enjoy each other. It's not a surprise to anyone here. Stop pretending there's nothing going on."

McCrae cleared his throat. "I'll save the two of you," he said to both Lawson and Clara as he leaned back in his chair. "I think maybe you all ought to hear the official word. Kane and Sharpe have been formally charged. We've got signed statements from other people whose land he's practically stolen. Even the banker has been implicated. " He paused. "Sharpe's admitted to poisoning your stock, and… the fire."

Evelyn felt both Travis and Royce tense at those words.

Lawson cracked his knuckles. "Don't matter if he meant to hurt anybody or not in that fire. He did what he did. Him tryin' it again by taking these girls was nothin' if it wasn't bragging."

"Well," McCrae replied, "he won't be bragging from behind bars."

Marigold sniffed. "Good riddance."

McCrae grinned. "Won't walk away from this one. Judge says there's enough evidence to lock 'em both up for a good long stretch. Years. Maybe more."

Relief washed through the room, and Evelyn felt grateful tears prick her eyes. It was news that they all needed to hear.

"Enough of that." Marigold finished the last scraps on her plate and set down her fork. "Where's that baby?"

Evelyn laughed. "He's in his room resting."

Marigold just gave a nonchalant shrug and pushed her chair back, letting it slide against the floor. "Well, I'm going to wake him up and see that precious face!"

"If you wake him up," Evelyn warned, "you're changing him and putting him back to sleep later."

"You say that like it's a bad thing," Marigold practically sang behind her. "Maybe my daughter will have a baby soon, and I can dote on another one!"

Clara groaned and put her head in her hands.

Evelyn laughed again, especially when she looked at Lawson, who'd turned pale. Fortunately for him, McCrae spoke up again.

"Oh, and Miss Evelyn, I'll be having some deputies out tomorrow to help take down some of these decorations from the fair."

"No," Travis said, shaking his head. "We'll leave them up for a bit longer."

Evelyn felt her heart leap. "You mean you want them to stay up?"

He nodded. "For a bit more."

For a bit more it would be, then. She felt happiness warm her head to toe.

"Well, with that leg, you won't be able to do much about it, anyway," Lawson said abruptly. "So when you're ready, will you let Cade know, so I don't gotta do it all alone? I've already gotta pick up the slack from an old man and now a cripple."

"I'll show you, old man!" Royce huffed, chortling.

"And I'll show you, cripple Lawson," Travis put in.

McCrae laughed. "I'll send help whenever you all are ready."

"That settles it then," Evelyn declared, standing up to grab plates. "Who's ready for dessert?"

***

When everyone bundled themselves back into coats and stepped out into the evening, Evelyn waved them off, feeling joy she almost couldn't contain. She watched Clara glance over her shoulder at Lawson and wink while he waved at her with bright, red-flushed cheeks.

She giggled, watching them.

She wasn't sure where they were at with their confessions, but the feelings were obvious. Cade tipped his hat, and Marigold and Mr. Price headed back to their wagon. "When he wakes up, you tell that baby boy I love him!" she called, and Evelyn nodded.

When the door closed again, Travis was standing in the doorway. "Travis, what are you doing?" she scolded, out to help him back to a chair.

He laughed and held a hand out to halt her before she could fully reach him.

"There's something I want to do," he whispered, then reached into his pocket to pull out a small wooden box.

Her breath seemed to catch in her throat. "Travis…?"

He swallowed, jaw working, eyes fixed on the box for a moment and then at her. "Lawson got this for me, couple days ago from town…"

Her heart flip-flopped, so crazily she could hear it in her ears.

He opened the box to reveal a beautiful ring—a gold band with a diamond that twinkled like a star—and she felt almost faint.

"Evelyn, we may still lose this ranch," he said slowly. "I don't know what will happen with that. We may have to start over somewhere else one day. We might have hard times over and over again. I can't promise you ease. I can't promise you anything except to love you and protect you. You came at a time when I thought I wasn't capable of loving anyone or anything, and I didn't want to. You surprised me in the best way, and this Christmas has been so special with you. And I know that I'll never want to spend Christmas with anyone else, as long as I live."

Tears spilled from her eyes, and she pressed a trembling hand to her mouth.

"So." He could scarcely meet her gaze. "Will you marry me, Evelyn Rhodes?"

Her answer broke from her like a prayer. "Yes. Oh, Travis—Yes!"

He smiled wide, sliding the ring onto her finger.

"I don't care where we live," she whispered, voice shaking. "I don't care if we're poor. I don't care if we start over with nothing. I've done that before. Just promise me that we'll face everything together. No matter what it is."

His thumb brushed her cheek, catching a tear. "I promise," he said.

"And I love you," she whispered brokenly. "More than I ever expected I could love anyone."

His breath hitched. His forehead dropped to hers. "I love you too," he said. "You and that boy have given me back my life. You've saved me."

"And you saved us," she said. "In so many ways."

She threw her arms around him, hugging him tightly—and didn't realize she'd pushed him to lean weight on his injured leg until he groaned.

"Oh, no. Sorry!" she squealed, easing back, but he only shook his head.

"No, no." He reached around and brought her closer. "You'll only be sorry if you pull away from my hug again." He chuckled. "Merry Christmas, my love."

"Merry Christmas," she whispered in his ear, her heart full. Healed. Whole.

Epilogue

One Year Later

The bell from the small white-steepled church chimed out all the way across the valley, so loud she half-wondered how she could never hear it from the ranch. It seemed so loud in town. But it was so, so beautiful.

She'd been coming to church quite frequently over the last year, just like she'd promised Reverend Ellis.

She glanced out of the frosted windows and watched as more people filtered in to gather. Families all bundled up in wool and galoshes. The lanterns on all the wagons outside, and throughout the church, glowed so beautiful on nights like tonight.

Christmas Eve.

She looked at her handsome husband, who shrugged off his coat as he settled in beside her. Mason reached eagerly with his little hands to sit on Travis's lap, and Evelyn just smiled wide. She was glad they could make it to church this year.

It seemed only right they give thanks where thanks was due. The reason for Christmas. Jesus's birth. Jesus' promise to the world He had come to save.

Evelyn felt tears fill her eyes as "O Come, All Ye Faithful" rang out across the congregation. She bowed her head at the sweetness of it all. A year ago, she had stood before this same Lord with fear and uncertainty filling every part of her. Tonight, she was filled with nothing except gratitude.

For safety. For warmth. For love. For family. For the man whose fingers were now laced with hers like he never meant to let go again.

As the final candle was lit and the church glowed gold and gentle, Travis leaned close enough to whisper, "Feels different this year."

She smiled softly. "Because God's been good to us," she said.

He nodded, eyes shining in the candlelight. "He sure has."

Truly, what a difference a year could make!

Evelyn couldn't help but think back to that last Christmas and just how magical it was. It was the first Christmas of the rest of her life. The Christmas where everything changed for her. For the better.

Now, she was married to the greatest man she had ever known, living on the best ranch she'd ever been on, raising the most beautiful boy she'd ever laid eyes on—with friends and a community more supportive than any she could have ever imagined.

Back when she and Arabella were just trying to survive, people shunned them. They looked down on them. But not here. Not in Evanston.

Here, the people loved unconditionally. Fully.

They'd all healed her in ways they'd never fully understand, but in ways that she'd prayed thanks over every night. The ranch looked different now. Happier. Brighter. Alive again, without worry of foreclosure.

Truthfully, that had been a bout of luck in and of itself.

The banker, Mr. Presley, had been implicated in some of Kane's crimes, so they'd been given an extension until spring—

just like everyone else got—to come up with the money they owed. But just as all the leaves came into bloom, Travis found the biggest gold nugget anyone had ever seen.

It had paid off the ranch in full, making it easier on Travis than she was sure he had ever had it before. He could stop worrying about all the bank notes against the place—finally—and just be at peace with his land. With his home. He was able to own it all, free and clear, and now everything he got from the sale of his horses was his alone.

The horse stock was doing well. None of the other horses got sick once they found the lye and cleared the streams. Even Duke had made a full recovery, and Travis had decided to keep him for Mason to ride when the boy was old enough.

The old wooden porch had been repaired, new shingles stood out proudly on the roof, and this Christmas, even more decorations than last were displayed across the entire property.

After the first Christmas fair, Evelyn had decided to take it on permanently. Travis had put up what she strongly suspected was a token grumble about it at first, but soon enough came around...

Christmas Day began in the usual busy way—with Mason's footsteps pattering irregularly behind her, as uneven as any toddler's, but quick and fiery. She turned just in time to see him barreling in her direction, arms outstretched, cheeks flushed pink with excitement, mouth wide open in a grin.

"Ma!" he crowed, as though he had not said the same thing sixteen times already that day. He still seemed delighted and surprised at his own voice as he toddled around.

Evelyn laughed and bent down, lifting him easily into her arms. He was getting big, with sandy-brown curls that stuck out every which way, cheeks round as apples, and one of the happiest dispositions she—or anyone else—had ever seen.

She didn't have a clue what she would have done without him. She missed Arabella, of course, and she wished every day that things had been different. That she would have made it. That they would be in Evanston together, somehow.

But still, she couldn't imagine not being Mason's mother now.

He pressed a sloppy kiss to her cheek and then reached for the wooden spoon she had been using.

"No, sir," she chided gently. "That's for stirring, not for chewing." Keeping things out of his mouth was a full-time endeavor.

He giggled, unbothered, and wriggled until his feet hit the floor again.

"I don't get why he can't say pa!" Travis complained, tongue in cheek, as soon as he walked into the kitchen.

Evelyn turned.

He leaned against the doorway, arms folded across his chest, watching their son. "*Ma* has been said probably twenty times today already."

She shrugged cockily. "I guess I'm just the favorite."

"Oh, really?"

He pushed off the door frame and walked toward her, the smile widening as he scooped her up in his arms. His fingers jabbed and tickled her ribs. She squealed. "Favorite, huh?" Travis asked, laughing as he continued to tickle her.

Mason squealed and all but ran at the two of them, clutching hold of their legs firmly.

"You want some tickles?" Travis asked him, scooping him up.

"Da!" Mason chirped with a laugh.

Travis froze and then blinked slowly, looking to Evelyn as if to ask if she heard it.

She nodded.

"Did he just?"

She nodded again, her lips curving upward. "Merry Christmas...Da."

"I'll be...!" he said quietly, kissing the boy on the top of the head. "That's right, son. I'm here."

Evelyn swallowed back the sting of tears just as a knock sounded from the front door.

"They're early," she said, wiping her hands on her apron and heading out of the kitchen.

"They always are," Travis said, setting Mason down gently. She could hear them both right behind her, until the toddler toddled ahead in the front hall, his arms flailing with excitement.

Evelyn could already hear them outside, laughing.

In love.

Engaged just recently, in fact. *About time.* When she opened the door, Clara exclaimed a boisterous "Merry Christmas!" and pulled Evelyn into a hug so forceful she nearly knocked her to the floor.

"Merry Christmas," Evelyn gasped.

Lawson stepped forward, standing a bit taller these days. Taller than the doorway seemed to allow. She tilted her head to take him in. "Feeling pretty confident now that Clara's said yes?" she joked.

He shrugged his shoulders with a shy grin. "Somehow I've convinced her that I'm worth spending her life with."

She didn't see much of him these days. He still worked the ranch with Travis and Royce, but he never came in for breakfast, dinner, or even supper. He was always off at the Price ranch, courting their daughter like a proper gentleman should.

It was nice to see him, though. And she told him so.

He nodded. "You too, Mrs. Baldwin."

She giggled. She wasn't sure she would ever tire of the title.

Marigold bustled in last, shaking snow off her cloak. "Evelyn, child, if there isn't enough food in this house to feed half the county, I'll eat my bonnet."

"I made your favorite," Evelyn said.

Marigold beamed. "I knew I raised you right."

Travis sighed heavily behind her. "Marigold, if you eat all the meat again, I'm going to steal some of your livestock."

Evelyn swatted his arm playfully as she turned and made her way back into the kitchen.

"You look good, Travis," Marigold said, patting his belly. "Looks like she's feeding you right."

"Remember last Christmas when his leg was all busted up? He gained about fifteen pounds from that, and it's just kept on ever since." Lawson laughed and Evelyn shook her head. The man hadn't gained more than a few pounds all year. They were just way too fond of teasing him.

But that was why she loved days like today. Days to get together. Sometimes, life got busy, and visits were further apart than they'd like, but days like this were reserved for family and friends—and it was something she would always make a priority.

"I guess if I found a big ol' nugget of gold, I would take it easy, too!" Lawson continued, already in the kitchen when Evelyn got there. He was eyeballing all the food, Marigold right next to him.

"Hard to keep a good man down," Travis replied, glancing at Evelyn in a way that made heat coil low in her stomach like it always did.

Truth was, that gold nugget had been a blessing.

"I searched that stream with you day in and day out after that son of a gun, Kane, put lye in the creek—just in case his pals came back. Where in the world were you hidin' it? It was as big as my fist!" Lawson held up his fist, along with a piece of bread that he stuffed forcefully in his mouth.

"I wasn't hidin' it," Travis drawled. "It was hidin' from me!"

Barrett barked a laugh.

"It was a blessing," Clara insisted firmly. "After last year? Huge blessing."

"That's right." Marigold tugged the bread out of Lawson's hand and smacked him in the back of the head. "Don't be rude! Leave that food until we sit and say grace!"

"I'm hungry!" he protested, through a mouthful.

Laughter erupted. Indeed, this is exactly what days like this were for. The Lord, friends, family—love. The celebration of it to its fullest.

***

After the guests left, the ranch fell quiet again. It was always a little jarring at first just how lively it got with their friends, but it was nice. And it was also nice when they left, and Evelyn and Travis were left with that quiet contentment. Of peace. Of home. And today, Evelyn didn't have to go into the dress shop to work, and Mason had already laid down for sleep after a full day of excitement. That meant the rest of the evening was completely theirs. And theirs alone.

Travis was still by the fire in the sitting room, warming his hands, when she walked up behind him.

"You look like you're thinking awfully hard," she commented.

"Thinkin' how different this Christmas is," he said. "How different everything is."

"I have something for you," she whispered, shyly handing him a box.

His brow lifted slightly. "Another gift?"

She nodded. "Just one more."

He took it with a smile, unwrapping the brown paper carefully before pulling the small toy from the box—and staring.

"A baby's rattle?" he asked.

Simple. Wooden. Softly carved.

He turned it over, confusion knitting his brow. "Evelyn... Mason's already got—"

He stopped. She smiled, hearing his breath catch. He looked at her, his eyes widening, searching for the answer that she knew he already knew.

"Are you—?" he asked, swallowing.

She nodded, tears filling her eyes. "Yes."

Quickly, he reached out, cupping her face gently in both hands—kissing her.

"You're sure?" he asked, pulling back just enough to rest his forehead against hers

"Yes," she breathed. "I'm sure."

He let out a choked laugh. one that broke into something suspiciously like a sob. He pulled her into his arms and held her tightly, burying his face in her hair.

"Thank you," he whispered, voice shaking. "God, thank you."

His joy moved her in a way that she hadn't expected. She clutched his shirt tightly, her tears wetting the fabric. He pulled back further, wiping them gently from her cheeks.

"A second child," he whispered in complete awe. "Our child."

Ours.

She nodded. Mason was his in every way that counted. She knew that. He knew that. But there was something special about creating a life. Evelyn felt that herself. She'd never carried one herself. She'd never grown one inside her.

This would be a whole new experience. A whole new journey. A whole new adventure.

"We're really buildin' a family," he said softly. "A whole new life." She watched a flash of poignancy roll over his face.

"Yes," she whispered. "Are you all right with that?"

He nodded. "I do miss them, but I love you more than anything in the world. And it makes me proud that I've gotten a second chance with you."

She smiled, tears falling freely once more.

He pulled her into another kiss. This was slower. Deeper. And more than anything, it overflowed with love. Outside, the snow kept falling, not nearly as intensely as it had the previous year. Inside, the fire burned with the warmth of family, more radiant yet.

Travis rested his forehead against hers once more

"I've got everything I ever wanted," he whispered. "Everything."

And Evelyn knew, with absolute certainty, that she did as well.

None of it had happened the way either of them thought it would, but life was funny that way. And it didn't change a thing about how blessed they were. In fact, Evelyn wondered if happily ever after felt even happier only after someone had experienced true and utter heartbreak and come out on the other side. God had made a way. God had been there with them, through it all—and they truly had come out on the other side.

A Christmas blessing.

A Christmas miracle.

HANNAH LEE DAVIS

THE END

Also by Hannah Lee Davis

Thank you so much for reading "**The Mountain Man's Christmas Bride**"!

I sure hope it brought a little joy to your day and a flutter to your heart!

If you enjoyed this story, you might like to take a peek at the rest of my **Amazon book collection** right here:

https://go.hannahleedavis.com/bc-authorpage

Every time you read one of my stories, you help me keep this ol' dream of mine alive—so thank you from the bottom of my heart! ♥

MERRY CHRISTMAS!

Printed in Dunstable, United Kingdom